the

Faded

Photo

ALSO BY SARAH PRICE

An Empty Cup

An Amish Buggy Ride

Secret Sister: An Amish Christmas Tale

The Plain Fame Series

Plain Fame

Plain Change

Plain Again

Plain Return

Plain Choice

Plain Christmas

The Amish of Lancaster Series

Fields of Corn

Hills of Wheat

Pastures of Faith

Valley of Hope

The Amish of Ephrata Series

The Tomato Patch

The Quilting Bee

The Hope Chest

The Clothes Line

For a complete listing of books, please visit the author's website at
www.sarahpriceauthor.com.

the Faded Photo

A NOVEL

SARAH PRICE

Waterfall
PRESS

Text copyright © 2017 Price Publishing, LLC
All rights reserved.

Published by Waterfall Press, Grand Haven, MI

www.apub.com

Amazon, the Amazon logo, and Waterfall Press are trademarks of Amazon.com, Inc., or its affiliates.

ISBN-13: 9781503938670
ISBN-10: 1503938670

Cover design by Shasti O'Leary Soudant

Printed in the United States of America

For the living know that they will die,
And the dead know nothing:
they have no further reward,
and even the memory of them is forgotten.

—Ecclesiastes 9:5

PROLOGUE

The fresh layer of snow—something that usually excited Frances more than anything—did nothing to cover up the fact that she would have to sit in an old-fashioned red sleigh next to a dying woman.

"Why me?" Frances turned from the window as her mother hovered over her, about to brush her brown hair. "No one else has to go!"

"Never ask 'why me.' You know I don't like that. Sometimes in life you just have to do what you have to do. Besides, you don't know the plans God has for you. Or for others, for that matter." Her mother jerked the brush a little too roughly through a knot at the nape of Frances's neck. "And what is with all of these questions? Why didn't you wear your Mary Janes? I specifically told you to put them on."

Frances winced as another knot was attacked by her mother's swift hand. "I hate Mary Janes. They're stupid-looking and too big anyway."

Her mother took a step backward and glared at her in the mirror. "You'll grow into them, Frances. Now, enough complaining out of you." Her mother leaned forward and turned on the water faucet, dampening the brush, which made it smell bad.

Wrinkling her nose, Frances leaned away from her mother. "I just don't understand why I have to go!"

"She's dying, Frances, and you know how much she loves you!" Her mother tried to slick down the cowlick at Frances's crown. "It's just one photo, probably the last one we'll have of her."

"I don't want to be in a photo with a dead person!" The thought had terrified Frances from the moment her mother had come up with the idea the previous week.

"Oh, stop it! She's dying, not *dead*. How would it appear to other people if you denied her this last wish? You know she has no children of her own." Tossing the damp, smelly hairbrush into the sink, her mother stood back and assessed the finished product with a half-pleased expression. "You look well enough, I suppose."

Frances made a face that did not go unnoticed.

"Honestly, have some compassion, Frances Lynn! Imagine how scared she must feel, poor Mrs. Bentley!"

But Frances didn't want to imagine how their neighbor felt. All Frances could imagine was having to stand in the freezing cold—something she hated more than anything!—for a photographer to take what might be the last photo of Mrs. Bentley for a Christmas card. *And why,* Frances wondered, *would Mrs. Bentley want a photo with me, anyway?*

The battle with her mother ended even before it began. At nine years of age, Frances couldn't possibly win, not against an adult, let alone her mother, who, it seemed, always won, regardless of the opponent.

Her mother glanced at the clock and made a noise of exasperation. "Let's hurry it up, Frances. I have a lot to do this afternoon. You know how your father likes his Saturday night pot roast promptly at five o'clock."

As soon as her mother invoked the father card, Frances knew better than to dawdle any longer. If her mother lived for social appearances, her other focus in life was catering to her husband.

And so, at eleven o'clock on a Saturday morning, Frances found herself sitting in the red wooden sleigh, her stuffed elephant tucked under her arm, trying to smile as she inched away from Mrs. Bentley, just in case whatever the woman was dying of was something that she could catch.

It was cold out, and the ground was now covered with at least two inches of snow. Even though she wore her blue coat and tan knit hat, Frances was freezing from all of the sitting around while everything was made "just right."

"Closer, dear," the photographer said, gesturing with his hand for Frances to move into Mrs. Bentley's arm that was wrapped around her. The elephant fell out of the sleigh, and as Frances moved to retrieve it, the photographer stopped her. "Perhaps you should stand next to her."

Glancing at her stuffed animal that lay in the snow, Frances sighed and stood up, hoping that her mother wouldn't step on it.

The photographer smiled. "Much better."

But Frances did not feel much better. In fact, she felt much worse.

Mrs. Bentley, however, did not seem to notice. At forty-two, she was still pretty. Frances liked her short black hair that framed her face. With her dark winter coat and red hat that sat just so on the back of her head, Mrs. Bentley did not look sick and, therefore, did not look like she was dying.

And that's when Frances did the unimaginable: she spoke without thinking.

"Mom says you are dying."

The second she heard her mother gasp, Frances knew that she was in trouble. But the words were out there; she couldn't take them back. *Besides,* she argued with herself, *Mom did say that!*

Mrs. Bentley, however, didn't seem to mind. She merely hugged Frances closer against her side and kissed the top of her head. "Aw, sweet Frances! How I love your honesty. It's so refreshing to have someone say what they are truly thinking! It's so much better than all of the whispers, side looks, and pity. I'd much rather people ask me what's on their mind than tiptoe around the subject. It's better than being seen as a pity case."

In Frances's mind, Mrs. Bentley's words vindicated her. To her further satisfaction, her mother had been unknowingly implicated by Mrs. Bentley.

"I have cancer, Frances."

"Cancer?" It was an unfamiliar word to her, and once again, she wondered if that was anything like a bad cold. She leaned away, just a little, and hoped that her mother didn't notice.

"It's a bad disease when your body starts fighting against itself. No one really knows how it starts. And the cure for it depends on the type of cancer and how long a person has had it before discovering it."

"What type do you have?"

"Breast. It started in my breasts," Mrs. Bentley said, gently placing her hand on her chest. "But now it has spread to other places in my body."

"So cancer is going to make you die?" Frances asked.

Her mother gave her a stern look. "Frances!"

But Mrs. Bentley didn't seem to mind. "It is, Frances."

"Are you scared?"

"Frances!" her mother said in a sharp tone. "That's enough!"

But Mrs. Bentley ignored her mother's reprimand. Instead, a smile spread across her face as she responded to Frances. "Am I scared? No. Not in the least. Crying about it or being sad will not change the fact that God wants me home, my dear child. My time on earth is finished. I have a much greater future ahead of me."

Frances did not know how to respond. If *she* had cancer, she knew *she* would be scared. And she certainly would *not* be taking photographs in a sleigh while it was snowing with a child that lived down the street! But Mrs. Bentley didn't have any children of her own, a fact that had made Frances's mother even more adamant that the photo shoot take place.

As she stood beside Mrs. Bentley, smiling for the photographer, she couldn't help but think that life without having children was even sadder than the fact that Mrs. Bentley was dying. After all, what was the purpose of life if you didn't have a family? Mrs. Bentley would die and be put into the ground without anyone to remember her years later. The memory of her life would fade away, probably by the time the first snow fell next winter. And by then, just as no one talked about Grammy or Grandpa anymore, no one would remember Mrs. Bentley or the silly photograph that she was posing for at the current moment.

"Smile now!" the photographer said.

Frances did as she was told, not just smiling but grinning for the photographer as she stood next to the dying woman in the old-fashioned red cutter sleigh for a Christmas card that no one would remember in years to come. The only thing Frances would remember about that day was that the ground was covered by snow and that she hoped, later, her father might take her sleigh riding.

CHAPTER 1

Please stop ringing. Frances navigated the narrow staircase while trying to slip on her shoes, no easy feat with three large dogs racing on her heels as if they were trying to beat her to the first-floor landing. The telephone, however, didn't seem to hear her wish, its shrill ring beckoning to her from the kitchen.

"Can someone get that?" she called out, irritated that, once again, everyone else in the house appeared deaf to the ringing nuisance. It was a bone of contention with her, a constant battle that continued to defeat her. With everyone having cell phones, including her twelve-year-old daughter, answering the house phone had become the sole responsibility of one person: Frances.

She survived the staircase and set down her laptop bag on the floor by the front table. Yesterday's mail lay heaped in a pile, something else she needed to sort through. She felt a tightening in her chest, a far too familiar feeling that forced her to shut her eyes while taking deep breaths. And then the phone rang, yet again.

Deep breaths are not going to help me today. She grabbed her purse from the floor. Another ring.

"Anyone?" She dug inside the bottom of her bag, looking for the little orange bottle of prescription pills. Dr. Morgan had instructed her to take one every six hours, but Frances had heard that Xanax could be addictive. Long ago, she learned that the only person she could depend on was herself. The last thing she wanted was to rely on something, never mind a tiny magic pill that kept her calm, so she restricted herself to "in an emergency only" mode. When the phone rang again, she knew this was one of those times.

"Fine! I'll get it!" There was no point in venting further, as she knew no one heard her, and if they did, they certainly didn't care about answering the phone anyway. Dodging Harry and Neville, both of whom bounded down the hallway toward Dory—all three dogs barking as they headed toward the back door—Frances narrowly escaped being trampled as she hurried into the kitchen to snatch the receiver from the charging station propped on the counter. "What?" she snapped as she reached over to open the back door and let out the dogs.

"Uh . . . Mrs. Snyder?" The woman on the other end of the phone sounded startled at the abruptness of her tone of voice. Immediately, she felt guilty. After all, it wasn't the woman's fault that everyone in her house ignored the call, unless, of course, it was another one of those annoying telemarketers.

"I'm sorry," Frances said, leaning against the counter and lifting her foot onto the nearby stool. She held the phone against her shoulder as she tried to straighten the strap of her black Coach heel. "It's been one of those mornings."

On the other end of the phone, the woman hesitated before she cleared her throat. "Dr. Steele asked me to give you a call."

Frances finished fixing her shoe and stood up straight. She wasn't really listening to what the woman was saying. Instead, she was going over a mental list of things she had to get done today: return Carrie's library books, shop for food, stop at the dry cleaner's, and go to that volunteer luncheon in Hoboken, not necessarily in that order. A routine follow-up call from her gynecologist's office wasn't on that list, but she briefly thought about adding it, just so she could cross it off when the receptionist, or whoever this was calling, gave her the all-too-anticipated news that her Pap smear was normal.

"That was nice of him," Frances said, walking over to the refrigerator. She needed to make sandwiches for Carrie and Andy. Otherwise, she'd be shelling out another ten dollars to cover their school lunches. Again. Most mornings, she felt like a walking ATM. Flinging open the refrigerator door, she quickly pulled out the lunch meat, cheese, and mayonnaise.

"You normally don't call after my exams," she mentioned. "Well, except that one time when we were in Jamaica." She laughed out loud as she began making sandwiches, the phone cradled between her ear and her shoulder as she worked. "That almost gave me a heart attack."

The woman didn't laugh with her. "Dr. Steele would like you to meet with Dr. Graham, one of his colleagues, over on James Street at the medical center."

"Oh?" Frances reached up to adjust her gold earring. "What for?"

Another hesitation.

Immediately Frances stopped fussing over the common everyday things that usually occupied her time. What seemed so important just moments ago was no longer on her mental to-do list. Feeling like a heavy weight in her chest, her heart started to pound as her palms began to sweat. Was it only last week that she had gone for her annual OB-GYN exam and biennial mammogram?

The woman finally responded. "There were some abnormalities on your mammogram," she said in a far-too-businesslike tone.

"Abnormalities? What kind of abnormalities?" Inwardly, she groaned. She knew far too well that abnormalities could be anything: a cyst, a shadow, a fibrous mass, even a bad reading by an inexperienced radiologist.

The sound of papers shuffling in the background made Frances wonder if the woman was looking through her file or merely glancing through a schedule, perhaps through her very own to-do list.

"I really couldn't say, Mrs. Snyder. I'm just relaying the information from Dr. Steele. Could you come into Dr. Graham's office this afternoon?" She paused long enough for Frances to picture her, a faceless person who didn't even have the courtesy of stating her name, looking at a computer screen, searching for an open appointment. "Say, two o'clock?"

"Today?"

"Uh . . . well, both Dr. Steele and Dr. Graham were fairly insistent that you come in today."

Frances heard the sound of heavy footsteps upstairs and turned her back to the open doorway that led into the hallway. "Why does Dr. Steele want me to see this . . . Dr. Graham?" Another question, and this time she suspected that she already knew the answer. "I have a meeting at noon. Can't this wait? I'm supposed to leave in a few hours for a luncheon in Hoboken. Traffic can be a killer . . ." The irony of what she just said hit her as soon as the words left her mouth. Lowering her voice, she asked, "If you don't mind my asking, what kind of doctor is this Dr. Graham?"

"He's a surgeon, Frances."

Frances? In almost twenty years of her going there, no one at Dr. Steele's office had ever called her by her first name with the exception of the doctor himself. Suddenly, she felt cold and began to shiver, her hand rubbing her arm as she stared at the far wall of the kitchen. "Is this something I should be concerned about?"

There was a very long pause. The silence answered her question. If she had answered with something light and airy like *It's probably nothing* or *Just being extra cautious*, Frances might not have felt that vise tightening around her chest for a second time that morning. But the woman didn't say any such thing, so Frances wasted no time popping off the top to her pill bottle and fishing out not one but two little white magic pills. Only this time, she wondered if two would do the trick.

"It's cancer, isn't it?" Frances glanced over her shoulder, hoping that her husband wasn't on his way downstairs yet. The last thing she needed was for him to overhear this conversation. She lowered her voice, then asked, "He found a tumor, didn't he?"

"I . . . I really couldn't say," the receptionist replied, stumbling over her words. "Is two o'clock OK with you, then?"

"Do you have anything earlier?" Suddenly that drive to Hoboken for the volunteer luncheon didn't seem so important. It didn't matter if they were finalizing the holiday fund-raiser and were already planning next year's Spring Fling. With her doctor insisting that she see this Dr. Graham right away, Frances knew that there was no way she could accomplish much of anything, not on a day that started like this one had. A morning that suddenly forced her to deal with panicking thoughts of breast cancer. Two o'clock sounded like far too long to wait. She immediately decided to send her regrets to the luncheon ladies because, without a doubt, she wanted to see Dr. Graham ASAP. No dillydallying. No delays. No wondering all morning what he would say to her. She needed to strive for efficiency. That's what Nicholas kept saying to her. Simply put, she did not have six hours to waste worrying about what she hoped was nothing.

But it seemed that this was just one more thing she could not control.

"Two o'clock is the earliest appointment that we have, I'm afraid," the still-nameless woman on the phone said in an apologetic tone.

When Frances hung up, she felt as if her entire future was being held hostage. She stole a quick glance at the clock on the microwave: 7:51 a.m. Over six hours. How could she possibly make the commute to and from Hoboken with *this* dangling over her head? She began to mentally reorganize her day, mapping out the logistics involved, despite the nagging suspicion that nothing would go right, regardless of how much planning and rearranging she did.

"Coffee ready?" Nicholas asked as he walked down the steps, heading through the hallway toward the kitchen. "What a day I have ahead of me," he complained. "Back-to-back meetings. Again."

Frances peered up. As usual, her husband looked especially polished in his custom-made gray suit and freshly ironed white shirt. He walked over to the back door and opened it for the patiently waiting dogs. "Who was on the phone?"

She didn't answer at first. Instead, she focused on getting his coffee. It would give her time to control her trembling hands.

When she turned around, the mug in hand, she noticed that he was struggling with his new red silk tie, trying to straighten the knot.

"Here." She handed him the coffee, and then without being asked, he lifted his chin and Frances took over the task of straightening his tie so that it lay perfectly flat and straight against his shirt, just the way he liked it.

"Dr. Steele's office," she responded at last. She hoped he wouldn't see through her calm exterior. The last thing she wanted was for him to witness her unravel. *Stay calm.* Her mind raced with the possibilities of what, exactly, could have triggered that early phone call.

Apparently, Nicholas thought the same thing as he looked at his wristwatch. "So early?" He raised the mug to his lips and carefully took a large swallow. "It's not even eight o'clock yet."

Frances didn't respond, focusing her attention on the tie.

"It's that lump, isn't it?" He reached up and grabbed her hands, stopping her from perfecting his tie. His face suddenly took on a more serious and concerned expression. "Frances, what did he say?"

For a few seconds Frances considered her options.

Nicholas hated it when she hid things from him. Still, he also hated it when she overreacted, always accusing her of blowing things out of proportion.

There are just some things that are better left unsaid, her mother had always proclaimed, usually when she was out shopping and buying, yet again, another dress that would hang in her closet, hidden from Frances's father. *A woman keeps the marriage together. That's our job. We*

have to reward ourselves with a little treat from time to time. You'll under-
stand when you get married.

Frances was sure that telling Nicholas would only irritate both of
them. He'd ask dozens of annoying questions and begin badgering her
for the answers, answers that she simply did not have. Yet. And *that*
would irritate *her*.

Besides, with the merger on the table, Nicholas was much busier
at work. This phone call with the little cryptic information that the
woman provided would certainly distract him and stress him out even
more than he already was. Even worse, he'd probably feel obligated to
go with her to Dr. Graham's office at two o'clock. That, too, would
turn into a problem since he always resented sitting around waiting for
doctors that wasted his time. During her first pregnancy with Andy,
Nicholas had grumbled and complained during every office visit, staring at his watch or tapping his fingers on the arm of the chair. It had
been even worse when she had Carrie. Everyone had thought Nicholas
was so adorable, pacing the floors and staring at the clock. Only Frances
knew the truth: he wasn't worried about *her*. Rather, he was worried
about being cut off from his clients and office when the nurse had made
him turn off his BlackBerry.

All of this went through her mind as he stared at her, waiting for
a response. His expression began to change from concern to irritation.
"Frances?"

Snapping out of her internal debate, she shook her head and forced
a smile. "He said nothing, Nicholas." She tried to reassure herself that
it wasn't a lie. In truth, it wasn't. After all, she hadn't even talked to the
doctor. "Everything's fine."

"You shouldn't have waited so long to get it checked," he scolded.
He finished the coffee and set the mug on the counter. He grabbed his
cell phone and began scrolling through his messages. "Any more coffee?"

The sandwiches forgotten, Frances walked over to the counter and
poured him another cup of coffee. She always put the timer on the night

before so that it would be ready and waiting when they both came down in the morning. When she handed him the piping-hot mug, he took it without thanking her.

"Don't forget that I have that meeting in New York later today."

His company's headquarters were in midtown Manhattan. However, they had a satellite office in Newark where he often worked. He usually had to commute into New York only to meet with clients when they were in town.

"Got it," she said. "So I shouldn't expect you until late, yes?"

He reached up and tugged at the knot of his tie, undoing what Frances had just done. He didn't answer her as he glanced down at his phone and then began answering early-morning e-mails.

"Come on, Rick!" he groaned.

"Something wrong?"

He shook his head as if her question was an inconvenience. "I told Rick to get the files ready for my meeting and have them couriered to the New York office. He's just now sending me a message asking me how many copies I need." A few choice words mumbled under his breath warned Frances not to ask any more questions.

"Mom!" Carrie called out as she and Andy began running down the stairs. The sound of four feet pounding on the hardwood steps interrupted any further conversation between Nicholas and Frances. It was always the same thing in the morning: silence, followed by an eruption of noise and energy as the children burst downstairs. When Andy reached the bottom of the staircase, he jumped over the last three steps and landed on the floor with a loud thud. Before Frances could say anything, Carrie tried to imitate her older brother, but instead of landing on the floor, she banged against the wall. Immediately, the three barking dogs joined in.

No matter how routine it was, the morning commotion always irritated Frances almost as much as the incessant telephone ringing. She leaned to the side and glared over Nicholas's shoulder at the children.

"Come on, guys! Let's go easy today!"

"Sorry, Mom!" Carrie said without any remorse in her voice as she darted past her mother and headed toward the pantry. As a tween, she was straddling the fence between child and teenager.

"Sorry, Momma!" Andy yelled. If Carrie did not sound remorseful, Andy sounded even less so. In fact, Frances fought the urge to cringe when Andy spoke: the more she had asked her son not to call her "Momma," the more he did so. To Frances, it sounded rednecky, as if they were living in the hollows of Pike County, Kentucky, and not in an upscale neighborhood in Morristown, New Jersey.

"Guess what?" Carrie asked as she slipped past her father. "Margot's having a party at the ice-skating rink, and she's not inviting Jade." She gave her mother a smug smile.

"I thought you were friends with Jade?"

Carrie scoffed. "Oh please! Like last year maybe!"

Andy pushed his way past his sister. "I seem to remember you crying last year when *you* didn't get invited to Jade's for a sleepover."

She raised her eyebrows and reached up to push back her shiny long hair. "Well, it's not me crying *this* year, is it?"

Over his sister's head, Andy glanced at his mother and rolled his eyes.

As if suddenly realizing that his children had entered the room, Nicholas looked up. "Hey, slugger. What's the good word?"

Andy grinned and puffed up his chest. "Starting quarterback this weekend at the away game. You gonna make it?"

"Wouldn't miss it for the world."

Andy looked at his mom again, and she knew that he was going to ask her the same question. But he hesitated too long. Carrie dove for the refrigerator and accidentally bumped into Frances.

"Easy, Carrie!" Andy snapped.

Instead of apologizing to her mother, Carrie yanked open the refrigerator door and pulled out the milk. Upon seeing it empty, she held it up.

"We're almost out, Mom," she said, waving the carton in the air. "Again."

Frances didn't need the reminder. "I know, I know."

"Did you remember to sign that field trip form?" Carrie slid the container of milk onto the counter and reached back into the refrigerator for the orange juice. "What the . . . ?" She looked at her mom and simultaneously shook the carton and her head. "Don't we have anything to drink around here?"

"I'm going food shopping today, Carrie."

"That doesn't help for now!" She slammed the refrigerator door and stomped to the other side of the counter. "Breakfast is the most important meal of the day!"

Andy reached out and pinched her.

"Ow!"

"Mom! What's up with the sandwiches?" he asked as he pulled his cell phone from his pocket to check the time. "You didn't finish them, and we have to catch the bus!"

She counted to ten. Twice.

"I'm finishing them now."

"Way to go, Mom." Carrie leaned against the counter and watched as Frances hurried to finish making their lunches. "It's your one job in the morning, Mom. Epic. Failure!"

Rather than get into a fight with her daughter, Frances bit her tongue at Carrie's irreverent and self-righteous statement. She reached into a drawer and pulled out the sandwich bags. Andy had already grabbed two bottles of water and set them on the counter, a small gesture of help, or perhaps an apology for his sister's attitude. So far, it was turning into a crappy Wednesday morning.

She needed the kids out of the house so that she could get ready for the day. Between cleaning and the ever-increasing pile of laundry, she had enough housework to keep her occupied all morning. At noon, she would meet with the fund-raising committee in Hoboken.

Her afternoon would consist of food shopping (*Thank you for the kind reminder, Carrie*), and then she would have to make dinner, a dinner that would be hastily swallowed by her two children without any consideration whatsoever for the amount of time she had put into cooking it. It would then be followed by a "Thank you, Mom" uttered out of habit rather than genuine appreciation.

And, of course, now she had that appointment with the surgeon. But she'd rather not think about that. It would distract her from her other tasks. The tasks that involved keeping her home in order and running smoothly, or, at least, attempting to achieve that lofty goal.

Home should be peaceful and calm, a haven of retreat and relaxation, her mother had always said. *Unless you want to work full-time and be away from your family, that's the job of the wife, Frances. Don't forget it.*

After so many years of listening to her mother and watching her cater to her husband and children, it had become the goal that Frances strived for on a daily basis. She was, after all, just a housewife, and just like her mother had told her, it was her job.

But no matter how hard she worked at it, she never quite achieved the ideal.

Nicholas glanced at his watch and lifted an eyebrow. "I've got to run. Traffic," he said. "You got these two?" He barely waited for an answer as he set his now-empty mug on the counter and walked out of the kitchen.

"Sure. Don't worry. I got it," she said to his back, not expecting an answer.

It was her standard reply to everything these days.

CHAPTER 2

She had managed to get into Hoboken and attend the luncheon, hoping that making small talk with five other women about the upcoming MoMA fund-raiser would distract her from thinking about her early-morning phone call from Dr. Steele's office. At a quarter to one, she had feigned a text message and excused herself from the table as if to make a phone call. When she returned, she apologized as she told them that she had to leave early to return to Morristown. All of this without demonstrating one ounce of the panic that had been building inside of her throughout the day.

A successful man needs a strong woman behind him, her mother had told Frances just before she had married Nicholas. *No one wants to be married to a hot mess. It just reflects badly on the entire family.*

Whether or not that was true, Frances knew better than to give anyone a reason to gossip about her. And, for the most part, she felt certain she succeeded. Long ago, she had mastered the stiff upper lip. She had, after all, learned from the best of them. The last thing she wanted was for Nicholas to hear otherwise from one of his business or golf partners via their wives.

Traffic back to Morristown wasn't half as cumbersome as she had expected, probably because the transition from morning rush to evening crush was yet to happen. While she waited to pay the toll on the turnpike, she listened to 105.5 on the radio, barely hearing the songs that were playing. When she realized that, her thoughts returned to the reason she was driving down the New Jersey Turnpike at one thirty in the afternoon. What were the abnormalities? Earlier in the morning she had forgone the cleaning and sat at her computer. Even though she knew she shouldn't, she spent an hour looking up mammograms and abnormalities. She knew it could be anything from nothing to a cyst to a clogged milk duct, although she doubted that last one. And, of course, there was always the possibility of the abnormality being the Big C. But cancer didn't run in her family, and she knew, just knew, that wasn't the problem.

She arrived at the doctor's office almost ten minutes early, something she hadn't planned on. Instead of entering the office and waiting inside, she remained in the car, her hands on the steering wheel as she stared at the front door of the building. People walked in and out, almost all of them elderly and with someone accompanying them, most likely a caregiver. No one appeared particularly happy, although there was one mother who smiled as her young son held her hand and skipped along the walkway. She wondered which one of them was the patient: mother or son.

That particular visual stayed with Frances for a few long minutes. Most likely, one of them was sick. Yet, from the outside looking in, everything appeared perfectly normal. There was no indication that anything was out of the ordinary. Frances wondered if, maybe, the little boy had just gotten a clean bill of health. Perhaps that was why the mother smiled. Or, if the mother was the one with the medical issue, perhaps she had just learned that the test results showed no sign of cancer.

But then why would she bring her young child with her?

No. Frances realized that the patient was most certainly the child, and therefore, the mother either was the greatest actress in the whole world or everything was as it should be.

Frances finally left her car, pausing only to lock the doors and glance at her reflection in the window. She knew she looked a bit tired. She *had* been feeling a bit run-down recently. She ran her fingers through her blond hair and frowned. Not only did she need a haircut, but her roots were starting to show. Just one more thing on her ever-increasing long list of things to do.

She took a deep breath and decided that she, too, would be like that mother: strong, defiant, and masked—no matter what the doctor said. After all, the odds were in her favor that it was, indeed, nothing. With a new sense of determination, she turned from the car and headed toward the building, wondering if anyone else was sitting in their car, their hands on the steering wheel, and watching her with the same questions she'd had just moments ago.

"So, Mrs. Snyder," Dr. Graham said as he entered the small examination room where Frances sat with a pink paper robe covering her naked chest.

He was an elderly man with thinning gray hair and faded blue eyes. The light-pink shirt and black tie emblazoned with the pink cancer ribbon screamed out that he was most likely married; how else to explain the perfectly starched garment and matching tie? One quick glance at his left hand told her that he didn't wear a wedding ring, but she could imagine that most surgeons wouldn't anyway.

He gave her a smile, a smile that was kind and compassionate as he asked, "How are you today?"

For a moment Frances merely stared at him, amazed at the irony of his question. *How am I? How should I be?*

However, she hadn't expected him to walk into the room and greet her with the one question that she didn't have an answer to.

Prior to a quarter to eight that morning, when she received that abrupt phone call from Dr. Steele's office, she'd had a full day of things to do, a schedule to follow, and a family to care for. Even though she had managed to muddle through the morning and keep her cool when Debbie Weaver remarked that Frances had missed the last two meetings—a not-too-subtle reminder that Frances was not pulling her weight on the committee—her mind had been secretly reeling with the thought that something might actually be wrong with her health.

Dr. Graham's smile caught Frances off guard, and for just a moment she thought that all of this was a mistake. Certainly he had reviewed her file and studied the mammogram images. He had good news for her. He wouldn't be smiling otherwise.

But just as fast as those thoughts went through her mind, she knew that it was just wishful thinking, something she wanted to hear: *This was all a mistake, Frances* and *Sorry for wasting your time and causing undue alarm.* However, she also knew that his smile and greeting were probably standard protocol for most doctors. Dr. Graham's calm demeanor might not mean that everything was fine; in fact, she suspected that it might mean the opposite.

"Well, I suppose I'd feel a lot better if I knew why I was here," she replied, hoping that her voice didn't sound as edgy as she felt.

He leaned against the counter and sink, leaving his hands folded in front of him. *A very nonconfrontational body language sign,* she thought, wishing that she could feel optimistic but knowing that the reality of the situation was quite different. Optimism would have required a *No need to worry, Mrs. Snyder; it's just a precaution to send you to the surgeon* from Dr. Steele's assistant when she had called earlier. Pessimism was sitting here in a strange doctor's office, waiting for him to explain the reasons for such an urgent appointment.

To her relief, he did not waste time in providing that answer.

"Your mammogram results came back, and Dr. Steele noticed an abnormality in your left breast."

The lump.

She had first felt it six months earlier, back in May. It hurt when she touched it. She hadn't thought much about it, especially since she wore only underwire bras, which she hated but never had time to replace. When she first felt the tiny lump under her left arm by the side of her breast, the wire had just broken free from the stitching and had been jabbing her. It wasn't until Nicholas touched her one night and she winced from the pain that she realized it hadn't gone away, even after she threw out the old bra.

"OK," Frances responded to the doctor, forcing herself to remain calm.

"You've been having some pain there, too, yes?"

She nodded once.

"The mammogram also showed some puckered skin at the site, so we'd like to do an ultrasound, and then depending on how that goes, a biopsy."

Biopsy?

"I'm prone to cysts," she quickly pointed out.

This time it was Dr. Graham who nodded.

"I saw that in Dr. Steele's notes."

"It's probably nothing, right?" She noticed a shadow cover his eyes. "I did research this morning while I was waiting. Breast cancer doesn't hurt, right? So it's probably just another cyst."

Dr. Graham contemplated her question. He stared at her with light-grayish-blue eyes for a moment too long, and Frances felt that racing feeling in her chest again. Why hadn't she thought to bring her Xanax? She hoarded them, always trying to talk herself out of using them until she felt as if her heart might explode. This, however, was the perfect moment to take one without feeling any guilt, and she had left them at home.

"Let's see what the ultrasound says before ruling anything out, shall we?" he responded at last.

Without waiting for her reaction, he opened the door and called for an assistant to come into the room. Frances couldn't even look at the woman who greeted her with a cheerful hello. Instead, she tried to find her inner place, the only place that she could retreat to when things became overwhelming. She focused on her breathing, feeling her chest rise and fall as the doctor told her to lie down. He was fumbling with a machine while his assistant flicked off the lights. She felt the doctor open the front of her pink paper gown and heard him ask her to raise her left arm over her head. With complete automation, Frances did as he instructed, still trying to steady the rapid rise and fall of her chest.

"You are going to feel something cold," he said, just before he squirted something from a clear bottle onto what looked like a wide probe. The thick gel looked just like what her doctor had used when she'd gone for her prenatal checkups and in-office ultrasounds. "This won't hurt at all, though," he added.

Frances remained silent, staring up at the ceiling and feeling herself slip into a zone. She was no longer lying supine on an examination table with a doctor gently pressing the ultrasound device against her skin, moving it around with one hand as he pressed buttons on the machine with the other. Instead, Frances was . . . nowhere. She felt weightless and free, as if she were floating through the air. She heard a ringing in her ears, which helped drown out the noises from the machine.

After no more than five minutes, Dr. Graham shut off the machine, and his assistant stepped forward to gently wipe the gel off her skin. Frances anxiously stared at him.

"Stay there, please," he instructed.

Dear God, she prayed. *Please. Not me. Not now.*

His assistant was rolling another cart from the far side of the room to the examination table. With her nerves on fire, Frances listened to the rattle of the metal wheels and then, once the cart was situated, to the sound of packages being opened and sterile utensils being laid out.

"Frances? You hanging in there?" Dr. Graham asked.

She turned her head, hating the noise of the crinkly paper coming from the table. "What did you see?"

He leaned over her so that she didn't have to strain her neck. "I want to do that biopsy, Frances."

Alarmed, she started to sit up. "What? Why?"

He pressed his hand to her shoulder and gently pressed her back onto the table. "It's standard procedure when the ultrasound shows something suspicious, Frances. We try the noninvasive methods first, but if we cannot rule out what we are looking for, then a biopsy becomes necessary."

She raised her hand to her forehead and shut her eyes. Dr. Graham began to explain what he was going to do, but she already knew. Earlier that morning she had read about biopsies, which were conducted when the other tests, such as the mammogram and ultrasound, couldn't rule out breast cancer. A needle would be inserted into her chest—and into what Frances hoped would prove to be a benign cyst—to extract tissue cells. A lab would test them and return the verdict, which was either immunity or a death sentence. At least that was how it felt as she straddled the fence between the two.

"Now, we're going to use the ultrasound as we perform the fine-needle aspiration. It will help guide us to the area in question," he said. "I won't lie and tell you that you won't feel anything . . ."

She started to jump up again.

"But it's only a slight pinch. I think most people are alarmed more at the idea than the actual feeling," he continued.

This is not happening. This is simply not happening. She shut her eyes and covered them with her forearm, willing herself not to cry. But as she heard Dr. Graham talk to his assistant, using medical terms that she couldn't quite understand, tears welled up through her eyelids.

The nurse pressed a tissue into her hand and tried to reassure her with some soft words that Frances didn't even understand. Her mind was tuned into one thing and one thing only: a strange doctor whom, until just half an hour ago, she had never met was going to insert a needle into her breast.

All her life, Frances had been rather prudish when it came to her body. In fact, prior to meeting Nicholas, she had been with only two other men, one of whom she thought she was going to marry. When she began dating Nicholas, a full two years after the tumultuous breakup with Sam, she'd refused to engage in any form of intimacy until the engagement ring was on her finger and a date was set.

For some reason, that had not discouraged Nicholas; instead, it had provoked his passion even more.

After six months of dating, they were engaged, and it was another six months until they were married.

Now, regardless of the fact that Dr. Graham was a doctor, to have a stranger probing at her breast was almost an affront to her sense of propriety. Like a tidal wave of mental angst, a dozen different thoughts crossed her mind: she should have told Nicholas the truth about the phone call, she should have asked for a female surgeon, she should have considered a second opinion of her mammogram records, she should have never been here in the first place. At least not without her husband at her side.

"Relax, Frances," the female assistant said. "If it helps, you can squeeze my hand."

"I don't understand any of this," she sobbed as she let his assistant take her left hand in hers, holding it tightly.

"You're going to feel the pinch now," Dr. Graham said in a soft voice.

Then she experienced the piercing sensation in her sensitive breast as it was penetrated by the needle. She cringed as every muscle tightened in her body, and then cried out as the pain didn't stop. In fact, unlike the regular shots she used to receive as a child or the blood draws she sometimes got as an adult, the needle continued to burrow even deeper.

Catching her breath, Frances squeezed the assistant's hand. She tried to think of something happy, to find a memory that would take her away from the current moment. But all she could think about was Mrs. Bentley and whether she had gone through something like this. It had been decades since she'd thought about that uncomfortable day when her mother made her pose next to their neighbor in that red sled for a Christmas photograph. *More than thirty years is a long time when it comes to medical advances.* Surely they didn't have such technology back then, technology that, today, might have helped save Mrs. Bentley's life.

"We're almost done, Frances. You hanging in there?"

She tried to nod, but couldn't. Instead, she murmured, "Mmm-hmm" to acknowledge his question.

After what seemed like another five minutes, but in reality was more like one, the doctor withdrew the needle and quickly put a bandage over the tiny puncture site. The assistant waited a few seconds before gently releasing Frances's hand.

"That wasn't so bad, was it now?" the woman asked.

More tears came to Frances's eyes. The biopsy was over, and while just having had it was bad enough, she knew that worse things might be ahead. She couldn't imagine losing her breast or going through chemotherapy. She knew she would have to pray to God that he take this cup away from her. She couldn't go through with the emotional and physical upheaval that cancer would throw into her life. Cancer was something that God would just have to give to someone else.

The doctor left the room to give her some privacy while she changed back into her clothes. Her side hurt, and her head was pounding with a dull ache that she knew wouldn't go away anytime soon. Stress had a way of doing that to her. And this was more stressful than anything she had been through before. Even worse, this time she had gone through it alone.

In hindsight, perhaps she should have told Nicholas. But she hadn't known that the procedure was going to take place. She had thought she was meeting with the surgeon to discuss the mammogram results. But apparently they wanted to do the biopsy right after the ultrasound, which was more than worrisome, to say the least.

For a moment she paused. She knew very few women who had been diagnosed with breast cancer, an oddity in itself since at least one out of eight women get it, according to that morning's hasty research on WebMD.com. Frances was relatively young; she had just celebrated her forty-second birthday less than a month ago. Most women seemed to get breast cancer at a much older age. She didn't know anyone in her limited circle of friends and acquaintances that had gone through it. *My God.* Her fingers paused over the last button of her silk blouse. *They wanted me to come so fast because they already* know *that I have breast cancer.*

The door opened and Dr. Graham walked in. He had an appointment card and reached out to hand it to her. "Friday at nine o'clock you should come in so we can go over the results," he said.

"You already know," she whispered.

His expression faltered for just a quick second. And then he shook his head, never once losing eye contact with her. "We won't know anything until the results come back, Frances."

She narrowed her eyes, distrusting him for the first time that day. She reluctantly accepted the card and slid it into the side pocket of her purse. *After all, what else could he have possibly said?*

As she walked out of the medical building, she inhaled the crisp autumn air and sighed. She had about forty hours until she would return to learn the truth—whether or not she was right and Dr. Graham was just putting her through the motions because he already knew what the answer was. Frances, though, had to wait until Friday at nine, and it didn't seem fair.

CHAPTER 3

"Cancer?" Despite being in public, Charlotte practically shouted the word, not caring if anyone overheard her.

In a panic, Frances started to wave her hands in the air and frantically glanced around, hissing, "Shh!"

Despite her attempt to quiet her friend, she saw that several people were already looking at them. They were sitting at a sidewalk table on South Street in Morristown, the restaurant overlooking the town square—the Green, as it was referred to. Being a late Thursday afternoon, and despite the fact that it was too late for lunch yet too early for dinner, all the outdoor tables were already crowded with people. Even though it was October, people tended to flock to the center of Morristown so they could enjoy coffee outside of Starbucks or a glass of wine at the numerous spots that offered outdoor seating on the extra-wide sidewalks. Ever since the real estate boom, Morristown had thrived and was now home to over fifty restaurants and bars.

Earlier that morning, and after much deliberation, Frances had texted her friend Charlotte, asking if they could get together in the afternoon. Simply put, Frances needed to confide in someone about everything that had happened in the past twenty-four hours. The memory of yesterday's biopsy was still raw, and the countdown to tomorrow's meeting, when she would hear the test results, kept her on edge. She needed a voice of reason, something that Charlotte Parker always had.

But she didn't want the entire town to know about it.

"Keep your voice down," Frances whispered.

Charlotte frowned and leaned forward, her black hair cascading over her face. Abruptly, she pushed it away, tucking a strand behind her ear. She was a pretty woman with deep chocolate eyes and perfect heart-shaped lips, which were currently pursed as she said, "You think you might have breast cancer, and you're worried that someone might overhear me? Something is wrong with this picture."

"I . . . I just don't want anyone to know. Not until I know what's going on." Maybe she should have waited to tell her best friend. Unfortunately, ever since she'd left Dr. Graham's office the previous day, she hadn't been able to think about anything else. All night she had tossed and turned, switching between total optimism that the biopsy would be benign and complete pessimism that her doctors already knew the truth and were just going through the motions, unable to change the course of the cancer. The former thought tended to lose out to the latter, and after a fitful sleep, Frances realized that she needed someone to talk to. Now she was worried that she'd made a mistake.

Charlotte shook her head, a strand of her hair falling across her forehead this time and casting a shadow over her eyes. It helped Frances to not be forced to look into her best friend's eyes. During their fourteen-year friendship, they had been through thick and thin. The one thing that Frances could count on was Charlotte's brutal honesty. Sometimes it was a blessing, other times a curse.

"You're kidding me, right? Please tell me you're not serious!" Charlotte took a long deep breath and leaned back in her chair. "You aren't going to pull one of your Carrie maneuvers, are you?"

Frances looked up and pursed her lips. "That's just not fair. You know how Nicholas felt about having a second child. I had no choice but to wait to tell him."

However, she knew that Charlotte wasn't likely to accept her complaint. And since her friend was also never one to keep her opinions to herself, Frances wasn't surprised when Charlotte responded in a terse tone.

"What's not fair is you taking on the world by yourself, Fran. This is complete baloney. You've gone beyond the call of duty, more than anyone should have to. Don't play the stoic soldier on this one."

Playing with the edge of her white cloth napkin, Frances stared at her untouched glass of chardonnay.

"It's early yet," she offered in a soft voice, still hoping that no one could overhear their conversation. Both she and Nicholas had grown up in Morristown. She never knew when someone might recognize her. "I'm probably jumping the gun anyway."

"I see." Charlotte drummed her fingers on the edge of the table, studying Frances's face with a strong, steely gaze. "And Nicholas? What does *he* think about all of this?"

"Oh, I . . . well . . ."

"Mmm-hmm." Charlotte then exhaled, a sound that reflected palpable frustration. She leveled her eyes at Frances. "You didn't tell him, did you? Why am I not surprised?"

Definitely a mistake. "You know how he gets, Charlie."

"No. No, I don't," she snapped back through clenched teeth. "And you know why? I'll tell you why. Because you take everything upon yourself. You think you are Wonder Woman. You always have, too."

This time Frances narrowed her eyes. "Again, not fair."

"Sure. Right." Charlotte reached for her beer and took a healthy swig before adding, "Sometimes you need to lean on someone else's shoulders."

When she set her glass back down, small droplets of condensation landed on the tablecloth. Frances watched as they spread out, creating a polka-dot pattern. Not one of them connected, and she couldn't help but recognize the irony.

"Look, I'm telling you because I . . . I just don't have anyone else to talk to right now."

And that was the truth.

Her parents lived in Florida, and she was estranged from her siblings, one of whom lived in New York City and the other, a struggling actor, in Los Angeles. It had been years since Frances had talked to either one of them. When her parents had lived in town, neither her sister nor her brother had done much more than call them, and that was only when they needed something, usually money. It irritated Frances how little respect they showed to the two people who had not only raised them and sent them to college (or, in the case of her brother, *offered* to send him—he refused but suggested they could fund his efforts in Los Angeles instead) but also never once turned them away when they needed financial assistance. It also bothered Frances that she worked endless hours to create that perfect balance in her life and had never once asked for a handout. Yet it was her, not her sister and certainly not her brother, who called and visited their parents on a regular basis and remained a concerned fixture in their lives.

"OK, OK," Charlotte conceded. "But you need to keep me in the loop, Fran. Not like the last few times."

The past. Always the past. Frances pressed her lips together and looked away. Just because they'd been friends for so long didn't mean she had to share everything with Charlotte, did it? Of course, Charlotte always had an intuitive way of sensing when things were out of sync. Perhaps that was both the best and worst part of having a best friend: they often knew more about you than you knew about yourself.

"I've never hidden anything from you, have I?"

Charlotte raised an eyebrow and gave Frances one of those looks that burned through her. "Really?"

"Really."

"Well, I suppose that's true, to some degree," Charlotte said, tapping her well-manicured fingers against the tabletop. "You might tell me everything; you just don't *volunteer* everything. It's like squeezing water out of a rock to get information from you."

"There are some things that should be kept private."

"That's your mother talking."

"No." But Frances leaned toward the possibility that Charlotte might be correct. It wasn't just that her mother did things in a certain way; it was that her mother did things so perfectly. Was there anything really wrong with trying to mimic her example?

Despite the serious nature of the conversation, Charlotte laughed. "When are you going to cut the umbilical cord and become your own person? You need to realize that your mother's way doesn't have to be *your* way." Charlotte's dark eyes started to soften. "Anyway, there's no privacy between us. We're sisters, remember? Or, at least, closer than any sister either one of us ever had."

At this comment Frances smiled. "Against all odds, right?"

Lifting her glass up, Charlotte held it out toward her friend in a mock cheer. "You got that right, sis!" She took a long sip and set the glass back down on the table. "Who would have thought that my ex-husband would have brought us together after he dated your sister?" Another laugh. "I don't know whether I should thank her or curse her for not having married him. She dodged that bullet."

Frances had never liked Gary. He was controlling, manipulative, and clearly unfaithful. At one point he had cheated on her sister with Charlotte and later cheated on Charlotte with her sister.

"She may have," Frances admitted slowly, "but at your expense, though."

Giving a casual shrug of her shoulders, Charlotte seemed unaffected. "Perhaps, but at least we found each other."

For a moment she remained silent. Frances watched as Charlotte seemed to ponder something, and knew that whatever it was, it wouldn't remain a secret for long. Her eyes drifted over Charlotte's shoulder to a woman who was walking behind a German shepherd with a leather harness. The dog stopped at the curb by the traffic light, waiting patiently for the light to change from green to red so that it could lead the woman across the street. Although it was a common sight in their town, it struck her differently today for some reason.

Morristown was home to the Seeing Eye, a nonprofit organization that bred and trained dogs for the legally blind. Carrie was always begging her parents to foster one of the puppies until it was ready to be trained and then paired with a blind person. They had finally agreed that, when Carrie turned sixteen and could handle the responsibility, they would take in a puppy. *That's just going to have to wait now. I guess everyone has problems. Why should I be any different?*

"We've been friends now for almost fifteen years, right?" Charlotte said wistfully.

Frances turned her attention back to her friend. "That's about right. Just after Andy was born."

"And I've been divorced for . . ." She squinted her eyes as she mentally calculated in her head. "Six years?"

"It was five years ago."

"That's it?" Her eyes opened and she stared at Frances. "Wow. Feels like a lot longer!"

That did not surprise Frances. Her friend's marriage had ended even before it began. Gary had been nothing short of a control freak narcissist since long before they said "I do." The only problem had been that, while Charlotte had stood by her vows, Gary had not. Over and over again, until his cavorting could no longer be ignored. Fortunately, they hadn't had any children. Unfortunately, they had amassed quite a lot of assets: properties, investments, even cars. Or so Charlotte had thought. The divorce had been messy and had dragged on far too long for anyone to make much sense of anything, especially with the way the judicial system worked, or as Charlotte would say, didn't work. What her experience had taught Frances was that "until death do us part" looked far easier than the alternative.

"But it took four years to finalize it," Charlotte said in a flat voice. "Don't forget that he left me with nothing. Sold the investments, bankrupted the properties, and ruined my car that night."

"What's your point?"

"They're bastards." She gazed at Frances. "All of them. Don't forget it. We can sugarcoat it, paint over it, pretend that things are peachy keen. But deep down, they're all the same, Fran. Unless, of course, you are one of the lucky ones who develops a thick skin and two blind eyes."

Her words sent a chill through Frances. She felt the fine hair on her arms tingle, so she rubbed them, hating the way her skin puckered into tiny goose bumps under her fingers.

"You aren't telling Nicholas for a reason." Her matter-of-fact tone said more than her words. "And that will come back to haunt you, Frances. Remember when you stopped taking birth control pills and didn't tell him?"

Frances bit her lower lip.

"Do I need to remind you how he reacted when he found out?"

She shook her head. That was a memory she wanted to forget and had worked hard, every day, to make certain that he, too, forgot.

"Do you really want to go through that again?" Charlotte raised an eyebrow. "Eventually all secrets are discovered, Fran. And this one is right up there with you hiding your pregnancy."

Lifting her chin, Frances refused to break Charlotte's gaze. Charlotte might be tough and may have suffered through more than Frances could ever imagine, but she knew that holding it together was some-times just as hard, if not harder, than fighting to escape.

"I have no idea what you are talking about," she lied. "Nicholas wasn't *that* upset when he found out about Carrie."

Charlotte averted her eyes. "You can pretend that your skin is thicker than most, but you are not impenetrable. I was there when it happened, Frances. I lived through it with you. And trust me, if you don't confront the mistakes of your past, you won't be able to move forward into the future," she said. "A cancer-free future, mind you."

The conversation ended abruptly—thankfully, as far as Frances was concerned—when the waiter came over to see how they were doing. Like always, the tension from the conversation quickly dissipated. After glancing at her watch, Charlotte asked for the check.

"I have to show a house in an hour," she said apologetically. "But we are *not* finished with this conversation." She handed the waiter her credit card and waited for him to leave. "When is your next appointment?"

"Tomorrow," Frances answered. "I'm meeting with this Dr. Graham on James Street at nine. He's going to discuss the biopsy results with me then."

Charlotte frowned. "Biopsy? That sounds serious."

"It . . . it wasn't pleasant." Her admission felt like the first step in a twelve-step program. The fresh memory of lying on that examina-tion table, her face to the institutional green wall as she cried from the pain, both physical and psychological, would haunt her forever. Out of all the things that she'd been through in her life, having a long needle shoved into the side of her breast ranked high on the list. "But, hopefully, everything will be fine. I mean . . ." She paused and finally sipped her chardonnay, which was, unfortunately, no longer chilled. "I had that cyst a few years ago, remember? It was in the same spot, so I'm sure that's just what it is." She looked over the top of her wineglass at her friend. "Right?"

Never one to mince words or play pretend in the midst of a crisis, Charlotte responded with a simple shrug of her shoulders. "I'm around tomorrow if you need to talk," she said as she signed the credit card receipt and shoved the waiter's pen in her purse.

Tomorrow. Frances gave Charlotte a quick hug good-bye and watched her walk down the sidewalk. She lifted her wineglass to her lips, choosing to sit and finish it rather than hurry home to the chaos that undoubtedly awaited her.

CHAPTER 4

As Frances sat, waiting, on the same table as she had on Wednesday, she felt depressed. An inevitable feeling of déjà vu had overtaken her when she stepped into Dr. Graham's examination room just a few minutes earlier. This time, however, she did not wear a pink paper gown. For a second she wondered why she had not been escorted into the doctor's office. *Isn't that where patients are told the test came back negative?*

Dr. Graham knocked, then entered the room, pausing to shut the door behind him. When he turned around, Frances was stunned. There was absolutely nothing she could read from his blank expression. No fear. No hope. No apology.

Instead, he met her eyes and simply said, "The biopsy results came back positive." No greeting, no inquiry as to how she was doing. He merely jumped right into the thick of things and got down to business. This, too, was something Frances figured was a learned behavior, from a man who most likely had said those exact words hundreds of times over the course of his career. She could only imagine that his experience had taught him the direct approach was the best course of action when delivering bad news.

"Of course." That was all she offered in response. She had expected to hear those words, spent the past few days preparing herself for this news. For some reason, she wasn't surprised, and she didn't feel a tightening in her chest. It was as if something switched inside of her and, suddenly, she was on autopilot.

Since Dr. Graham didn't sugarcoat his words, she wasn't going to sugarcoat hers, either. Despite the fact that she had hoped for a better outcome, she had prepared herself for the worst.

He raised an eyebrow at her response. "Of course?"

She nodded her head, adding, "I anticipated that." She paused, thinking for a minute. "Maybe I already knew you'd say that since Wednesday. There was a look on your face. In fact, I bet you already knew, too, didn't you?"

He didn't respond to her question. She suspected that her reaction was unusual and caught him off guard. That, too, she expected. After all, she imagined that most of his patients, upon hearing *We found cancer cells*, did not surrender to the verdict without a fight. But she had already accepted the inevitable, long before she actually heard the words.

She felt nothing. And *that* was a change from the daily stress and panic that she felt.

With a tinge of curiosity, she watched Dr. Graham's reaction, but he was very adept at masking his emotions. Perhaps he was wondering how she could react with such composure, not with tears or bargaining or even disbelief. The answer was simple: time was of the essence. The longer patients fought the diagnosis or waited for second opinions, the longer it took to begin treatment. And Frances knew that too much of a delay could make treatment more complicated and less efficient. Without immediate intervention, a patient's condition could reach a more critical stage.

Complete acceptance was an important element of the healing and recovery process. It took a healthy mind for a sick body to regenerate.

"Even though it doesn't run in my family," she said in a flat voice, "I'd like to run a genetic test for my daughter's sake."

He nodded his head. "That's the BRCA test. We can arrange for that."

For a moment she sat there, realizing that everything she thought she knew about her future had just changed. And while a thousand questions slowly began swirling around inside of her head, she knew she must stay focused. She'd have time to digest this news later.

But there was one question that she needed answered.

"Dr. Graham, how far along is it?" She braced herself for the answer.

He gave her a look, his eyes full of empathy for her unspoken fears. "I don't know, Frances. Not yet."

She nodded in understanding, even though she didn't understand. How could a doctor state that she had cancer but not know what stage it was? The staging of the tumor would determine not just the possible treatment but the outcome. "Could you at least speculate?"

He sighed and crossed his arms over his chest. "Just from speculating, from the size of the lump on the initial ultrasound, it appears to be stage two. Until we remove lymph nodes, we won't be able to officially stage it. However, there were definitive cancer cells in the tissue. Malignant cancer cells."

Malignant cancer cells. Something that Frances had never expected to hear, even after the biopsy and the two restless nights that followed two very unproductive days. *Cancer.* Such an ugly word. A word that changed lives as much as a new baby or divorce did. However, cancer was uninvited, more like the latter than the former. Nobody was ever excited about either one of them.

For a while she didn't know how to respond. The memory of the painful biopsy quickly faded away as the fear of what lay ahead presented her with a new challenge. Would there be surgeries? Chemotherapy? Radiation? Would it go into remission? What if it returned?

She felt that all-too-familiar tightening in her chest and knew that she'd need to take a Xanax when she got home. Suddenly, all the things that had felt so important, such as making certain Andy didn't wrestle with the dogs in the living room or monitoring Carrie with her obsessive texting and tweeting, to her very own fixation regarding the lights being turned off in the entire house before bedtime, no longer mattered. Even Nicholas's constant late nights and MIA weekends didn't matter. Instead, she could think of only one thing: fighting this unfair verdict.

"I've always been healthy, Dr. Graham," she said at last. "Taken care of my body."

He stood in front of her, an empathetic look on his face. She couldn't help but wonder if this was a practiced response on his part: waiting for the patient to process such unfortunate and unwanted information. Certainly he must have said those same words—*There were definitive cancer cells*—to hundreds, perhaps thousands, of women over the past few years and obviously knew the importance of giving the patient time to process the news before discussing treatment options.

Time. It was a small gift, so she took what she could of it.

"I . . . I have two children, and I volunteer at the Museum of Modern Art in Manhattan. My kids have activities. My son plays football. My daughter, Carrie, likes ballet." Her hands trembled, and she slid them under her thighs so he couldn't see them shaking. If Frances was modest about her body, she had learned long ago to keep her emotions in reserve, an emollient that seemed to help thwart disappointment over the years.

As she sat there, she realized that there was an invader in her core, an unwelcome guest who'd snuck into her life and was threatening to steal her chance of achieving the perfectly manicured balance that was expected of her. And even if she hadn't yet achieved it, she knew that her children needed her. Her house needed her. She had been the pillar sustaining her family, perhaps not financially, but at least on the home front. Without her, things would inevitably crumble. Food wouldn't get ordered. Dry cleaning wouldn't get picked up. Children would miss after-school activities. Family vacations wouldn't get planned. That was her role, the one that she had accepted after the birth of her firstborn, even if Nicholas had not been thrilled about shouldering the brunt of the financial responsibilities.

"And my husband . . . he has a job. An important job. And he hates going to doctors. There has to be some sort of a mistake. There isn't any way that I can have cancer." She paused, removing her hands and nervously placing them onto her lap. Her wall of fortitude was cracking. She willed her hands to stop shaking while fighting the urge to cry. Shedding tears was something she simply did not do. Crying would not make the diagnosis change. Instead, she took a deep breath and met the doctor's concerned gaze. "I'm sorry. I didn't mean . . ."

Dr. Graham gave her a compassionate smile. "It's a lot to process. This disease makes people emotional. An apology is not necessary."

Frances straightened her shoulders, grateful that she had caught herself before she lost it completely. "I want you to understand that you are treating me, the person, not just the disease."

"Mrs. Snyder . . ."

She held up one of her hands, which, mercifully, had stopped shaking. "My family is busy. Work. School. Sports. So this needs to be as minimally invasive as possible for their lives. I don't want to distract them. I can't be a burden to them."

"I understand how you feel . . ."

"No!" Then, taking a deep breath, she slowly counted to ten. Her coping mechanism. Losing control was also something that she rarely did. It was unproductive and a bad example for her children. She'd learned to control those impulses, just like her mother had. In a much calmer tone, she said, "No, you don't understand how I feel. You aren't me."

He reached for the tissue box and handed it to her, but she waved it away. Certainly offering a Kleenex was part of his normal protocol with newly diagnosed breast cancer patients. Frances didn't need to ask how many women cried after being told they had cancer. He seemed surprised that she didn't need a tissue. There would be no tears from her.

"Mrs. Snyder, I understand that you are going to need some time to digest all of this. Perhaps it's better if we reschedule our meeting until your husband can—"

Frances interrupted him with a soft one-word response: "No." The last thing she wanted was to include Nicholas in any of these preliminary discussions. To begin with, he'd want to know why she hadn't told him the truth about the phone call on Wednesday morning. If she had to explain the delay, she might as well find out more about the treatment first. Then there was the issue with the acquisition of the Chicago company. He had trips coming up and meetings. Always the meetings. If she could just shield him from having to reschedule those, at least for a short while. And, of course, the real reason was something she didn't want to share with Dr. Graham. Not now. Probably not ever.

"No, Dr. Graham," she repeated in that calm, composed voice. "You can talk to *me* about the options."

Dr. Graham's eyes narrowed, and for the first time, he glanced down at the manila folder that contained her paperwork. Frances wondered how thick it would become by the end of this ordeal. For now, it contained only a few documents, the first one filled out in her own handwriting. It was the document that contained her insurance information, health history, and emergency contact information.

"I'm sorry." His eyes scanned the paper as if searching for something. "I thought you had indicated you were married."

"I am."

Dr. Graham looked at her again, this time with a look of confusion on his face. "Then I don't understand. Shouldn't your husband be part of the decision-making process?"

"No."

One word. No explanation. She had none to give, not that he would understand anyway.

"No? Just no?"

When she didn't respond, the doctor gave her another questioning look.

Frances shook her head. "Not yet. Not until I know more. There's no point in getting everyone all topsy-turvy until we have all the facts."

He set down her file on the counter and crossed his arms in front of his chest. Leveling his gaze at her, he studied her face for a long moment. "Frances, I don't think you understand. This will go fast. Very fast. There will be breast MRIs, CT scans, and probably a PET scan, too. We'll need these tests in order to determine a treatment plan."

She knew all this from her online research.

"You are also going to need some moral support," he continued. "And it's always better to have a second set of ears to hear what we are telling you. Sometimes emotions can get in the way of decision-making . . ."

"I can assure you that won't happen." But, even as she said that, her mind was whirling with a hundred different thoughts. *Cancer.* How could she possibly fit cancer into her busy life? How could she juggle everything if she had to face a life-threatening illness? And the most important question: How could her marriage possibly survive something as awful as breast cancer?

But then her conversation with Charlotte flickered into her mind.

"I do have moral support," she heard herself say. "At least enough until there is a plan."

"I really think that it's best . . ."

But Frances didn't acquiesce.

There was nothing wrong with her simply going through those tests and waiting until the doctor knew more about her treatment program, she reasoned. Why upset the children just yet? Why get Nicholas involved, especially when he was so busy right now, until she had more information about her treatment? She needed the complete picture before she told Nicholas, and only then would they tell the children, together.

She remembered far too well how people tended to treat cancer patients from her own experience. Her childhood neighbor, the woman at church, even the woman at Nicholas's work. It became all about everyone else, people lobbying to start food chains and help with childcare, all the while gossiping behind the patient's back, speculating about her survival rates. Even her own mother had taught her that cancer patients were to be pitied, and that was something Frances couldn't fathom.

"What's best, Dr. Graham, is that we figure out the strongest course of treatment and discuss all the options available to me," she said. "The least invasive preferably. Then I will discuss it with my family."

He shook his head and glanced down at his notes. Clearly, he was not happy with the way things were going. Frances realized that he probably hadn't encountered such a reaction from his hundreds of other cancer patients. But he really had no choice at this point. She was his patient, and she hadn't signed a HIPAA waiver. Legally, he could not contact her husband nor could he discuss anything with him. For now, this would remain a discussion between Frances and Dr. Graham. No third parties would be involved unless it was a specialist offering medical treatment.

And, for now, she intended for it to remain so, at least until she decided differently.

CHAPTER 5

"And then Betsy started crying at the lunch table!" Carrie shoved a forkful of pasta into her already full mouth. "Can you believe it? Crying!" She chewed for a few seconds before shaking her head and adding, "I can't believe you used to make me play with her!"

"I can't believe anyone names their kid *Betsy!*" Andy chimed in with an unkind laugh. "What kind of name is that, anyway? It sounds like an old lady's name!"

Frances stood on one side of the counter, her head pounding and her nerves just about shot as she watched her two children eating their dinner. They'd been home for less than an hour, and already she was counting down the minutes until she could retire to her bedroom for some peace and quiet.

"I don't think it's nice to laugh at someone who cried," she heard herself say.

"What?" Carrie dropped her fork onto her plate, which sounded like nails on a chalkboard to Frances. "Are you kidding me? She's the silliest creature in the world! She cries all the time, Mom. She's in eighth grade for crying out loud! Eighth grade!"

Trying to maintain her composure, Frances looked at her daughter. "You don't know what's going on in her life, Carrie. Maybe you could be a little more compassionate."

With a roll of her eyes, Carrie showed what she thought of her mother's comments. "You just don't get it, Mom. She's a geek. A total nothing. A big crybaby. And you wanted me to be friends with her?" Then she shuddered in a dramatic way, as if the thought of them being friends was beyond her comprehension.

. "Yeah, and you used to have a crush on Johnny Farmer! I'd be more embarrassed about that!" Andy said, then laughed as Carrie punched him in the arm. When he lashed back at her, Carrie jumped back and let out a screech, knocking over her water glass, which shattered on the tile floor.

The sound of the glass hitting the floor shot through Frances's head like an exploding cannonball.

"Could the both of you knock it off?" Putting her hands up to the side of her head, she squeezed her fingers hard against her temples. The constant noise, persistent bickering, and inconsiderate self-focus were more than she could handle tonight.

For a brief moment the kitchen fell silent. Andy gave his sister a look of disgust before getting up to retrieve the broom and dustpan from the pantry. Frances moved her hands and covered her face, not caring that her children were staring at her. She could imagine that they were probably wondering why their mother would lash out over something as simple as a petty argument for once. After all, there were so many other times that she hadn't reacted that were far more disruptive than the small squabble she'd just witnessed.

"Jeez, Mom," Carrie finally said in a softer voice. "Take a chill pill. Andy will clean up the mess."

Frances dropped her hands, completely depleted. She had not an ounce of energy left to deal with her children. Not tonight. Her eyes drifted to the digital clock on the microwave. Seven forty-five. She grabbed her cell phone from the counter and began scrolling through her e-mails. Nothing new. Voice mail? Empty. But there was one text message. She opened it, and her heart began to pound as she read the message:

Home late. Don't wait up. N.

She took a deep breath, hoping to calm her nerves. But she knew it was useless. They were on fire, and her entire body felt as if ten thousand needles were piercing her skin.

"I have to go out," she mumbled.

Andy looked up from the sweeping. "We're sorry, Momma." She cringed. "We didn't mean to upset you, did we, Carrie?" he said, giving his sister a death stare.

Without giving further explanation, Frances headed toward the door that led to the garage. "Make certain you clean up properly. If one of the dogs steps on a shard of glass, they could get really hurt." She hurried into the garage and pressed the garage door opener. The sound of it opening almost sent her over the edge.

For some time she sat inside the car, both hands set firmly on the steering wheel. She didn't know where to go; she just knew that she had to get out of there. She wasn't a person who visited bars, especially by herself, and currently she had no patience to sit through a movie. All that she knew was she couldn't sit in that house for one more minute. Not. One.

The problem wasn't necessarily the children. No, Frances was well aware that they were just one of the symptoms of the real problem. Most of the time, she blamed herself. It was the role she'd adopted to survive the pain of knowing that something was terribly wrong in her life. And it wasn't just breast cancer. The pain had been present long before her diagnosis.

As her eyes began to flood with tears, she tried to jam her keys into the ignition. On the third try, she managed to make a connection. She wiped at her eyes with the palm of her hand, then shifted the gear into reverse and pulled out of the garage. Not caring that it was dark and raining, or that she'd left her children home alone, she backed down the driveway. The exterior of the house was dark, and the empty trash cans were upended, with the lids strewn about the front lawn. How many times had she asked one of the children to bring the empty cans from the curb to the garage? And how many times had she asked Nicholas to fix the timers on the outdoor lights? Come to think of it, how many times had she asked Nicholas to fix anything? His answer was always one of two things: he'd fix it later, or he'd hire someone to do it. Neither ever happened.

Frances drove down her winding street toward Interstate 287 and noticed that all of her neighbors' homes looked welcoming and well tended. The word *prideful* came to mind as she gazed at their custom in-ground lighting casting perfectly orchestrated shadows over their brick or stone exteriors. A few had spotlights aimed at their front doors, where holiday wreaths with perfectly placed bows would soon be hanging. No doubt, there would be tiny white lights—not colored ones, which most of the neighborhood frowned upon and considered classless—covering the perfectly shaped bushes, too. Fake candles would be placed on the windowsills, and almost every house would have a lit Christmas tree, visible through one of the many large picture windows that faced the street.

Frances could only hope that this year she could convince Andy and Carrie to help her set up the Christmas tree and, if she was really lucky, string some lights on the boxwoods that lined their front walk.

She was tired of courting that horrid feeling of inferiority, especially since it didn't travel alone. Instead, it seemed to drag along its preferred companion: self-inflicted guilt. After all, whenever she complained, she learned firsthand from Nicholas who was to blame for their family's social inadequacies. Although he never came right out and said the words, she could tell by his attitude that he felt she could do more. Everyone always wanted more from Frances; even Frances wanted more from herself. Gritting her teeth, she knew she had to tell him. And she couldn't wait for him to come home and tell her, yet again, that he was tired and they could talk in the morning. She was well aware that the morning conversation would never come.

Her car seemed to take on a life of its own, driving itself along the highway, heading in the direction of I-280 East. While she hated driving, especially at night, she had to face the truth. There would be no more burying her head in the sand about Nicholas's late nights, weekend commitments, and lack of interest when it came to anything that had to do with her.

It was time to face the truth. And time to tell him the truth.

When she pulled into the parking lot, it was almost nine o'clock. Lost in her thoughts, she'd missed the exit and had to make a U-turn to backtrack. The last thing she wanted was to take the wrong exit. Despite the mayor's claims that he was cleaning up the city, Newark still remained a scary place at night, and she didn't want to get lost.

When Frances pulled up to the building, she could see that there were a lot of lights on for that time of night. She'd been to her husband's office only a handful of times, but she remembered well enough where his reserved parking spot was located and knew that his office was on the fifteenth floor, just one floor beneath the top executives.

Despite the many lit floors, the underground parking garage was mostly empty. She drove down two levels and looked for spot number 324. Confident that the employee assigned to number 325 wasn't going to show up anytime soon, she pulled in next to Nicholas's black Audi.

Her hands shook as she put her car keys into her purse and headed toward the door. She knew that security would have to buzz her in, so she pulled out her wallet to have her ID ready. Still, she had a surreal feeling when she crossed the empty parking lot and reached for the buzzer, glancing up at the camera so the security guard could clearly see her face.

"May I help you?"

"Frances Snyder, visiting my husband, Nicholas, on the fifteenth floor," she answered, surprised that her voice remained calm and steady. That certainly wasn't how she felt.

A buzz and a clicking noise alerted her that the door had been unlocked. She opened it and passed through. The elevator door opened, and a uniformed man stepped outside, using his hand to keep the doors from shutting so she could enter.

"Good evening, Mrs. Snyder," he said, stepping back inside to accompany her up to the fifteenth floor. Using a key, he unlocked the panel of buttons and then pressed the button for her husband's floor. "Still raining out there?"

She nodded her head, but remained silent, not wanting to engage in conversation.

"Almost makes me wish it was colder," he continued, staring up at the panel of lights above the door. "I'd take snow over rain any day."

Frances made a noise of acknowledgment, which he thankfully seemed to take as a hint to stop the small talk. When the doors opened, he stepped aside, waiting for her to exit before escorting her down the long corridor toward the back offices.

Her hands began to shake, so she put them in her coat pockets, not wanting the guard to see that she was nervous. She wished the security guard would let her walk the rest of the way unaccompanied. The last thing she wanted was for a stranger to bear witness to whatever she might find behind the closed door of her husband's office. On the other hand, maybe it was better this way. The scene might be less dramatic when she walked in on Nicholas and whoever was with him.

But his office door was closed. And locked.

"No light on. You said he was expecting you?" the security guard questioned.

She nodded, even though she didn't remember having said any such thing.

"Maybe the conference room, then?" The guard didn't wait for her answer. Instead, he led her down another hallway and toward a room that, indeed, had light coming from underneath the door.

What, exactly, was she doing here? What would she say when she confronted him? How would he react to being spied on by his wife? Caught doing whatever it was that he did on all those late nights when he told her he was working late?

The security guard didn't seem concerned as he reached out for the doorknob and turned it, slowly pushing it open and stepping aside.

Frances took a deep breath and brushed past him into the room.

The conference room was lit up, the table littered with papers and files. Her eyes swept the room, which appeared empty, despite two cups of coffee and a tray of food that littered the mahogany conference table. There was another door at the back of the room that was slightly ajar. From the small opening, she could hear voices. It felt as if someone else were directing her, as if she were a puppet on strings and an invisible hand were guiding her toward that room.

As she neared it, the voices grew louder, which made her stop.

Two men appeared in the doorway, so deep in conversation they didn't notice her standing there for a few moments. But when they did, surprise registered on their faces. Behind them, a third man emerged. He carried a round plate with two sandwich halves on it. When Nicholas caught sight of Frances, his initial reaction was confusion, but almost as quickly it turned to irritation.

"Frances? What are you doing here?"

For a moment she couldn't respond. While she hadn't expected to find Nicholas alone, she hadn't expected to find him with two other businessmen, either. She tried to collect her thoughts, to wrap her head around the scene before her, which was so different than what she'd anticipated.

Nicholas set down his plate and crossed the room. He took her arm and quickly led her back to the hallway.

"Are you checking up on me?" he asked, even though they both knew the answer. "What are you thinking?" He glanced over his shoulder.

"I . . ." She didn't know how to respond. What was she thinking? "I . . . I was concerned," she finally said.

"What did you think? That I was having an affair?" he whispered in an angry, hoarse voice.

"I . . . I just needed to see you, Nicholas," she responded. It wasn't a lie. She did need to see him. Even more importantly, she needed to know the truth. "You're never home anymore."

She was tempted to tell him about the test results having come back positive. At least it would justify the fact that she'd come to his office at this time of night. But wouldn't that be a cop-out? Just as she decided to tell him, Nicholas interrupted her thoughts.

Running his fingers through his thinning hair in a familiar gesture of exasperation, he looked away from her and uttered, "It's called work, Frances. *Work*. You know that word, right? It's the word that puts food on the table and pays the bills. Work."

"But I needed to talk to you about something."

"Well, this certainly isn't the time or the place, is it?" he snapped. "And who's home with the kids? Obviously not you." He stared at her. There was an intense emotion in his expression. Irritation? Annoyance? *No,* she thought. More like disgust. He glared as he shook his head. "You're really something else, Frances. I can't believe you drove all the way out here. That you have such little faith in me!"

She lowered her eyes, staring at the floor, her shoulders hunched forward. If her heart had felt as if it were in her throat before, she now knew it was in her chest, pounding hard. Shame washed over her, and she could barely talk as she whispered, "I'm so sorry."

"You should be!" he replied sharply. "You know we have this big deal on the line, and I really don't have time for your emotional theatrics right now. So go home, Frances. I'll be there when I get there."

He looked up and saw the security guard standing at the end of the hallway. Motioning with his hand, Nicholas called out, "Would you mind escorting my wife back to her car?"

Without so much as another word, he turned and walked back to the conference room. She stared after him until the security guard approached. Her cheeks felt warm. She couldn't hide her humiliation. Fortunately, the guard did not so much as look at her, providing the distance Frances needed as they walked back to the elevators.

During the drive home all she could think about was one thing: How could she possibly burden him now when he was so angry with her, thinking that she had suspected him of cheating when, in truth, she just needed to talk with him?

CHAPTER 6

"You do realize, Frances, that what you are suggesting is rather unconventional?"

During the course of the week, Frances had met with several doctors to better understand her cancer and her options. An MRI and a CT scan had preceded two reluctant meetings, first with a medical oncologist, then with a radiation oncologist. After she declined to schedule an appointment with a plastic surgeon, Dr. Graham requested another meeting.

Sitting across from him, his large mahogany desk littered with files and papers, Frances did her best to maintain her poker face. Despite the disorganized chaos that she witnessed, she knew from her research that he was, in fact, very organized. Not only had he attended the top medical school in the country, he'd also been listed as one of the top doctors in his field for five years in a row. Dr. Graham was clearly the best that Morristown Memorial had to offer when it came to treating breast cancer.

Which is why she needed to remain calm and focused.

"I do realize that, yes," she said. "But my research has pointed to other options that I'd like to explore."

"*Your* research?" Dr. Graham lifted his hand to his forehead, removing his glasses as he did so, in a gesture of disbelief. "That darn Internet."

She laughed, the first time since their meeting the previous Friday. It felt good to laugh.

"That's not it, Dr. Graham," she said. "I'm not researching alternatives to be one of those patients who are afraid of chemo or chemicals or surgery. It's just exactly what I told you last week: I don't have time for cancer."

"Well, it found time for you," he replied.

Frances felt her spine straighten as she repeated his words to herself. Whether cancer had found her was not the issue. She knew she needed to remain strong and stoic to battle whatever lay ahead. But she also needed to maintain a balance in her life; she needed to maintain control.

"Well, too bad," she said.

This time it was the doctor who smiled at her rebellious disregard of cancer's grip on her life. It was the first time that she felt a connection with him. His smile enlightened her, allowing her to look at the situation through another set of eyes. Frances hadn't felt this hopeful since her diagnosis, and she was depending on Dr. Graham to help her keep the faith. However, she had every intention of implementing her plan, with or without his support.

"Ah, Mrs. Snyder . . ."

"Call me Frances," she said. "I think you and I should be on a first-name basis at this point."

"OK, Frances," he said, never offering his own first name. "So, what we are suggesting is a double mastectomy with chemotherapy and radiation to follow."

But that was not part of her plan.

"No."

He blinked his eyes. "No?"

"No." She said it with such conviction and strength that he sat up straighter. "I don't want a double mastectomy. Too many women are having that done. It's overkill. In fact, lumpectomies have the same statistics for recurrence and survival rates as double mastectomies. So I say no to the double mastectomy. It's not something I want to invest my time in, the recovery is just too long. And then there's the reconstruction to think about, which can take twice as long to recover from."

Dr. Graham made a disapproving noise that sounded like he was sucking air through his teeth. "Mrs. Snyder—"

"Frances!" she snapped. His patronizing tone had suddenly irritated her. She was tired of being doubted, of being second-guessed. She wasn't an unintelligent woman. And it was, after all, *her* body.

"Frances," he patiently corrected himself. "You are really taking a chance here."

"What about those cases where they get chemo and radiation first?" She leaned forward in her seat and poked her finger against the top of his desk. "Those women don't get their breasts chopped off!"

"It's not chopping—" he started to argue.

"Please!" She leaned back and ran her fingers through her hair. She almost laughed at the doctor but didn't want to upset him. After all, he was her medical savior. "Will I lose my hair?" she asked.

"I . . . uh . . ."

"I'll take that for a yes." When she said the words out loud, it suddenly didn't feel as bad as she had imagined over the past forty-eight hours. "So what do I do? Shave my head?"

"That's a little drastic," he managed to say.

"Not any more drastic than removing both of my breasts."

He conceded with a simple "Touché."

His stone-faced expression told her all that she needed to know. Dr. Graham had his own ideas about what she needed to do to beat the invader in her life, and she had her own. Unfortunately for him, they were both very different.

"I need the least disruptive way to get rid of the cancer, Dr. Graham."

Pushing back his chair, he stood up while shaking his head. "That's not the way it works here, Frances."

"So how, exactly, does it work? Every cancer is different. I learned that from my research. For some women, their cancer is genetic. For others, it's environmental or even caused by stress. Hormones can influence its growth. Cancers are all different: different types, stages, and causes. So if it's true that there are different causes and even types, then tell me, Dr. Graham, why are all of the treatments the same? Why aren't treatments tailored for the woman?"

He took a deep breath and walked toward her. Gently, he placed his hand on her arm and stared into her face. He wore an expression of compassion that, she could sense, also included a tinge of superiority.

"Frances, I know you think I don't understand how you feel, but I do. Even though I've never had breast cancer, I certainly can understand your frustration." He gave her an empathetic smile. "These cures, these treatments, however drastic they may seem . . . they are the best the medical field has to offer right now, and statistically, they give you the best chance of living a long, healthy life."

She lifted her chin and stared at him. For a week, she'd studied everything she could about lumpectomies and mastectomies. There was no way that she could go through either of those surgeries without Nicholas and the children finding out. Hospital stays, drains, and painkillers would not mask the truth. And she *needed* to mask the truth. Just for a little while longer until Nicholas forgave her. Besides, more than anything, she didn't want to be *that* woman who became the focal point of pity within the family. She didn't want to interfere with their lives. And she already understood the psychological ramifications of breast cancer for herself, so she could imagine how her children might feel if they knew about her illness.

Dr. Graham sighed and rubbed the bridge of his nose. She felt sorry for putting him through the stress of keeping her secret, but it was only to protect her family.

"Chemotherapy will shrink the tumor, I'm sure. But you'll need surgery, Frances. Without it, the cancer will grow stronger." He leaned against the edge of his desk. "To try and avoid surgery is simply not an option."

Frances digested his words. *Surgery.* They wouldn't know whether she would need a lumpectomy or a mastectomy until after chemotherapy. The idea of losing her breast—one or even both!—made her feel like running away.

An image came to her mind of a red sleigh on a snowy day. Mrs. Bentley had had a double mastectomy with no reconstruction. Frances could now see her face as if it were just yesterday, and not thirty-some-odd years ago. Mrs. Bentley had been matter-of-fact about dying. She'd answered Frances's questions on that snowy day when they posed for that photo. Mrs. Bentley had seemed to appreciate Frances's innocent candor, a rare treat when most people avoided the subject entirely.

Frances's mother, however, felt only pity for the woman. Even though her mother had smiled to Mrs. Bentley's face, she had also talked about what a pathetically frail creature she was to anyone who would listen. Her mother had organized food drives to help with meals, but never contributed any time herself. Instead, she made quite a lot of fanfare over delivering the meals to the Bentley home as if she, and not others, had cooked the meals. Frances often wondered if her mother organized the food drives to help Mrs. Bentley or merely to appear like a good Catholic woman among her social circles.

Unlike candor, pity was an ugly gift.

Frances shuddered at the memory. She didn't want to be pitied by anyone, especially by her own family.

"How soon does all this begin?"

"I want you to start your first round of chemo on Thursday. It will be a two-week cycle: one week on, one week off. So every other Thursday you'll come to the chemotherapy center."

"But Thanksgiving is coming up."

Dr. Graham glanced at the calendar on his desk. He flipped over the page to look at November. "You should be fine, Frances. Your chemo will start October 20 and then again on November 3, November 17, and December 1. Perfect planning to avoid Thanksgiving!"

He sounded quite pleased, as if she'd purposefully scheduled her cancer diagnosis to avoid the upcoming holiday. Now, however, she had to figure out how and when to tell Nicholas. She knew she couldn't go through chemotherapy alone. And while she was certain he would be upset she hadn't told him already, he would understand once she explained that she hadn't wanted to distract him from work.

"You will need to come in next week to have your Port-a-Cath inserted," he added, switching back into doctor mode. "And I want you to have a tour of the chemotherapy center. My assistant will get all of this scheduled for you."

"Port-a . . . ?"

"Port-a-Cath," he repeated as he pushed his chair backward and reached into his file cabinet for something. What he withdrew was a shiny piece of laminated cardboard with a medical diagram. He set it on the edge of his desk and reached around the side to point to different illustrations of parts of the body. "It's a catheter connected to a portal—this round device with a silicone septum here—that gets inserted into your chest."

"My . . . my chest?"

He pointed to his own body, just under the collarbone. "Here, Frances. And the catheter will run up a vein and into your neck."

Instinctively, her hand fluttered to her throat.

"It sounds worse than it is, trust me."

She grimaced at his words. "Have you ever had one?"

"No. No, I haven't."

"Then please don't tell me that it sounds worse than it is."

He bit his lower lip and slowly nodded his head. "Fair enough. How about this? I've dealt with hundreds, maybe even thousands of patients who've had this device installed. They all say it's not as bad as it sounds."

She could accept that.

"Why do I need it?"

He nodded his head once. "Good question. When chemotherapy is administered, the nurse will puncture your skin with a needle here." He pointed to the circular silicone part of the portal. "It doesn't hurt at all." Before she could comment, he quickly added, "Or so my thousands of patients have told me."

She couldn't keep herself from smiling. Despite the circumstances, she was beginning to appreciate this Dr. Graham.

"The reason you have it, Frances, is because the chemotherapy is too strong for your veins. There have been instances where veins have collapsed and shut down. The port provides a more direct pathway, thus allowing us to get the drugs into the main artery in a safer manner by lowering the risk of damage to the veins, skin, and muscles."

"Wow," she said drily. "Sounds like a party, doesn't it?"

This time he smiled. "I can assure you that it's no party, but it's the best treatment we have. I will not try to sugarcoat it, Frances. Sometimes the treatment will feel far worse than the disease. But in the long run, chemotherapy can give you back your life, the very thing the cancer wants to rob from you."

"If the treatment doesn't kill me."

"And *that* will not happen." He set down the diagram and folded his hands on top of it. "I promise you that."

There was a moment of silence that befell them while Frances stared at his folded hands. He wasn't wearing a wedding ring, and she wondered if that was by chance or by choice.

He cleared his throat. "How did your family take the news?"

"I . . ." She averted her eyes, too embarrassed to admit the truth. She hadn't told her husband, because he had been too busy to spare the time for a discussion, a simple conversation that revolved around her for once, and not him. It was far too painful to acknowledge. So she chose the lesser of the two evils, which was to tell Dr. Graham a lie. "They were concerned, of course. But I reassured them everything would be fine."

"And you believe that, don't you?"

For a moment she was confused, wondering whether he meant that they were concerned (or would be, anyway, if she had told them) or that everything would be fine. She decided on the latter. "Yes, Dr. Graham. I do."

He gave her a broad smile, in acknowledgment. "That's what I like to hear. You know, a positive, upbeat attitude does wonders when going through treatment. With a good attitude and a good support team, you'll be amazed at how strong a fighter you truly are. While I haven't personally experienced it," he added with a soft smile, "I have seen it over and over again."

"A thousand times?" she asked in a slightly teasing tone.

He laughed. "Yes, at least."

Dr. Graham stood up and motioned toward the door of his office. "Now, let me get you scheduled for the tour of the chemo floor as well as the Port-a-Cath surgery. It's an outpatient procedure, Frances, so your husband should be prepared to take you home and let you rest until the anesthesia wears off. No driving and no strenuous activities, understood?"

She nodded, barely listening when he introduced her to his assistant. Her mind reeled as she came to the realization that now she would have no choice; she would have to tell Nicholas. After what she'd heard, she knew she would need the support of her husband during the upcoming months. This time, there was simply no way that he could avoid being by her side. And once she told him what was going on with her health, surely things would finally change and he would want to put his family before anything else.

CHAPTER 7

The second floor of the Carol G. Simon Cancer Center was more intimidating than Frances had imagined. A young man took her on a short tour of the chemotherapy center, pausing to explain the different areas. But Thomas's explanations fell on deaf ears. Frances stared at everything and nothing at the same time, his words simply not registering with her. The conflicting emotions that welled up inside of her hindered her ability to comprehend anything.

She had a "welcome" folder pressed against her chest as she followed her "tour guide," which was a horrible way to think of him. Tour guides were supposed to show people historic sites or take them on adventures through exotic attractions, not through the institutional wing of a cancer center. In all her years, Frances had never put *chemotherapy center* and *tour guide* in the same sentence. The former brought fear along with visions of death, while the latter sparked dreams of curiosity and exploration of exotic locations, none of which she had in regard to her upcoming cancer treatment.

Surely, this was going to cause an upheaval in her otherwise well-organized routine and methodical approach to her roles as wife, mother, and homemaker. She had embraced those roles since way back when, after the birth of her first child, and as with other aspects of her life, had always approached them with poise and conviction. While she often liked to initiate changes in her home life, such as redecorating, organizing, and gardening, she was adamant about not making changes to her personal life, especially when these changes might disrupt the routine of her family life.

Thomas walked her through the process of how to check in at the front desk and where to wait for her turn to be called. Prior to each chemotherapy session, she would first need to have her blood tested in order to make certain her blood cell counts were high enough to handle chemotherapy.

"What happens if they aren't?" she asked.

He shrugged. "Then you wait another week."

The casual way he answered her and the nonchalant shrug of his shoulders irritated her. This wasn't a sold-out movie on a Friday night. It was cancer, and it deserved more respect than a disinterested shoulder shrug. "Does that impede the progress of the treatment?"

"Not at all," he said as he guided her across a hallway and through a large door. "It's cumulative."

Why did that word disturb her so? *Cumulative.* Was it because it conveyed a feeling of an accumulation of poisonous substances inside her body, a body that she'd always taken great care of? What would all these chemicals do to her? Sure, she knew these were substances carefully monitored and administered to combat and kill an uninvited invader. But she'd read throughout her research that the chemicals could also precipitate some unwanted—perhaps even dangerous—side effects. How would she, or even worse, her family, be able to deal with these? It was not just the fact that her appearance would be affected, but what about the prospect that she would become unable to care for herself? Would her mental health be affected as well? What about clinical depression? She'd also read that cancer treatment often caused emotional unbalance, frequent thoughts of death and suicide, and trouble focusing as well as remembering the simplest things. Would she find herself standing in the kitchen and forgetting what, exactly, she had intended to cook her family for dinner? Her sleeping patterns would inevitably change, too. Would she have trouble falling asleep or wake in the middle of the night for no reason at all? How would her children and husband deal with all of these changes and disruptions?

"Cumulative? I don't know exactly what that means," she replied, dubious as to whether she really wanted him to answer her.

Thomas gestured toward a large reception desk in the middle of the room where they now stood.

"It doesn't leave your system," he explained, with no further comment or attempt at alleviating her concerns. "Now, you will sign in here and then see Eddie over there. He'll take your vitals and record them in the computer system. After he's finished," Thomas said, motioning for her to follow him as he walked by a long row of gray leather chairs that lined the back wall near the windows, "you take a seat and wait here."

"Where?"

"Anywhere. Just pick a chair that isn't taken."

As they continued on, Frances looked at the other patients. Right away she noticed that no one looked happy. Not that she expected them to be smiling, but she certainly hadn't expected the doom-and-gloom expressions on their faces. There was a definite feeling of resignation in the air. There were no nods or waves to Thomas from the two dozen patients who were quietly undergoing their treatment. She hadn't been expecting high fives, or even a thumbs-up, but surely a nod or small smile, as he must have been their tour guide, too, she thought.

Most of the patients had someone with them, a person who sat in the chair by their side, a husband or a sister most likely. Or perhaps an older son or daughter. She didn't see any young kids or even teenagers, like her own. This was certainly not the best place for someone as vulnerable as a child. Almost all of the people wore something covering their heads: a scarf, a cap, or a wig. Only the men sat there with their bald heads exposed. Frances swallowed as she followed Thomas. These people were, for the most part, older patients who seemed resigned to be there and were just going through the motions. In just a few days, she would become one of them. From the expressions on their faces, the ones who did glance up when she walked by, she realized that they must have been thinking the exact same thing about her: *Soon she, too, will become one of us.*

When Dr. Graham scheduled the appointment for her to meet with the chemotherapy staff, Frances suspected that Nicholas would not be able to come with her. And then she reflected on the debacle of the previous week, when she'd driven to his office. He'd barely spoken to her since then, returning home well after ten o'clock and leaving even earlier in the morning than he usually did. Between his indignation at her intrusion and his focus on work, life seemed far too chaotic to even consider telling him.

She had, however, sent him an e-mail. A simple message that said:

I need to talk to you. F.

The read receipt never came. He hadn't even opened it!

When they reached the end of the corridor, someone called out to Thomas. He glanced at Frances. "Can you give me a minute?"

She nodded, watching his back as he walked away.

Now, standing alone, she crossed her arms over her chest and turned, her eyes skimming the faces of the patients sitting in the recliner chairs. Some appeared to be sleeping, while others just stared blankly at the wall in front of them. Instead of focusing on them, Frances looked out the window, wondering how the center had created such an inviting garden. There were trees, bushes, and even benches for people to rest on. She tried to envision what was beyond the garden. Probably the entrance atrium. And she realized how clever the center had been to create something so bright and full of life just outside the windows, in a section of the building where people felt the complete opposite.

"Welcome to the club!"

Frances was startled by the voice. She glanced over her shoulder and saw an elderly woman who was seated in the corner. She had a cap on her head and a big smile on her lips, which seemed an incongruous divergence compared to the other patients in the room.

"Excuse me?"

The woman raised her eyebrows, or what was left of them, and grinned. "I said, 'Welcome to the club.' You know, the Cancer Club."

This time Frances hugged herself tighter and looked around for Thomas. "I . . . uh . . ." She didn't know how to respond. "Thanks." She paused before finally adding, "I guess, anyway."

The older woman laughed. Once again, Frances's senses were struck by an apparent discordance, this time between what she heard and where she was. Laughter did not belong in the chemotherapy treatment center.

"True, true," the woman said as her laughter subsided. "It's a club that no one wants to be a member of. Unless, of course, you're old man Henry."

"Old man Henry?"

The woman pointed a wrinkly finger with chipped pink nail polish at the chair next to her, where an older man was snoring softly. He wore a cap on his head, similar to the ones she often saw golfers wearing on the rare occasions that Nicholas was home and camped out on the sofa in front of the television. "That's old man Henry. He likes being here, I think."

Frances wasn't certain what to make of that comment. How could anyone enjoy chemotherapy?

As if reading her mind, the woman gave a soft snicker. "Guess there isn't much else for him to do at Pine Acres."

Glancing around again for Thomas, but not spotting him, Frances felt compelled to ask, "What's Pine Acres?"

The woman made a noise in her throat, almost like a harrumph, as if Frances should know the answer to her own question. "Pine Acres. You know, the place across the street?" She stared at her expectantly as if her explanation would jar Frances's memory. "The nursing home?"

"Oh!" she said, even though she still had no idea what Pine Acres was or why, for that matter, she should have.

The woman narrowed her eyes and studied Frances. "You probably never even heard about the place," she went on, pressing her lips together in disapproval. "Why would you? Let me guess. Married, two children, and no thought that one day you might be forced from your home to live with old coots like that poor Henry!"

Frances felt her heart beat rapidly as a lump invaded her throat. Was that what could be in store for her: an early retirement into what constituted, more often than not, the last stage in a person's life? Would she be forced into a home, should the side effects of her treatment be so incapacitating that her family wouldn't be able to care for her? She started to harbor doubts about the wisdom of undertaking chemotherapy. Becoming a burden to her family was not part of her plan. There was no way that she would allow herself to become dependent on them. She was the caregiver of her family, not the other way around! Preserving her self-reliance was her objective. It was not negotiable, but that place, a . . . *nursing home*! Perhaps she would be better off letting nature take its course, after all.

Thankfully, before Frances could respond, Thomas appeared from around the corner.

"Sorry about that, Mrs. Snyder," he apologized, then paused, looking over at the woman. "Oh, now let me guess: Madeline, you sharing your war stories with our new patient?"

The older woman waved a hand dismissively at him and turned around to look out the window.

"That's what I thought," Thomas said, but not unkindly.

"You go on with your tour, Thomas," Madeline replied without looking at him. "She'll learn the truth soon enough."

That was a bittersweet comment that did not sit well with Frances.

Thomas turned back to Frances and made a face, rolling his eyes in a manner that reminded her of Carrie. The only difference was that Frances couldn't quite interpret the meaning of his gesture. Was it irritation or impatience? Did that Madeline woman make the same comment all the time? Did the rolling of his eyes express his genuine disapproval or was it just a learned response, a routine comeback to her behavior?

"Come along, Mrs. Snyder, and I'll show you where to go for ice pops, water, and coffee. Or, better yet, you can have your husband or friends fetch them for you. You'll need lots of fluids while going through your chemotherapy sessions. Your mouth and tongue will become dry, and you might want to chew on something cold or wet, even ice cubes, to fight the sensation. Cold water or coffee will help, too."

Thomas took her elbow and guided her to another area of the center. Frances, however, couldn't resist one last glance at Madeline, who was now staring intently at her hands folded in her lap. She could only imagine that Madeline was the favorite Walmart greeter of the Chemo Cocktail Lounge, welcoming new patients and giving them the dark, seedy gossip even before they learned the routine. Upon their return, they would most likely avoid her, which explained why every chair in the room was occupied except for the one to the right of Madeline.

A part of her felt sorry for Madeline, with no one seated beside her (except Henry, who was still asleep) to fetch her ice pops or coffee.

Clearly, there was more to Madeline's story than met the eye. But Frances had as little interest in learning her story as Thomas had in telling it. At least not on that day. Her mind was focused on her own story, one that, at the present moment, was filled with fear and anger.

It took her a minute to come to grips with the reality that she, too, would be alone in a recliner. That is, unless she managed to find the courage to tell Nicholas. One look at the other patients and Frances knew that she had to share her diagnosis with her family. Everyone was right: she simply couldn't go through this alone. The past weeks had been hard enough. Frances needed to start thinking a little less about others and more about herself. And it was high time that they, too, considered her needs over theirs.

For once.

CHAPTER 8

Frances stood before the mirror and put the wig on. Her own hair was pulled back in a tight bun. Dr. Graham had given her a prescription for the custom-made wig, but Frances hadn't wanted to wait until her hair started to fall out before trying some on. She wanted to be ready.

"That looks nice," Charlotte said.

Frances thought it looked terrible and knew her friend was just trying to be nice. She could tell by the reserved tone of voice Charlotte had used that it looked awful.

"Let's try a different style," Frances suggested, pulling the wig off and placing it on the stand. "Something just . . . crazy!" Her eyes scanned the items on the faceless mannequin heads. "Oh! What about this one?" She pointed toward a short, spiky styled wig. It was completely different from the one she'd just tried on and nothing like her own conservative hairstyle. "That looks like fun!"

Charlotte gave a short laugh that expressed no mirth. "I would find it fun if you weren't going to lose all of your beautiful hair."

Frances let her hand drop. She swallowed, her mouth suddenly dry. In two short days, she would be starting her first chemotherapy treatment. While she'd hoped, against all odds, that she wouldn't lose it, Dr. Graham had compassionately told her that with Adriamycin and cyclophosphamide, or AC as the medical people called it—a very potent chemotherapy cocktail that she would be receiving for the first four treatments—she would indeed lose her hair. She hadn't cried, just merely pushed the cold harsh reality into the recesses of her mind. She had tried not to imagine the day she would stare in the mirror and see the inevitable. But the idea frightened her.

Hair. One of the symbols of femininity. Women spent hundreds of dollars at hair salons each year attempting to hide their grays and shave the years from their appearance. Frances knew only too well how others made snap judgments about women based on their hair. Too many roots? Oblivious. Outdated style? Lazy. Perfectly coiffed? On top of her game.

"That's why we're here," she said in a soft voice. "Find a short wig and then get my hair cut to match, right?" She looked at Charlotte, hoping to get some reassurance. A word of comfort when she was beginning to feel weak. "I mean, it's only hair, right?"

Charlotte did not respond at first. She just stared at Frances. "You don't have to do this."

"I do have to do this." She reached out and touched one of the wigs. "It'll make the transition easier."

Charlotte reached out and touched Frances's arm. "I know you don't want to feel sorry for yourself. You're trying to be in control. But life has just dealt you a bad hand, Fran. It's OK to acknowledge that."

Lifting her chin, Frances walked past her friend, her eyes assessing the other wigs on the wall. Then she glanced back. "Remember what I said. Positive thinking, Charlie. I don't want any negative vibes sent my way."

Rolling her eyes, Charlotte began strolling down the aisle while Frances took a step back and scrutinized the many different choices.

A mother and her young daughter walked into the store, the little bell over the door announcing their entrance. The daughter looked to be the same age as Carrie. Her long blond hair loosely framed her face, and she was wearing a simple white leotard with matching stockings. A dancer, no doubt. As the daughter walked right beside her mother, with her head bent over her cell phone, Frances heard her laugh. Then she grabbed her mother's hand and showed her a picture on the screen. Her mother smiled, and they started to chat as if they were good friends. It was such a comfortable exchange between a mother and a daughter.

If only Carrie would talk to her like that. Frances watched them, imagining the days when Carrie had held her hand and drawn her pictures. But unlike the young dancer girl, Carrie had turned into a sassy teenager far too early, leaving Frances with only memories and the hope that her daughter might one day become more friendly.

As they passed Frances, the mother glanced down at the wig in her hands. Immediately, sympathy crossed her face and she looked up to meet Frances's gaze, giving her a tight smile of silent support.

Frances felt short of breath as her heart began to palpitate. That smile had reminded her of her own mother. She could almost make out her voice in her head.

Poor Mr. Bentley! her mother had said, with the phone pressed tightly to her ear. *I'm not sure how well he's coping with his wife's illness. I just dropped off a meal for them this afternoon, and when he answered the door, he looked as though he hadn't slept in days. Such a patient man!*

As if he should be any other way, Frances wanted to yell at the memory of that day.

"Charlotte!" she called out. "I'm going to take this one." She held up the short spiky wig and stated, "I'm ready for a change."

At their next stop, Frances heard the bell ring when Charlotte opened the door to Supercuts, but she hesitated before stepping inside the salon. It was all so unsettling and yet, at the same time, necessary. Charlotte had been correct: Frances was intent on controlling what she could, and this was another step that needed to be taken. All of her research on the Internet had said so. Women going through breast cancer often felt better when they took this step rather than waiting for chemo to steal their hair.

Still, she was suddenly having second thoughts. How could she just cut off her hair? See it piled in long, loose curls on the floor to be swept up and thrown away?

"Come on, Frances!" Charlotte snapped. "It's cold outside!"

Frances took her time entering the salon. "I . . . I was just thinking—"

Charlotte interrupted her by gently prodding her. "It's a haircut, not a death sentence, for crying out loud! You said so yourself when you told me you wanted to do this. Now, let's get this over with. Then we can go next door for some coffee."

But it's my hair, Frances thought, subconsciously lifting her hand to run her fingers through it, perhaps for the last time. In the past eighteen years, she'd not once changed her hairstyle, or even her hair color. Nicholas loved her long blond hair. He always had. And he also liked things to stay the same. *Consistency,* he always said, *makes for perfect happiness in a marriage.*

Funny. She shook off her black jacket and hung it on the coatrack. *That's the same thing my mother used to say.*

"How can we help you ladies today?" a young woman behind the cash register asked. With her blue hair cut in a pseudo-punk style, she reminded Frances of a modern-day Cyndi Lauper, a throwback to the eighties. The nose ring and wrist tattoo helped to complete the transition into the twenty-first century.

Charlotte stepped to the side, making room for Frances to approach the check-in desk. With a nervous flutter of her hand, Frances gestured toward her hair. "I'd like a haircut."

"A trim or . . . ?" The woman hesitated and waited for Frances to complete her sentence.

"Something different."

"OK, then. Did you have something in mind?"

Frances swallowed and nodded her head. "I . . . well . . . I want to cut it all off."

The woman blinked and glanced at Charlotte. "All of it?"

"Short. Very short."

"I see." But it was clear that she was taken aback by the request. Even she could tell that Frances was not enthusiastic about it. How could she be? After all, she had such beautifully thick, long hair. "Well, then . . . let's get you situated; then you can tell me what you have in mind."

Frances took a deep breath and followed her to the closest chair. It was burgundy, thankfully. Had it been gray, like the recliners in the chemotherapy room, Frances might have been tempted to run out of the salon. Instead, she sat down and let the woman put a cape around her shoulders. Once she'd snapped it, she spun the chair around so Frances could look in the mirror.

"How short were you thinking? Two, three inches?"

"One inch, maybe two at the most."

The woman breathed a sigh of relief and laughed. "Oh! I thought you meant you really wanted your hair cut off!" Another laugh. "Two inches shorter isn't so bad! You have such beautiful hair anyway!"

"No, I meant I only want it one or two inches long." She fumbled in her purse and withdrew the wig to show the stylist. When she held it up for her to get a better look at, she was met with complete silence.

This was the moment Frances had wanted to avoid. She didn't want to tell her story, didn't want to see a look of pity on the woman's face. She knew that this first time would be the worst. *I just have to get used to the idea of people feeling sorry for me.* She pursed her lips and exhaled. "I have breast cancer. It's going to fall out anyway. I'd rather it be on my terms, not the cancer's."

"Oh."

That one word said it all. It was soft and quiet, a moment of understanding that, despite Frances's wishes, was filled with compassion, empathy, and alarm. Frances understood all of those emotions, especially the last one. How many times had she heard bad news about a friend or acquaintance? She remembered when she first learned about her friend Jane's divorce and her neighbor Stephanie's illness. She had not only been worried about them but also for a flash second worried that she, too, might one day face a similar problem. And then, after that feeling passed, Frances would hide a sigh of relief that it was someone else's problem to deal with, not hers.

"I'm . . . I'm terribly sorry," the young woman said.

"It's OK," Frances replied before quickly adding, "I'm OK with it. I just don't want clumps of hair to fall out. That would be more shocking than cutting it off. So do whatever you can to make it look good. Chic, sassy, anything. Just keep it as short as possible." She averted her eyes and stared at the floor, where long, dark curls from a previous customer lay scattered and forgotten.

The woman placed her hands on Frances's shoulders and, despite her youth and outlandish looks, suddenly turned into a comrade. With an understanding smile, she nodded her head.

"You'll look beautiful when I'm done with you. I have just the cut in mind. And if you want, we can save your hair to send to Locks of Love. Sometimes helping others makes it less . . . shocking."

Frances could barely respond. She wished she had thought of that herself. Everyone was always talking about "paying it forward," and donating her own hair was the perfect way to help someone else.

"That would be nice," she answered, feeling a little bit better about sitting in that chair.

Charlotte sat down in the empty chair beside her and swiveled around to face her friend. "Don't get all weepy-eyed on me now," she proclaimed in a strong enough tone to make Frances almost laugh out loud. "I can think of twenty other things worse than getting a haircut, and I don't think I need to remind you that cancer is one of them!"

"You're such a good support," Frances teased back, hoping that the threat of tears had passed.

With an exaggerated air of vanity, Charlotte glanced at her fingernails, perfectly manicured and painted a bright red, and sighed. "I know. That's what friends are for, right?"

The stylist paused and looked over Frances's head into the mirror, their eyes meeting in the reflection. "You ready?"

"No."

The woman gave her an empathetic smile. "Your friend is right, I think, and, if you don't mind me saying so, doing something good with your hair will help you feel better."

Frances nodded and blinked her eyes, trying to hold back the tears. Her hair. Her beautiful long blond hair. The color that Nicholas preferred, even if it meant frequent trips to the salon to touch up her dark roots. She hated the idea of having it shorn off, but she knew she had no choice. It was better to cut it on her own terms. At least there was something she could finally control.

The woman began to section Frances's hair and clipped each one to the side. For a moment she had to shut her eyes so she couldn't see what was going on. *This is not happening. This is not happening,* she told herself. But when she heard the first snip and felt the gentle tugging on her scalp, her eyes flew open and she began to cry.

For once, Charlotte dropped the bravado and stepped to the side of the chair. She reached down for Frances's hand and clutched it tightly.

"It's going to be fine, Fran. You can do this."

Through her tears, Frances somehow nodded her head. She *knew* she could do this; the only problem was she didn't want to.

Twenty minutes later, Frances walked out of the salon, her blond hair short and spiked in a sassy way and her long locks tucked safely in a plastic bag. The salon had refused to charge her for the haircut, which made Frances feel even worse. The last thing she wanted was to feel like a charity case. But when she realized that arguing was fruitless, she accepted the generosity of the hair salon with a forced smile that hid her tears while she secretly decided to make a financial donation in the name of Supercuts to the Susan G. Komen organization.

A vision of Mrs. Bentley crossed her mind. That was just how her mother had seen their dying neighbor: a charity case. And in her mother's eyes that meant Mrs. Bentley was someone to be pitied, a tolerated burden at best. Just the condescending tone of voice that she had used whenever she brought a pan of lasagna or a chicken casserole to the Bentley house had been enough to embarrass Frances when she was a child.

They walked next door to the coffee shop. Frances sat down, the plastic bag still in her hand. She was staring at it, wondering why the locks looked so thin, when in real life, her hair had always been thick and full. *Or* maybe *it's just my perception.*

"Here you go," Charlotte said, handing Frances a coffee.

Shoving the bag of hair into her tote, she took the drink with her free hand. "Thanks," she said.

"I like it." Charlotte sat down across from her. "It's really cute."

Cute. At forty-two years old, cute was not what she wanted to be. Sexy. Refined. Sophisticated. Beautiful. Not cute.

"Nicholas is going to hate my hair," she whispered.

Charlotte raised an eyebrow. "I hope that's not the reaction you get when he sees it. I'm sure you both have more important things to think about than your haircut, which looks adorable."

Frances hesitated. How could she confess the truth? Admit that she hadn't even told Nicholas yet? After thinking about it for a bit, she decided that, with Charlotte, a direct and honest approach was the best approach. Taking a deep breath, she looked up and met her friend's concerned eyes.

"I haven't told him," she admitted.

"Come again?" An incredulous Charlotte leaned forward.

"Please, don't make me repeat it."

Shaking her head, Charlotte leaned back and studied Frances's face. Her eyes clouded over, disappointment mixed with distaste. She scowled. "How is that even possible? I mean, you have cancer, Frances, not a broken fingernail!"

Frances rolled her eyes. "I know that I have cancer, Charlie. You don't have to remind me of *that*."

"It's real simple, Fran. You wait until he walks through the door, and you say, 'Hi, honey, I have cancer.' The thing is that you have to do it before he asks you what's for dinner or if you picked up his dry cleaning."

"Ha-ha," Frances deadpanned. "I don't know where you got the idea that he's so narcissistic."

"Narcissistic? More of an egotist!"

Running her middle finger up and down the side of the plastic cup, Frances felt the heat of her pumpkin latte, too hot to drink just yet. Suddenly, she wished she had suggested they stop for a glass of wine. "I really wish you'd ease up on him," she managed to say, avoiding eye contact.

"I'm sure you do," Charlotte quipped. "That would be fantastic to let up on him, because it would mean he finally got his act together and realized that, contrary to his personal beliefs, he's *not* the center of the universe and you, in fact, don't exist just to serve him."

"That's not fair."

Leaning forward, Charlotte pointed at Frances. "No, what's not fair is that you're shoved into a corner and can't even tell him that you have cancer! Let me guess. Work?"

"Work."

Frances could tell that Charlotte was trying to keep her temper in check, trying hard to not explode. "When are you going to grow a backbone, Fran?"

"Stop. This whole thing is hard enough to deal with. I don't need more reminders of what's wrong from you."

But Charlotte pressed forward. "A marriage is a *partnership*, Frances, not indentured servitude. What, exactly, has he done for *you* lately?" She paused and narrowed her eyes. "Or, for that matter, ever?"

Part of Frances felt as if she needed to defend Nicholas, that Charlotte's attack on his character was uncalled for. But as much as she wanted to pretend that Charlotte's criticism was not true, she couldn't deny that her friend's brutal honesty stung. There was no salve for the wasted years of open wounds from the silent battles she'd fought.

"Look, we've talked about this before—"

"Too many times, I might add!" Charlotte shot back.

"When he finishes with that contract, I'll tell him."

From Charlotte's expression, Frances knew that her words were falling on deaf ears. "It's not like the time he blew off that appointment for your family's holiday photo. Or when he spent the better part of the day in his office instead of mingling with your guests at your Labor Day barbecue." Once again, she leaned forward and leveled her gaze at Frances. "You are starting *chemotherapy* on Thursday, Frances. Your husband should be there to support you."

"I told you," Frances said in a stern voice, hoping to put an end to the conversation, "I'll tell him."

"You should have told him already."

Frances glanced at her cell phone to check the time. "I have to go, Charlie. I need to run to the grocery store and get dinner started."

Charlotte made a disapproving noise deep within her throat.

"Thanks for the coffee," she said as she stood up and grabbed her purse from the back of the chair. "I promise. As soon as I get the chance, I'll tell him."

"I can't go with you. You know that, right?"

Frances leaned forward and kissed her friend's cheek. "I'll be fine."

"You shouldn't be going alone."

Perhaps that was true, but Frances knew that she *was* going alone. It wasn't worth feeling sorry for herself. "He promised to be home tomorrow night. I'll talk to him then."

"I'd bet you he'll be late, but I don't like cheating people out of their money."

Frances laughed at her friend's joke, even though she suspected Charlotte hadn't intended it to be funny.

"What happened to your hair?"

Carrie stood in the doorway, staring at her mother with her mouth hanging open and her eyes large and wide. She hadn't even stepped over the threshold.

Nervously, Frances gave a little laugh and lifted her hand to her short haircut. "Don't you like it?"

"No!"

Andy walked up behind his sister and gave her a shove into the foyer. But he, too, stopped short when he saw his mother. "Whoa!"

Frances took a deep breath. The truth was that she knew it would take time to get used to it. For all of them. But it had been the only way she could deal with the reality of eventually losing her hair.

"You look"—Carrie said as she dropped her backpack and crossed her arms over her chest—"old."

"Carrie!" Andy pushed her again.

"Well, it's true!" she cried out in defense. "Why would you do that, Mom? Your hair was so pretty."

Frances shrugged her shoulders. "Time for a change, I guess."

Making a face, Carrie started to walk down the hallway toward the kitchen but not before she added another quick cutting remark over her shoulder. "Dad's going to hate that."

One, two, three. Frances began to count under her breath.

"Don't listen to her, Mom," Andy said as he placed his hand on her shoulder. "It's just different, and that's not a bad thing. We just have to get used to it."

She managed to smile at him. It was always Andy who calmed her down when his sister was acting out. Her daughter's verbal arsenal knew no level of restraint. For as long as she could remember, Carrie had had a sharp tongue with no inner sense to curtail her snide remarks or insulting observations. If she became a lawyer, she might do well. Otherwise, she was going to learn a tough lesson later in life when the rest of the world would make her realize that her brutal honesty crossed the line of appropriate social behavior. Frances just hoped she was around to pick up the broken pieces when her daughter learned that lesson.

For once, the house was quiet. After the kids finished their homework, Andy asked if he could play basketball with some of his friends and Carrie went outside to skateboard. Frances was relieved to have this downtime, a time to think and plan how, exactly, she was going to tell Nicholas.

She sat on the sofa, nursing a chilled glass of chardonnay. She didn't normally drink unless she was out with Nicholas or Charlotte. Tonight, however, she needed to muster the courage to finally tell her husband the truth. She thought the chardonnay would help calm her nerves.

It was almost eight o'clock when she heard the front door open. She easily identified the heavy footsteps as belonging to her husband. He dropped his briefcase on the floor in the foyer and exhaled loudly.

"Nicholas? I'm in the living room," she called out.

At first, there was no response. Thinking he hadn't heard her, she stood up, carrying her wineglass to the doorway. She was surprised to see him standing there, glancing down at his cell phone with a concerned look on his face.

"Nicholas? Is everything all right?"

He looked up at her, and his eyes fell from her new haircut down to the glass, a momentary frown crossing his face before he returned his attention to his phone. "Yeah, just work." He looked back at her face. "You cut your hair."

"I did."

He made a noise, almost a grunt, but said nothing further. No comment, whether good or bad, about the change. Instead, he walked away from her, heading toward his office.

"I wanted to have a word with you," she said, trying to stop him from retreating.

"Did you pick up my dry cleaning? I have an early meeting tomorrow and want to wear that blue pinstripe." Without waiting for an answer, he reached down for his briefcase and started to head upstairs.

"In your closet," she answered. "Nicholas? Did you hear what I said? I need to talk to you."

He sighed and stopped walking, but didn't turn around. He had been avoiding her even more ever since she had shown up at his office that night. "Fran, I'm exhausted, and Jeff just e-mailed me some files I need to look over. Can't this wait until tomorrow?"

She pressed her lips together. Another delay? "It's important, Nicholas."

"So is my meeting. You know, my work? The thing that keeps a roof over our heads and food on the table? Unless, of course, you don't believe me again," he snapped.

She knew that he was still sore with her, upset about her showing up at his office. In hindsight, she should have waited. Now, however, he was throwing another delay into her plans. "Nicholas," she said, softening her voice. "When? When can we talk? I haven't had time to talk to you in weeks."

"Don't be so dramatic," he said. "Whatever it is can wait, can't it?" He didn't wait for a response. Instead, he continued moving, his phone ringing and his attention diverted to answering it.

Alone in the foyer, Frances shut her eyes and took a deep breath as she realized that, whatever her intentions, sharing the news would *have* to wait.

CHAPTER 9

Frances stood in the doorway to the dining room and assessed the table. Between the linens, the china, and the floral arrangement that she'd carefully placed as the centerpiece, it was just the way she wanted it: a perfectly set table.

Growing up, whenever her mother was entertaining at home, she would focus as much energy on setting the table as she would on preparing the meal. To Frances, it often seemed as if her mother's culinary efforts took a backseat to the oohs and aahs she expected regarding her finely crafted table. Once it was set, she would stand back and admire it as if it were a work of art and not a place to enjoy a meal and share family memories.

Sharing memories. That was the reason why her mother said she did it.

Frances often wondered if that was truly the reason.

She remembered all too well how her mother would stress over every last minor detail. Her father would quip that no one would care, or even know, if something wasn't exactly right. But Frances's mother ignored his comments as she focused on placing the candles among freshly cut greenery so the wax would not drip onto the tablecloth, folding the napkins into decorative shapes, and adding subtle decorations that complemented whatever holiday they were celebrating, whether it be Christmas, Easter, or even the Fourth of July.

"Don't listen to your father," her mother always told her. "When our guests compliment the decorations, he's just as proud as I am."

But there was one thing she hadn't learned from her mother: how to set a before-breast-cancer-talk table.

Frances purposefully overlooked pink linens, which she suspected her mother would have suggested she use. Instead, white linens adorned the cherrywood table, hiding the chips and scratches from so many family meals. Her plain white-and-gold-trimmed wedding china looked especially graceful on top of the gold chargers it sat on. In the center of the table sat a bouquet of white and red roses, the white of the roses so deep, they appeared to match the napkins perfectly.

"Well done," she whispered to herself. Even her mother would have been proud.

The phone rang, and she hurried to the kitchen, where she had set it on the counter. Glancing at the screen, she saw it was Charlotte.

"Hey, Charlie," she said as she held the phone to her ear. "Everything OK?"

She heard Charlotte give a little laugh. "I suspect I should be asking you that question. How are you feeling?"

Frances glanced at the clock. She still had two hours before anyone was due home. "I feel fine. Thanks again for being there for me." She raised her free hand to gently touch the bandage under her right collarbone. "It hardly hurts at all." That wasn't entirely true. There was a dull ache where the doctor had inserted the Port-a-Cath, and she couldn't touch the thin plastic tube that ran under her skin and up her neck.

"So tonight's the night, right?"

Frances rolled her eyes, glad that Charlotte wasn't there to see. "Yes, tonight."

"You're telling them tonight."

Just the fact that Charlotte was repeating her irritated Frances, but she checked her temper. "I told you that today. Dinner is cooking, the table is set . . ."

"Sounds like the perfect party setting for sharing such joyous news," Charlotte stated in a flat voice. "Are you trying to impress them before you depress them? Is that the game plan?"

Leave it to Charlotte. If she didn't know better, she would have thought that Carrie was taking lessons from her on the proper use of sarcasm. "I'm not trying to impress anyone." She turned around and glanced at the timer on the stove. "I just . . . I just want to do it my way. They're going to have a lot of questions. Besides, after tonight I don't know how I'll feel, and this might be the last family sit-down in a while."

Her comment was met with silence.

"Charlie? You there?"

Frances heard her friend sigh into the other end of the phone. "Yes, I'm here. And I'll be waiting for you to text me later. I want to know how they take the news."

"Thanks, Charlotte. I'll be sure to let you know. Now, if you don't mind, I want to lie down for a little bit." The truth was that she wasn't all that tired, but she needed to relax for a moment. She knew that the evening would be long and stressful. And there was no amount of decorating that could make that feel any better.

She was standing in the dining room when the front door opened. As soon as Nicholas entered, he jiggled his keys, then tossed them onto the front table and set down his briefcase. For once, she had managed to place the mail there, sorted into three piles: bills, junk, and other miscellaneous items. Even after all these years, she could never be sure if some of the sports-related magazines or catalogs might be of interest to Nicholas. Rather than discard them outright and risk upsetting him, which had happened on more than one occasion, she left everything perfectly organized on the hall table for him to sort through. She justified it as being one of the ways to show him how much she cared.

"Frances?" he called out, walking past the staircase toward the kitchen. As he passed the open doorway into the dining room, he stopped short and peered into the room, a concerned look on his face. "What's this? Company? Tonight?"

Her smile faded. She glanced at the grandfather clock in the hallway and saw that it was only ten to seven. Nicholas was home early. However, it wasn't because he remembered her request. In fact, he clearly forgot that she'd told him she needed to talk to him. Again.

Forcing a small smile, she shook her head. "No. Only us."

He frowned as if searching his memory for something that he might have forgotten. "It's not Carrie's birthday, is it?"

Trying to be upbeat, Frances walked toward him. Placing her hand on his shoulder, she leaned over and gently kissed his cheek. He smelled like a weaker version of the musky scent from earlier that morning. She could always recognize it: his day-old office scent. "No, it's not her birthday."

"So . . . ?"

Leaving her hand on his shoulder, she pulled back and gazed into his face. "So nothing. It's a 'just because' dinner."

"Just because?" He repeated the words in a suspicious manner that made Frances fight the urge to cringe. "Just because of what?" he asked.

"Just because I felt like it." She paused, wishing that he would lean forward and kiss her, gift her with a small token of his affection.

"Remember, I told you I needed to talk to you? I asked you to come home early? I thought we'd have a nice family dinner. It's been a while."

For a long moment he seemed to consider this. She could see him trying to determine whether something was amiss. The dining room was usually reserved for holidays and company, not a simple family dinner on a weeknight. But the look on Frances's face must have convinced him that nothing was wrong, because he finally forced a small smile back.

"I suppose 'just because' is a great reason, then," he said wearily while tugging on his tie. "Although it *has* been a long day."

His comment irritated her. Every day was a long day for Nicholas. Seeing him return from work before nine o'clock was shocking. During the week they rarely sat down together as a family. Frances had given up on that long ago. The more she pressured him to cut back his hours, the more time he seemed to spend at the office.

He glanced over her shoulder toward the door that led into the kitchen.

"Smells like you've been cooking up a storm. What's for dinner?"

"Lamb."

He raised an eyebrow. "Lamb?"

It was his favorite, mostly because she usually served it only on Easter and on Christmas Eve. His schedule was too chaotic to make such elaborate meals on a regular basis. Tonight, however, she'd decided to make everyone's favorite—mashed potatoes for Carrie, corn casserole for Andy, and a Caesar salad with anchovies for herself. And she even picked up a bottle of wine, which was uncorked and breathing on the center of the table next to the fresh flowers.

With a little shrug, Frances looked away, focusing on the kitchen rather than the quizzical look on Nicholas's face.

"Something you want to tell me?" he asked. His voice was flat and emotionless. She should have known that he would react this way:

defiant, concerned, untrusting. Only, deep down, she'd hoped that he would go with the flow and enjoy the surprise. After all, it was the last supper they would share before she started to fight her battle with cancer. Frances didn't know how long it would be before she would feel well enough to try to pamper her family again.

"Later, Nicholas. Why don't you go change," she suggested, "while I finish up in the kitchen?"

Perhaps she had gone too far. She had no idea what the future held, how her body would react to the chemotherapy. Her plan to try to maintain balance could abruptly end at any time. All she wanted was to have one more night of *normal*, even if her idea of normal wasn't normal at all.

Her thoughts were interrupted by the sound of footsteps coming down the stairs, followed by the patter of dogs' feet. Not surprisingly, Frances heard Andy jump the last few steps, pounding onto the landing. Despite wanting to, she didn't call out to reprimand him. Not tonight anyway.

"Whoa! What's this for? Carrie's birthday?"

"I must be a sorry excuse for a mother if everyone thinks it's someone's birthday when I cook a special meal for my family!" She swallowed the bitter irony that no one ever remembered her own birthday.

Andy leaned against the counter and dipped his finger into the bowl of mashed potatoes. Playfully, she slapped his hand away, but not before he got a heap.

"So, what's the big deal, then?"

She shook her head. "Nothing in particular."

"Did we win the lottery or something?"

She laughed. "You know I don't play that."

He shrugged. "Hey, I can always dream! After all, you gotta be in it to win it!"

She tossed a towel at him, which he caught.

She couldn't help but wonder when the last time was that she'd spent a few minutes alone with Andy, casually bantering back and forth. He was usually busy after school with sports and friends, too old to be bothered with his parents, unless he wanted something. And she was usually too tired to deny his requests, no matter how great or small.

But standing in the kitchen together, talking about nothing, meant everything to her. It was exactly what she needed tonight: a happy memory to hold on to before she began the day-to-day journey of defeating cancer.

If she could only have this one last night of normal. A night where she could pretend she didn't feel as if she were standing on the edge of a canyon, waiting for the wind to shift and push her forward into the abyss of the unknown. She only hoped and prayed that there was a bridge across that canyon, one that she could cross to reach the other side.

She knew she would have to tell them after dinner. She wanted the dinner to be special, a time of sharing and laughing. Only then would she be able to break the news to Nicholas. After the kids went to bed, they would discuss how to tell Andy and Carrie. She hoped to be able to wait until after she started her chemotherapy.

"Dad said to come downstairs," Carrie said as she walked toward the kitchen. She stopped in front of the dining room. "Company?" She looked irritated and turned to glare at her mother. "Seriously, Mom? I have a test tomorrow, and I don't feel like being all blah blah blah with your friends."

"Relax," Frances said. "You'll be happy to know that you only have to 'blah blah blah' with us, your family."

The expression on her face said it all. She frowned in disbelief. "What?" She looked around at the beautifully set dining room table and the lovely bouquet of flowers. "All of this for us?" When she returned her eyes to her mother's, Carrie grimaced. "That's almost as bad as company!"

"Carrie!"

Her daughter seemed unfazed by Frances's response. "I really need to study, Mom. Can't I just take a plate upstairs?"

Frances winced as if she'd been stung. She had hoped to avoid just such a reaction from Carrie. Just once. Instead, Carrie had remained consistent in reminding Frances that, despite her own dreams of family, her daughter was still a product of the "generation of entitlements" with unrealistic expectations and very little consideration or compassion for others. It seemed that most of the teen generation felt as if the world revolved around themselves, with little respect for the hopes, dreams, and needs of others. Just their own demands.

"You most certainly cannot." Frances didn't care. Not tonight. Not on *her* night. "You can study afterward. You can spare an hour to be with your family."

"An hour?" She sighed and then leaned against the counter, hanging her head forward so her hair covered her face. In a typical teenage fashion of overdramatizing everything, she mumbled, "I can't. I just can't."

"You will, and stand up straight, please. You can start by carrying these into the other room." Frances pushed two bowls, one filled with creamy garlic mashed potatoes and the other with an oven-baked corn casserole, toward her daughter. "Now."

With a huff and a puff, Carrie stomped toward the dining room, carrying the bowls and practically slamming them onto the table. Andy rolled his eyes and looked away.

Frances did a quick count to ten, willing herself to remain calm. Up until Carrie's outburst, everything had been going quite well. She couldn't—no, she wouldn't—let Carrie's attitude ruin what would most likely be one of the last ordinary nights for a very long time. And even if

Carrie normally behaved in an ornery and sassy manner, Frances would not permit it. Not tonight.

With everything ready, Frances called up the stairs for Nicholas to come down when he finished changing. Andy took a seat while Carrie furiously texted on her phone, most likely complaining to one of her BFFs that she was being forced to join her family for dinner. Frances had to remind herself that, when she was twelve, she, too, often rebelled against her mother's attempts at unifying the family around her ideals. The only difference was that *her* mother hadn't been as patient with her as Frances was with Carrie. That was something Frances had always vowed to do better: create a unified family without being the family bully.

Frances gave her daughter a stern look. "Phones off, Carrie."

With a groan, Carrie slammed her phone onto the sideboard and slid into her designated seat across from her brother. In virtual silence, the three of them waited for Nicholas. Almost five minutes passed before he finally joined them. He gave a quick, tense smile to Frances and took his place at the head of the table, but she could tell that he was somewhere else. The way that he served his food, barely looking at Andy when he passed the casserole to his left, clearly indicated he was still at the office.

"Everything OK, Nicholas?" Frances questioned.

"Huh?" He looked up and met her gaze. "Oh, yes. Just thinking about something that happened today at work is all." He glanced at the children, then added, "I'll talk to you about it later."

She knew what *that* look meant. He didn't like to talk about work in front of the kids. She never understood why, but as with other things, she didn't challenge him.

"So how was everyone's day?" she asked. Her voice sounded forced, the question rehearsed. She imagined it was a normal topic of discussion most families talked about while they sat around the dinner table. But for her family it sounded . . . artificial. This type of dialogue was reserved for other families, families that didn't have competing schedules and self-serving interests that interfered with—no, superseded—the attention and concern most households shared. Regular families like the one Frances always dreamed of obtaining.

"You'll never guess what happened at school today!" Andy offered enthusiastically. "That Michael kid got busted for having Xanax!"

Carrie's eyes widened. "The same one that called in the bomb threat last month?"

"What bomb threat?" Nicholas asked.

"Dad! Don't you remember?" Carrie rolled her eyes. "It was in the paper."

With his lips pressed together and a scowl on his face, Nicholas shook his head. "I don't understand why that kid hasn't been kicked out of school. He's nothing but trouble."

Andy made a face. "It's because he's white. If he was Hispanic or black, they'd have expelled him long ago."

"Racist!" Carrie shouted.

"Am not! It's just the truth. Everyone knows that." He poked his fork at the mashed potatoes. "Doesn't make it right, and I don't agree with it. But that's the way it is."

Inwardly, Frances groaned. When she planned the meal, she'd envisioned the children sharing details of their day. Now, however, Andy had given Carrie the fodder she needed to begin jumping onto her typical platform for social reform.

"That's disgusting," Carrie said. "And we just sit by and let it happen? Might as well go back to the days of segregation and different water fountains for different colors!"

"Carrie . . ."

Her daughter looked at Frances, a fierce and determined expression on her face. "No, Mom. If we don't stand up for the rights of others, we're basically condoning oppression."

Nicholas reached for the wine and poured himself a healthy glass. He set the bottle back onto the table and then, as an afterthought, grabbed it again to pour a glass for Frances.

"Can we change the subject, please?" he asked.

"Why?"

Nicholas leveled his gaze at Carrie. "We aren't going to solve the wrongs of the world in this room. Not tonight, anyway." He let his words sink in, then reached for his wineglass and took a sip. "Besides, your mother made this lovely meal, and I don't think she intended that the dinner conversation revolve around social issues that are outside our purview."

"I don't get it." Carrie sank back into her chair and crossed her arms over her chest. "You two always act like everything's just fine, shutting your eyes to things that are happening all around us."

"Dad said to stop," Andy cautioned.

Clearing her throat, Frances turned her attention to her husband. "Everything all right at work? You looked a bit"—she hesitated, trying to find the proper word, one that wouldn't irritate him—"preoccupied when you got home."

He set down his wineglass, a few red drops spilling onto the white tablecloth. Frances fought the urge to grab the salt and shake it over the spots to prevent staining. But she didn't want to call attention to it.

"The Brineman deal is back on the table. I've got two really long days ahead of me," he said. He lifted his glass to his lips and took a long sip. "I might as well just tell you." Another quick glance at the children. "I have to go to Chicago for all of next week."

Chicago. Frances knew what that meant. For over a year his company had been trying to acquire the Brineman accounting firms in Chicago. Its acquisition would propel Nicholas's company to a whole new level, making them the largest independent firm in the country. It was a big deal.

But it also meant that Nicholas would be traveling more than ever, and apparently that was starting next week. The timing of the acquisition couldn't have been worse.

"Is that what you wanted to talk to me about later?" she asked.

He nodded. "Not only will I be traveling more, they're even discussing setting up an apartment there."

"What?" Andy dropped his fork and stared at his father.

"Don't worry. I'll be home on the weekends." Nicholas gave his son a reassuring smile, one that was full of affection. "It will only be until everything's finalized."

"You'll miss my football games!"

"Only during the week," he reassured Andy. "And I wouldn't miss your big Thanksgiving Day game for anything. You know you're my number one priority."

Frances glanced at her daughter, too aware that she was watching the exchange. If Andy was the number one priority, who was number two? And the even bigger question: Who was number three? As much as Carrie bemoaned social injustice and how no one was doing enough to help the downtrodden, poor, and uneducated, Frances often wondered how her daughter expected any of them to address those particular issues when they couldn't confront the preferential treatment prevalent in their own home.

"Well," Frances said slowly. "I'm sure your father will make time for both football and ballet when he's home on the weekends."

For an excruciating moment no one spoke. Andy stared at his plate, focusing on shoveling food into his mouth. His appetite seemed to be growing as fast as he was. Nicholas reached for his wineglass again, and Frances waited, hoping that someone would say something, anything, to ease the tension that had filled the room.

Taking advantage of the break in conversation, Carrie cleared her throat. "Mom, don't forget about that field trip on Friday," she said as she dished a second helping of mashed potatoes onto her plate.

"Field trip?"

With a heavy, exaggerated sigh, Carrie rolled her eyes and set down the serving dish next to her plate. The spoon slipped and fell onto the tablecloth, so this time Frances quickly reached over to pick it up and wipe away the food before the butter could stain the fabric.

"Honestly, Mom! Don't tell me you forgot!"

Frances shut her eyes, just for a second. In truth, she had forgotten. So much had happened over the past weeks. And now, with chemotherapy, she would have to reconsider chaperoning the class trip to the American Museum of Natural History in New York City.

She looked at her daughter and was met with angry eyes.

"You always do this! You forget the most important things!"

"Carrie, that's not fair—"

But Carrie cut her off. "How many times did you forget about Halloween? We had to scramble to get costumes at the last minute! I was always the laughingstock of the entire class!"

"Carrie." That was all the warning that Nicholas gave, but it, too, went unheeded.

Frances felt as if the floor had fallen out beneath her feet. "That's not true. You know I always help you with your costumes. You just can't decide until the last minute."

But her words fell on deaf ears. "I don't get it!" Carrie shoved her plate away in disgust. "It's not like you actually *do* anything. Isn't that the point of being a stay-at-home mom? To take care of your kids? Well, you sure do everything for Dad!"

His fist came down on the table. "That's enough, young lady!"

"Well, it's true!"

He leaned forward and pointed a finger at her. "One more word and you're going to your room!"

"That's what I wanted in the first place."

Frances cringed as Nicholas narrowed his eyes and glared at their daughter. "You don't speak to your parents that way. Go on upstairs."

"Gladly!" She shoved her chair back and stood up, but not before picking up her plate.

"Leave it! Just go upstairs."

"I was taking it with me."

"I said, 'Leave it,'" he snapped at her. "And you're grounded until next weekend."

"What?" Carrie's eyes grew wide as she looked back and forth from her mother to her father. "*She* forgets my field trip and *I* get punished?"

Frances grimaced. The one thing she hadn't wanted had just happened: Carrie had ruined the dinner, and faster than usual. If only she could learn to control her tongue. Unfortunately, the older she became, the saucier her tone of voice and biting comments. Having a strong opinion without life experience to justify it could be a dangerous thing.

Nicholas shoved his plate forward and reached for his wine. This time, he drained it. Like oil and water, Carrie and Nicholas had clashed the moment she was born. The fantasy of Daddy's Little Girl had disappeared when Carrie came home from the hospital and cried for hours on end. She was inconsolable. Unlike with Andy, Nicholas rarely lifted a finger to help with her midnight and early-morning feedings. While Nicholas wouldn't leave Andy's side when he was an infant, it was a constant struggle to get him to even hold his daughter, let alone help with bathing or diaper changes.

"That's just great, Frances." He stood up, shoving the chair backward. "Like I needed this tonight?" Abruptly, he crumpled his napkin before throwing it onto his chair. "I have work to do. I don't need these distractions. When are you going to learn?"

Dumbfounded, Frances stared at him as he stormed out of the dining room, grabbed his briefcase, and headed into his office. The door slammed shut. She heard the lock turn and realized that, once again, she'd missed the opportunity to tell him. Her shoulders slumped forward as she stared at her half-eaten plate of food.

"Hey, Mom."

Andy's soft voice broke through her troubled thoughts. She looked at him, and he offered her a compassionate smile.

"I'll help you clean up, OK?"

All she wanted was to be alone. She needed time to wrap her head around what had just happened. But the look on her son's face touched her deeply. So rather than decline his offer, she merely nodded her head and knew that she would have plenty of time later, when she was alone in her room, to release the flood of tears that were building up inside her. And not just from tonight, or even the past few weeks, but from the past few years.

CHAPTER 10

Standing in front of the nurses' station, Frances hesitated.

She couldn't quite remember where she was supposed to go: to the gray chair or the nurses' station? Everything that had been discussed with her during her tour had simply evaporated from her mind. She remembered nothing: not the sequence of events, not the name of the nurse who had spoken with her, not even the reason why she was standing there at that moment.

Oh, she knew it was because she had breast cancer. *That* was something she couldn't forget. But why was she *here*? And on top of that, why was she *alone*?

She stared down the corridor along the wall of windows, taking in the lounge chairs, all of them gray and occupied, at least the ones that she could see from her vantage point. The people seated in them varied in age, gender, and ethnicity. Clearly, cancer did not discriminate. The main thing they all had in common, however, was that they each had a clear tube that ran from a machine into their chest or arm, and the machine was pumping toxic medicine into their bodies.

The second thing that they all had in common was the desire to live etched onto their faces. Even the more solemn expressions and haggard faces told a story of survival—or at least the will to still try.

Despite the different stories each face told, the patients had similar traits in common. Their skin appeared to be almost translucent, and their eyes were sunken into their faces, already looking as if they were half-dead. Frances wondered why they were even there. Clearly, their chances of survival were limited at best. Was the minute gain of a few extra weeks or months worth the suffering that was so obvious? Why didn't they just give up? More importantly, why didn't she?

I'm here because of my family: Nicholas and Andy and Carrie.

Frances blinked her eyes and gave her head a little shake. At least the family she hoped they would one day become. Whether they knew it or not, they *needed* her. Even if they didn't appreciate her, especially lately.

The realization made her take a deep breath and straighten her shoulders. She would not be one of those people in the gray chairs with ashen faces and parched lips, falling asleep during treatment with mouths hanging partially open and heads tilting to one side. She shook her head and did another scan of the room, hoping to see something more encouraging. But all she saw were wives or husbands who sat in a chair beside them, busily ignoring the patient while they tapped at a cell phone or read a magazine. Was that true love? If so, perhaps it was better that she had not forced Nicholas to find the time to listen to her.

"Excuse me," Frances said, leaning over the counter. "I . . . uh . . . I'm here for my first treatment."

The woman seated behind the desk looked up and smiled at her, her dark eyes peering over the top of her eyeglasses.

"You must be Frances!" She stood up and said, "We've been waiting for you."

Frances raised an eyebrow as she met the woman's gaze.

"You can just sign in here," she said, pointing to a clipboard on the counter. "Eddie will be along in a moment to fetch you." She gestured to a short brown-skinned man who was busy taking the blood pressure of another patient across the room. "He'll take your vitals, and then you can have a seat in one of the reclining chairs." She glanced around the room. "Hmm, we have a full house today, eh? I think there are some open chairs toward the far wall."

"And then what?"

The woman gave her a compassionate smile. "We'll come find you, Frances."

Frances contemplated this. *We'll come find you.* Like cancer had found her. Instead of commenting, she picked up the pen and scribbled her name on the sign-in sheet. Her eyes skimmed the list of names ahead of her: Marion Riley, James Johnson, Rita Sanders, Rod Bernard, Madeline Cooper, Steve Kapp. All people who, like Frances, were battling cancer. All of them were fighting for one reason or another. In that regard, they were all the same. Except not one of them was really like Frances. Not one of them was fighting to live for the same reasons.

Not. One. Of. Them.

"Mrs. Snyder?"

Frances jumped and turned around, startled by the man standing behind her.

"Oh!" Her hand pressed against her chest as she nodded her head. "That's me."

"Let's get your temperature, blood pressure, and weight so we can get you situated, yes?" His accent was so thick that she almost didn't understand what he'd said. He motioned with his hand for her to follow him around the nurses' station and toward a scale in the back. "Shoes off, then step onto the scale, please."

"Hundred and fifty pounds," she said, not wanting to see the numbers on the scale, a reminder of the ten extra pounds she had wanted to lose but hadn't. Just one more thing she hadn't been able to achieve. Just one more reminder that she was not infallible, even though she tried.

Eddie stared at her as if he didn't understand.

"I . . . I don't need to get on the scale," she explained, then nervously sat down. "I . . . I just weighed myself this morning."

"I see." He didn't argue with her. "I'll make a note of that, then." He scribbled something on a white piece of paper and asked her to roll up her sleeve.

While he was taking her temperature and blood pressure, Frances glanced at the rooms that were curtained off from the rest of the center. Older patients who were bedridden lay there, white blankets covering their bodies. All of them wore simple caps on their heads. Frances assumed they had lost all their hair from the chemo.

Instinctively, she reached up and touched her newly shorn hair.

How long will it take?

"OK, Mrs. Snyder, you're all set." Eddie handed her a slip of white paper and gave her an encouraging smile. "Go find a chair," he said.

When he motioned toward the row of patients receiving treatment, Frances nodded and, with the paper clutched in her hand, walked away from him. Each footstep felt heavy, and her heart began to pound. She felt as if she were floating above herself, watching as she walked past all of these people. She tried to place the names from the list to the faces, wondering if one of the men was Steve or Rod and the next woman Marion or Rita.

Just as she had been told, there were a few empty chairs toward the back of the room. Frances sighed, then selected one closest to the window. Setting her bag on the floor, she eased herself into the chair and shut her eyes.

Relax. Cancer, not chemotherapy, kills people.

Still, when she opened her eyes, she was struck, once again, with cancer's commitment to equal opportunity selection.

A few of the patients looked at her, or perhaps they'd been watching her all along. *Chemo Chick Walking,* she'd thought in a lame attempt to ease her palpitating heart. Now, as Frances caught them watching her, she could see sympathy in their eyes. Perhaps a few of them felt as if they were the lucky ones because they'd lasted as long as they had, escaping the cancer diagnosis until they hit sixty or seventy. At forty-two, Frances was, without a doubt, the youngest patient in the room.

Should she feel pride in that distinction? She didn't.

In the next chair, an older woman turned toward her. It was the same woman that she'd had a conversation with during her tour of the chemotherapy center. Somehow, she recalled that her name was Madeline. That was what the man had called her during Frances's tour of the Chemo Cocktail Lounge. Her tired blue eyes gave Frances the once-over, as if she were sizing up her new neighbor. Right away, Frances knew that the woman was a busybody. It was all too obvious by the way her eyes inspected Frances's handbag and shoes.

"First time?" Madeline said.

Frances responded with a muffled "Mmm-hmm" that she hoped would indicate her disinterest in socializing.

Apparently not. The woman gave her a quizzical look, the wrinkles under her eyes becoming even deeper. "First time and you're alone?"

For a split second Frances contemplated moving to another chair. The last thing she wanted was to turn her chemotherapy treatment into a social event. Instead, she concentrated and tried to get into her zone, the place where she always sought refuge when things were too unpleasant to face. She had the ability to retreat into her mind, envision happier days, and remove herself from almost any situation. When she was younger and in church, she taught herself to appear to be actively listening while escaping to her zone. Now, if she could only find it today, the chemotherapy could begin and end without unnecessary stress on her mind. And then she could get home and begin her new normal.

Despite having booked her appointment for early morning, she knew she'd only have a short time to rest before the children returned home from school. And then it would be back to smiles and listening to stories about their day. For everyone else, it would be a normal day in the Snyder household. With Nicholas leaving for Chicago soon, she had decided to wait, yet again, to tell him until he returned. Telling him now would mean that he would have to cancel his trip. At this point, she just didn't want to deal with the ramifications. Not right now. So, for today, there was no time for cancer to derail Frances's plans. This was just one more event, a thing that she knew must be dealt with—no matter how unpleasant—a scheduled appointment that she could cross off her list the moment she walked out those double doors, heading into the crisp autumn sunshine.

A nurse in pink scrubs walked over to her. Unlike the other people that Frances had encountered, she did not smile, nor did she greet her with a cheerful tone. Instead, she hastily clipped a clear bag of fluid to the pole behind Frances's chair. She pressed a few buttons and then began removing sterilized items from a plastic container. After putting on purple latex gloves, she grabbed a plastic tube with a round end on it.

"Your port is on the right side?"

Frances nodded, her hand instinctively rising up to cover the area where her port had been surgically implanted. The skin was still sore, and she dreaded the thought of the needle being inserted into it.

"It's not that bad," the nurse said, patiently waiting for Frances to remove her hand. Then, the nurse pushed Frances's blouse to the side and assessed her chest. "Ah, yes. There it is." She began swabbing the area with antiseptic before she lifted the round object toward the port. "You ready?"

"For what?"

There was no time for the nurse to answer a routine question. She pressed the round piece that was connected to a needle into Frances's chest and, breaking skin, snapped it into her port.

Frances grabbed the arms of the chair, her hands clawlike in their grasp, and winced at the pain. It was sharp and unexpected. The suddenness of the piercing felt invasive, spreading a new sense of reality through Frances.

"Sorry," the nurse said as she ripped two pieces of medical tape to cover the needle. "Trust me. If I give you a warning, it's worse."

"I bet!" Frances wasn't certain if she was grateful or irritated. Her skin stung and her heart began to race. *This is happening. It's really happening.* For a moment everything felt surreal, and she prayed that she would wake up and all of this would be just one long nightmare. But then it dawned on her that she really had cancer.

"Now, when I flush the line, you might taste something metallic in your mouth," the nurse said after drawing a tube of blood, which she promptly put aside. "Nothing I can do about that."

Frances shut her eyes and waited, knowing the exact moment when the nurse started and finished her next task. True to her word, a strange taste flooded her mouth, and she couldn't help but rub her lips together. She could taste it, smell it. No one had warned her about this during her meetings with doctors or tour of the chemo center. Somehow it had been overlooked. There was never any mention that the medicine would affect her taste buds. Having the chemicals in her body was bad enough; tasting them was even worse.

"There. It should go away in a little bit, the taste," she said. "Now, let me get your medicine while the line drips. You just stay there and try to relax."

"What's in that bag?" Frances hadn't wanted to inquire, hadn't wanted to know. At least, not on a conscious level. But the question had slipped out before she could stop herself.

"Benadryl and an antinausea medicine." That was it. No further explanation was given before the nurse turned and walked away.

Frances took a deep breath, leaning back and shutting her eyes once again. Instead of thinking about the upcoming slow drip of chemicals that would join her blood to fight her cancer, she focused on images of her children. She remembered Andy as a toddler taking his first steps, refusing her help as he let go of the living room chair and took the three steps necessary to reach the sideboard. His pride in doing something so important alone, without her help but with her applause, made Frances realize then that he needed her to be his constant cheerleader from the sidelines.

And Carrie had always been independent. Even when she was her most difficult, she still needed to know that her mother was there for her, an invisible wingman to catch her in the unlikely (but inevitable) case that she should fall.

Frances tried to imagine them as young adults, going to college and getting married, becoming parents and making her a grandmother. Those were the thoughts that she hoped would take her away from the chemotherapy center of Morristown Memorial Hospital.

She remained like that for a good twenty minutes, willing herself to keep her eyes closed until the nurse returned and fiddled with the apparatus. She must have thought that Frances was sleeping, because she didn't say a word. It wasn't until after the nurse left that Frances's curiosity got the best of her. Opening her eyes, she looked over at the machine. Two large plastic syringes had been pushed into the dispenser, one full of red liquid and the other clear.

"The red one is the nasty one."

Frances glanced to her left and saw that it was Madeline.

"It's called Adriamycin. That's the one that makes everyone sick."

Frances lifted both eyebrows. "I thought all of this made everyone sick."

The woman laughed, and when she did, her eyes crinkled into half-moons that were supported by a lifetime of wrinkles.

"That's true." There was a long moment of silence. Frances was just about to shut her eyes again when she heard, "I'm Madeline. What's your name?"

Inwardly, Frances groaned. Now would come the polite airplane talk that she dreaded. Whenever she flew somewhere, she avoided speaking to the person seated next to her. Just listening to random people who insisted on striking up situational conversation irritated her. Empty dialogue about careers, family, or banal topics that neither person cared about seemed like a waste of time. Even worse was the exchanging of contact information, as if either person had any intention of further communication.

"Frances," she heard herself respond in a quiet voice, hoping that the woman would get the hint that she wasn't interested in trifles. "We met the other day."

Madeline tilted her head, appearing to search her memory. And then she smiled. "I remember you, yes! You were touring with Thomas." She leaned over and, in a hoarse whisper, said, "He's a real stinker, that guy. I once sat here for over an hour before he unhooked me! More interested in that blond nurse over there than taking care of the patients, if you ask me."

Something about the unexpected insight into the social dynamics of the chemotherapy center made Frances smile. No matter where people were, there was always something to gossip about, regardless of how trivial it was.

Sitting back in her chair, Madeline frowned, the wrinkles around the corners of her eyes deepening as she watched Frances.

"You should really ask for some ice pops."

Ice pops? Vaguely she remembered that Thomas had mentioned them to her during the tour.

"Why?"

With a wrinkled finger, Madeline pointed to her mouth, which she proceeded to open, then stuck out her blister-covered tongue. "Mouth sores."

None of Frances's research had mentioned mouth sores. And from the look of Madeline's tongue, Frances could understand why. There was nothing Frances hated more than canker sores. Whenever she caught a cold, the inevitable canker sores inside her cheeks made talking painful, and she found herself irritable under the best of circumstances.

"Thanks."

She wanted to ask Madeline why *she* wasn't sucking on an ice pop. But Frances refrained from prying.

From the looks of the older woman, she was a chemotherapy veteran, a woman who had such severe cancer, it required multiple sessions a week. Perhaps it had metastasized, spread to her other organs. Whatever type of cancer it was, Frances didn't really want to know, and she certainly didn't want to know how advanced it was. The last thing she wanted was to get close to the woman, or anyone else, for that matter. In her mind, the chemotherapy was going to kill her cancer and she wouldn't need to have the double mastectomy that the doctor had recommended. And if that was the case, she wouldn't be returning to the Chemo Cocktail Lounge ever again.

What she needed was one thing and one thing only: distance. Keep your distance. As far as she was concerned, this ugliness would be over in eight weeks, and she would never have to return.

And no one would be any wiser about this unfortunate blip in her life.

No one.

CHAPTER 11

"Can I get you anything?"

Frances hung her head over the toilet bowl, wishing more than anything that Nicholas would just go away.

"I'm fine," she managed to say, but only seconds later she began vomiting again.

The previous day, when she'd left the hospital, she felt fine. One of the nurses had handed her several slips of blue paper, prescriptions for medicine that Frances needed to get filled, with a warning to watch for fever. But Frances had merely shoved the papers into her purse and hurried out the door to get as far away from the chemotherapy center and the hospital as possible.

Instead of stopping at the pharmacy on her way, she headed straight for home. She tackled her afternoon as she normally did: doing a load of laundry, preparing the evening meal, and making certain that everything was tidied up before anyone came home. By the time Carrie and Andy descended upon the kitchen for dinner, she still felt fine. In fact, Frances had silently laughed at cancer and all the people who complained about the toll it took on their bodies.

However, all of that changed when she sat down for dinner. The food tasted bland, and her stomach started to react. She had to push away her plate and lean back in the chair. Carrie merely glanced at her once, but Andy eyed her suspiciously.

"You all right, Momma?"

She winced. "I hate when you call me that," she mumbled.

He laughed. "I'll take that as a yes!"

But she shook her head. "It just hit me," she said. "I'm going to excuse myself and ask the two of you to clean up when you're done."

As usual, Carrie made a face but Andy nodded, watching as Frances left the table, her arm clutching her stomach. She retired to the bedroom and, for once, was thankful that Nicholas was working late. When he finally got home, well after ten, she pretended to be asleep.

He never tried to wake her.

Throughout the night, the pains and cramping continued. It wasn't until after two o'clock in the morning that she finally conceded defeat and raced to the bathroom. When she hovered over the toilet, vomiting what little she'd eaten, she knew that karma had just called her out for having mocked the power of chemotherapy.

From two o'clock until six that morning, she slept sporadically, occasionally getting up to sneak into the bathroom and, as quietly as she could, hang her head over the toilet. The last thing she wanted was to wake up Nicholas. But as usual, he slept soundly and noticed nothing peculiar about her absence, if he noticed anything at all.

In the morning, however, he heard her retching from the other side of the bathroom door.

"Frances?"

She managed to flush the toilet before he opened the door. The sound of the rushing water hurt her head.

"I'm fine," she mumbled, although she knew she looked anything but fine, especially when she stood up and peered into the mirror. She appeared worn-out. *How long have I been in here?* There were ridges in her right cheek that felt oddly like the pattern of the tile on the bathroom floor, which led her to believe that she must have fallen asleep in between bouts of nausea.

Nicholas stepped forward and touched her shoulder, but she pushed his hand away. She hadn't meant to react so sharply, and for a brief moment she caught his eyes in the reflection of the mirror.

Nicholas stared at her as if burning a hole into her soul. Not only was he seething that she'd pushed him away, but he was most likely angry that she was sick to begin with.

"I know, I know." She reached for the faucet and turned it on so that she could splash water on her cheeks. "You need the bathroom to get ready for work."

"What's wrong with you?"

She contemplated telling him. It was the perfect opportunity. She envisioned his response to her blurting out *I have cancer, Nicholas, and yesterday I had my first chemotherapy treatment, but you've been too busy, as usual, for me to even tell you.* He'd be silent for a minute as he digested her words, and then he'd realize how distant he had become in the past few years. How work had replaced his focus on the family . . . on her.

But when she assumed that he hadn't asked her that question—*What's wrong with you?*—out of concern, which she so desperately wanted to hear, but anger from her having shoved his hand away, she realized that she couldn't tell him. Not now. Not like this. Besides, he was leaving for Chicago in a couple of days, and she knew how important that work trip was.

"It's just a bug, I'm sure." She reached for a towel and covered her cheeks, the pressure from her fingers helping her focus on the here and now, not on the what-should-have-been. "It's that time of year, and the kids probably brought something home." She lowered the towel from her face and stared at him in the reflection of the mirror, half hoping that he would call her out on the lie. But he didn't.

"A bug," he repeated skeptically.

When she heard his terse tone, she realized the truth. He hadn't been concerned that she was sick; rather, he had thought she might be pregnant. Again. She felt her chest tighten as another wave of nausea overcame her. He was, yet again, oblivious to her needs. Only this time it wasn't a second child. This time it was simply the loving arms of her husband, reaching out to comfort her. A husband who would, without complaint, push aside meetings and obligations to tend to his wife during a time of distress.

But that was not the husband who stood before her now, watching her with suspicious curiosity.

"I'm fine," she repeated again.

"Well, let me get you some water at least," he offered.

It was the last thing she wanted, but she nodded anyway. She would have agreed to anything to make him go away. She didn't need to resurrect the past. Instead, what she needed were those antinausea pills that the nurse had prescribed. Why had she been too stubborn to fill the prescription? Now it was the one and only thing that she wanted. She would take anything to make the nausea go away.

When Nicholas returned, he handed her a glass of water and leaned against the wall, his arms crossed over his chest as he watched her.

She felt as if she were under a microscope. She knew that he was waiting for her to drink the water. Despite having no idea whether her stomach would tolerate it, she took a long sip from the glass.

In their eighteen years of marriage, she'd been ill only one time. It was during a business trip to Mexico soon after Nicholas had started working for the firm. She hadn't listened to everyone's advice about avoiding the drinking water, although she hadn't realized it at the time. One salad, with lettuce that presumably had been washed in tap water, became her Kryptonite. She spent three of the five days in the hotel room, and Nicholas had shown her no compassion.

"How could you have eaten a salad? What were you thinking?" he yelled at her. "These meetings and dinners are important. It's for both of us; that's why you were invited, Frances. It could impact my promotion, you know? We are being judged to see if we fit in with these executives and their wives!"

She hadn't responded. Instead, she lay in bed with a cool cloth on her forehead. The last thing on her mind was fitting in with executives and their wives. Silently, she prayed that he'd just go away and do whatever he needed to do. Anything as long as he stopped talking and left her alone.

Which he'd done.

After that experience, she remained healthy and strong, at least on the surface. If she ever felt poorly or knew a cold was coming on, she kept it hidden from him. Clearly, illness was something outside of his purview for compassion.

Now, she tried to push away the memory of Mexico. At least he wasn't yelling at her. She didn't know if she would be able to handle that. Not this time.

"I take it you weren't able to pick up my dry cleaning yesterday," he said.

Frances fought the urge to yell at him. Here she was, sick to her stomach, and his main concern was his dry cleaning? "It must have slipped my mind, Nicholas. I'm sorry."

He sighed and shook his head. "That's rather inconvenient, Frances."

She wanted to throw the glass of water at his head. And yet, because of her, he wasn't aware of the true depths of her sickness. She couldn't blame him for thinking this was just another passing bug. So instead of snapping at him, she merely gestured toward his closet. "You still have clean shirts from last week."

"Will you be able to pick them up today?"

This time, she hesitated before answering him. She felt a flash of anger and fought to quickly compress it, to tuck it away into the recesses of her mind, along with the other moments of anger that she too often felt.

"Yes, of course, Nicholas." She didn't know how she would do it, but she would. "Thank you for the water. That helped." Forcing a smile, she handed him the half-empty glass.

When he took it from her, he held it without retracting his arm. His face darkened as he studied her face, and she could see the wheels of his mind moving at a hundred miles per hour. He put the glass down on the bathroom counter.

"Change in seasons, I suppose. Or maybe I ate something that doesn't agree with me."

"Food poisoning?" he said, with his arms crossed over his chest.

"I had seafood for lunch yesterday."

He raised an eyebrow. "Food poisoning usually hits fast and furious, Frances."

"It was a late lunch," she snapped at last, irritated at the inquisition. "Don't worry, Nicholas. It's nothing."

In order to avoid his dark gaze, she leaned over the sink and splashed some water on her face. It felt cool against her warm skin. With her stomach empty, she knew she wouldn't vomit again anytime soon. If she could just get back to bed and sleep, she'd hopefully feel fine by midafternoon.

When she turned off the water, Nicholas handed her a fresh towel. She took it and covered her face, patting her cheeks as well as hiding her eyes. If only she'd told him. The moment had been there, presenting itself once again. But the irritated look on his face had angered her, and now the moment was gone.

She'd have to find another one. But when?

She shut her eyes and leaned against the sink. The deception had gone on far too long to simply confess the truth. It reminded her of the weeks after she'd learned about another life change: her second pregnancy. His reaction, her cover-up. It wasn't supposed to be this way.

"I . . . I just need to catch up on my sleep," she said. Dropping the towel, she looked at him, thankful to see the shadow of distrust dissolve from his face. "Maybe you could make sure the kids get to school this morning? Oh, and Carrie needs money for that school trip."

Nicholas gave her a look, out of either concern or irritation. Truth be told, at the present moment she didn't really care.

"Well." Nicholas glanced at his watch. "I'm sure I can get the kids to the bus."

Frances was certain that he was suppressing irritation.

"Don't forget that money for her field trip," she managed to say as she shuffled past him and crawled back into bed. Without him there, it felt warm and welcoming. She snuggled into the down comforter, pulled it up under her chin. She could hear him getting ready for work and knew he wasn't going to question her further, his focus most likely having shifted to work, the more important of his two problems. That left Frances the freedom to shut her eyes and slip into her zone once again. In those moments she could shut out the rest of the world and simply exist, as if she were suspended in air and floating through life with no worries or cares.

If only . . .

For the rest of the morning she remained in bed except for an occasional trip to the bathroom to hover over the toilet. She slept as much as she could and thanked God more than once that the children were at school and not home to witness her condition.

Perhaps it was time to figure out how, exactly, to tell Nicholas. She'd have to wait until he returned from his trip. Then she could sit down with him, explain what was going on, and answer his questions. She would know enough to be able to answer his questions without feeling ignorant. She would be facing her second treatment.

Together, they would tell the children. She'd have to figure out how to explain why she had kept it from them in the first place, without making Nicholas feel any worse for not having made the time. Would they accept her explanation that she hadn't wanted them to worry? That everything was going to be fine? But knowing the children, they would see through that. How would she explain the fact that their father had been too busy, too irritable, too Nicholas to have a moment's time for her to tell him? What she had started, a simple delay in discussing the situation, he had unwittingly continued.

It was almost noon when her phone rang. She reached for it, half expecting it to be Nicholas checking in on her and only half surprised when she heard Charlotte's voice on the other end of the line.

"Hey, girl. How are you doing today?" The concern and empathy in Charlotte's voice touched Frances.

"I think I lost five pounds already."

Charlotte gave a hollow laugh. "That's some diet."

"I don't recommend it."

It sounded as if Charlotte shifted the phone. Frances could envision her holding it to her ear with her shoulder while doing something else with her hands. Charlotte was, after all, a perpetual multitasker. "Look, I'm running out for a few things. I plan on stopping by, so what can I bring for you?"

"I . . ." Frances hesitated.

"Don't start that with me, Frances," Charlotte blurted out. "If you need something, let me know. That's what friends are for, right?"

Even though she was alone in the room, Frances shut her eyes and nodded.

"Yes, you're right. Of course," she said. Then she took a deep breath. "I have a prescription here, Char. I really could use it filled. It will help with the nausea."

"Easy enough. I can swing by in a little bit to pick it up."

"It's in my purse. In the kitchen, I think."

"Got it. Anything else?"

"And Nicholas's dry cleaning . . . it's at Willow's on Elm Place."

Charlotte sucked in air as if she had been caught off guard. "It's one thing to help you, Frances," she said in a slow, even voice, "but quite another to ask me to be a personal assistant to Nicholas."

Frances raised her free hand to her forehead and rubbed at her temples. "That would be helping me, Charlie. Please?"

"Fine!" But her tone didn't sound fine. In fact, she sounded as irritated as Nicholas had that morning.

"Thank you." Frances knew that it sounded meek, but it was the best that she could offer.

"You get better, and then you owe me, girlfriend."

She managed a small smile, even though Charlotte couldn't see her.

"Yes. Yes, I do," she whispered as she heard the phone click on the other end.

Two hours passed before the front door opened and she heard the sound of a woman's shoes clicking against the floor. The dogs didn't bark, which surprised Frances. She had managed to fall asleep after she'd spoken to Charlotte. Now, as she tried to sit up, her body ached and her head felt as if someone were twisting a vise around it.

"Charlie?" she managed to call out, her voice barely audible. "I'm upstairs."

Within minutes, Charlotte poked her head around the bedroom door.

"You look awful!" she announced as she pushed her way into the bedroom and marched over to the bed. "You should call your doctor, Fran."

But Frances wasn't about to do that. "It's nothing, really. All the research I did said that it's normal. That's why they prescribe the medicine." At the mention of the medicine, she glanced at Charlotte's empty hands. "You did get the medicine, right?"

"Relax. Yes. It's downstairs." She sat on the edge of the bed and reached out to touch Fran's forehead. "You don't have a fever, but you look horrible."

"You already pointed that out." She pulled the comforter up, tucking it farther under her chin. "I really could use that medicine, Charlie."

"Right."

Frances watched as she hurried back into the hallway. Her heels made a sharp clicking sound on the steps, and Frances shut her eyes, willing the pain in her head to disappear. She needed to feel better to face the weekend; there was too much that needed to be done. Carrie had ballet practice, and Andy had two football games. Nicholas would want to play golf on Sunday morning before he flew to Chicago later that evening. She needed to feel better to face the upcoming week. There was only so much she could ask him to do until he had to leave for the airport; then everything would fall back onto her shoulders.

She would have no backup.

"Here's some ginger ale," Charlotte said as she reentered the room, carrying a glass. "No ice. It will help you feel better." She handed it to Frances and then dropped a white bag on the bed. "Some of those medicines . . ."

"What?"

Charlotte shook her head. "I asked the pharmacist about them. You really need to talk to Nicholas. He shouldn't be going on that trip, Frances. You could have severe reactions to them."

But Frances didn't want to hear that. She didn't want to think about what might happen. She recalled when her sister had attended Alcoholics Anonymous meetings during her late teenage years because she'd hung out with a bad crowd and got arrested for underage drinking. Her mother, appalled at the social stigma of having a troubled teenager—with an arrest record!—made the entire family shuffle into church. One by one, they had gone into the confessional to admit their sins, and then, as if that wasn't enough, her mother had made them attend family counseling with Father Pat for six months.

If her mother had wanted to scare the rest of the family into walking the straight and narrow, it had worked.

But there was one thing that Father Pat had said that still resonated with her. "With any addiction," he had said, "you take it one day at a time."

At the moment, even though she was battling something other than addiction, that was exactly how Frances felt. It was the most that she could do: take one day at a time.

"Look, Charlotte, this isn't so bad." Frances wondered if she sounded convincing. "I mean, what's the point of upsetting everyone in the family, anyway? What purpose will it serve?"

Charlotte cocked her head, staring at Frances with a mixed expression: one part awe and one part disbelief. "Am I hearing you correctly?" she asked. "Are you saying that you don't intend to tell them? That you want to go through this without them knowing?"

Frances played with the napkin under her glass. How could she explain that, for once, she felt in control of something? "I'm . . . I'm considering it."

Charlotte's expression changed from incredulity to concern. "Frances, you have to tell your husband!"

"Do I?" Frances felt emboldened. "Every time I try to talk to Nicholas, something comes up." She ignored Charlotte's eye roll, so reminiscent of Carrie. "Maybe God wants me to walk this journey alone."

This time Charlotte's mouth fell agape with incredulity, and her eyes grew wide. "That's the most insane thing I've ever heard!"

"Is it?"

Frances had given it a lot of thought and had even prayed about it. When the idea first struck her, she took comfort in the fact that, perhaps, that *was* the plan: fighting cancer alone. And while she knew she would have preferred the support of her family, in many ways it was easier without their involvement. She didn't have to worry about being pitied or talked about behind her back. She didn't need to fear turning into Mrs. Bentley, with self-absorbed church members competing to see who could do more for the Snyder family while Frances was undergoing treatment.

Charlotte shook her head and stood up.

"We'll see how this pans out, Fran. I'm not certain you're thinking clearly. But I'm not going to tell you how to live your life." She started walking toward the bedroom door, pausing to look back. "Why don't you rest a bit? I'm fixing supper for everyone, and I'll leave it in the refrigerator. One less thing for you to worry about, OK? We can talk about this more next week when Nicholas is away. You just don't know what's ahead of you. You've only had one treatment after all."

Frances hesitated. In her mind, she knew what she intended to do. But Charlotte's words were marked with wisdom.

"Fair enough," she said.

"Good!"

As Charlotte left the room, Frances called out, "Oh, and Charlotte?"

"Hmm?"

Frances gave a soft smile. "Thank you."

CHAPTER 12

"I spent most of the weekend in bed," Frances confessed to Charlotte. She sat across the café table from her friend, toying with the white paper napkin next to her coffee cup. "It was awful."

Admitting that the weekend had been horrible was almost as painful as having lived through it. Between the vomiting, dehydration, and stomach pains, Frances could do nothing more than suffer on her own.

"Even with the medicine?"

She nodded. "Even with the medicine."

"And what did Nicholas say?" Charlotte asked.

Averting her eyes, Frances tried to find the words to respond. How could she admit that, after dropping both kids off at their respective sports, her husband had gone to the office on Saturday, where he spent the entire day, then woke up at the crack of dawn on Sunday to play a round of golf with his country club buddies? Frances knew he had plans to play golf but had hoped he would cancel when he saw she was still feeling sick. But with Nicholas, there was no such thing as being inconvenienced, and he had gone anyway. He hadn't even acknowledged that she had spent most of that night wrapped around the toilet bowl.

"It was better that no one was home all weekend," she finally said, avoiding the truth.

Charlotte's mouth fell open as she stared at Frances. "Are you seriously telling me that he still doesn't know?"

"I've tried, Charlotte. It's just not that simple."

"No, it *is* just that simple. You tell him. No excuses. Because if you don't, I will."

Frances sighed. "He's away, anyway."

"Away." It wasn't a question, just a flat statement. "Even with you so sick."

She didn't want to go into details with Charlotte. She didn't feel like having every comment dissected and torn apart by her friend. It wasn't as if Charlotte's opinion fell on deaf ears. It was just that Frances was tired of hearing what she already knew. Long ago, work had become Nicholas's lifeblood, his means of escape. And while it hadn't happened overnight, it had evolved to this point, the point of her not being able to attract his attention long enough to tell him that she was in the midst of a battle for her life.

"I think"—Charlotte began slowly, taking her time to choose her words carefully—"that you're afraid to tell him."

Frances laughed. "Afraid? Oh, *this* is interesting! Please. Do tell."

"You might laugh, Frances, but it's not funny. In fact, I'm starting to realize just how sad this situation has become. It's pathetic."

Pathetic. The one word that Frances despised almost as much as the word *pity*. Her heart beat rapidly, and every nerve in her body felt as if it were on fire. No, she wasn't particularly liking the direction of this conversation. After their discussion on Friday, Frances had thought they'd come to an agreement, that Charlotte understood her dilemma, but clearly that was not the case.

"I think you don't want to tell him because you're scared of his reaction. Or, rather, the possibility that he *won't* react."

Frances caught her breath.

Charlotte arched one of her eyebrows. "That's right, Frances. When, not *if*, you tell him, what will you do if he doesn't react? If he doesn't offer you the support that you need?" Charlotte leaned forward and grasped her hand, holding it between both of hers. "Have you considered that?" There was a long pause. "Is it possible that's the real reason why you haven't told him? Let's face it, Frances. You married your father, and you've become your mother."

If they hadn't been out in public, Frances would have jumped to her feet and walked away. However, she didn't want to make a scene. Besides, she hadn't driven. She'd be stuck walking home, and despite feeling a little better, her body still ached and she was plagued with terrible fatigue.

So instead of walking away from her friend and the offensive line of questioning, Frances lifted her chin and replied, "My mother has nothing to do with it."

Charlotte leaned back and withdrew her hands. "I think she has everything to do with it."

How dare she? While no marriage was perfect, at least Frances tried. And Nicholas wasn't anything like Charlotte's ex-husband. How many years had Gary cheated on her? Lied to her? Used her for her paycheck while berating her for not making enough money? The truth was that Gary had spent both of their incomes faster than either of them could make the money, using it to fund his philandering ways instead of paying the bills or investing in their future. And when he was fired from his job, he hadn't even told her. Instead, he simply pretended to go to work all day when he was actually out carousing with his harem of paramours or hitting up his parents for loans. All of Charlotte's dreams were shattered by his opportunistic focus on his own needs.

No. My marriage is not perfect, but I am not as blind as Charlotte was.

"I haven't had time to tell him, Charlotte. It's that simple." She narrowed her eyes. "Cancer didn't come at a convenient time for us. He's been working long hard hours." She paused before she added, "*Really* working."

Charlotte flinched.

"And when I was going to tell him, the Brineman deal came through. He was *busy*, Charlotte."

She raised an eyebrow. "Too busy for you to talk to him? I find that hard to believe."

"Once he finishes that merger, he'll be promoted to vice president. How can I let him be distracted after all of the years he sacrificed trying to get ahead? His goal is finally within his reach, Charlotte. And he's doing it for us. For the entire family, not just himself. Only a self-centered person would be selfish enough to prevent their husband from achieving his dream." This time, it was Charlotte who looked as if she might stand up and walk away.

"You aren't thinking clearly," she whispered. "You have cancer, not a migraine headache. You say that he's doing all of this for the family, and I say to you, 'What family?'" She dabbed at her lips with her napkin before setting it down on the table. "There's a difference between being truly altruistic and being extremely naive. You might want to reflect on that just a little."

Neither woman spoke as they left the café and walked to the car. Charlotte grabbed the little white ticket that one of the traffic police had stuck under her windshield wiper and crinkled it into a little ball, which she promptly tossed on the sidewalk. Frances fought the urge to pick it up, too angry at her friend to care if she didn't pay for the violation.

By the time Charlotte dropped her off, Frances couldn't get out of the car fast enough. She barely said good-bye before slamming the car door and hurrying into the house. Once inside, she shut the door and leaned against it, closing her eyes and letting the tears fall down her cheeks. The last thing she needed was to lose the only person she could count on. If it weren't for Charlotte, she would have no one.

Still, she couldn't take any more of the constant criticism. Her marriage was her own problem, not Charlotte's, and she planned on dealing with it the best way she knew how. She hadn't put her nose in Charlotte's marriage when it was going to hell in a handbag. In fact, she'd gotten involved only when her friend asked her to, and even then she was careful not to cross any lines. Every marriage had its ups and downs.

People changed and grew, sometimes closer together but oftentimes not. Neither she nor Nicholas was the same person they'd been almost twenty years ago. They'd both grown over the years, and their focus had shifted: hers to the children and his to his career. But she had to believe that deep down they still loved each other.

She pushed away from the door and set her purse on the table in the foyer. Slowly, she walked toward the kitchen, pausing to open the back door so the dogs could run outside. For a while, she stood and watched as they chased each other around the backyard.

Did they still love each other? She believed she still loved him. It wasn't anything like Charlotte suggested; she wasn't afraid of losing him, or that he wouldn't be there for her once she let him know. No. Not at all. Besides, even if she was, didn't that prove how much she loved him?

Frances had taken their wedding vows seriously. For richer and for poorer, for better and for worse, in sickness and in health. The only problem was that Nicholas wanted only the richer, better, and health. When times were tough and they were faced with poorer, worse, and sickness, he didn't seem to remember his commitment to love, honor, and cherish her.

"Mom! What's for dinner?"

She was in the laundry room, trying to get caught up on the housework. If she didn't stay on top of the dirty clothes, it was as if they bred by themselves, like those gremlins on TV. After cleaning the lint out, she shut the dryer door, then leaned over the machine and turned it on.

"Mom!" Carrie bellowed again.

"I'm in the laundry room," Frances responded, before picking up a basket of clean clothes and walking into the kitchen. "There's no need to scream like that."

"Well, you didn't answer!"

Her daughter's sassy tone didn't sit well with Frances any day, but lately she was too tired to fight that battle. She put the basket on the kitchen table and began sorting the socks.

"We're ordering in tonight." Frances tried to find the mate to one of her knee-highs.

"Again? You never cook anymore!"

Abruptly, Frances stopped folding the laundry. She tried to count to ten, but her blood pressure was rising far too rapidly.

"And there's like no food in the house," she added.

Spinning around, Frances glared at her daughter. Her chest tightened, her anger taking over her body. Pressing her clenched fists against her thighs, it was all Frances could do to control herself. What she wanted to do was cross the floor and shake her daughter. Why the constant complaining? The snarky comments and criticisms dug beneath her skin. She had always known that raising teenagers was hard. She just hadn't realized that it would start so early with her daughter. And now, with Frances dealing with her own problems, making life-threatening decisions that she hadn't been able to discuss with Nicholas yet, her fuse was shorter than ever. Carrie was only going through a phase, and it wasn't her daughter's fault that she didn't know about the cancer. Still, Frances was tired of the constant verbal attacks.

"I'm getting a little tired of your attitude, Carrie. It's time you realize that the world doesn't revolve around you."

The clipped, even way she spoke seemed to be effective. Carrie stared at her, her eyes wide and the color draining from her cheeks.

"Mom . . . ," she stammered in a shaky voice.

An apology. That was all that Frances wanted. That and a little more respect from her daughter.

"Yes?" She waited for that apology, wanting it more than she had realized.

But it never came.

"What is wrong with your hair?"

Frances lifted her hand to her head and touched her hair. When she drew her hand back, she saw strands of blond hair on her fingers. Quickly, she met Carrie's gaze.

"You have a bald spot," she whispered. "By your ear."

If just minutes ago her blood pressure had been sky-high, she now felt as if her heart had stopped beating entirely. *No, no, no,* she thought as she hurried over to the mirror that hung in the hallway. *Not so soon.* But when she looked at herself, she saw exactly what Carrie had noticed: a patch of bald skin about the size of a quarter by her right ear.

In the reflection in the mirror, Frances saw Carrie standing behind her, her arms crossed protectively over her chest as she met her mother's gaze.

"Are you OK?" she whispered. Her cheeks were pale, her eyes filled with concern.

Frances forced a smile. "I'm . . . I'm fine, sweetheart. I forgot that I banged my head on the washer lid," she said quickly. "It banged down and . . ." She glanced at the bald patch again. She could see that the rest of her hair was thinning, too. "It must have scraped my ear."

They looked at each other. For the first time in a long time, Carrie did not have a smart retort. Instead, Frances saw worry etched in her daughter's face. She appeared unsettled by Frances's explanation. "Are you sure you're OK?"

Frances tried to laugh lightly. "Of course. I told you . . ." She let her fingers touch the spot on her head. "Just a bad scrape," she added, hoping that she was convincing enough. But the truth was that the concern her daughter had just expressed, the yearning Frances saw in Carrie's eyes for reassurance that everything was, indeed, just fine, proved that it wasn't.

"I . . . I have homework to do." Carrie backed away, still watching her mother in the mirror.

Frances waited until Carrie disappeared upstairs before she turned her attention back to her hair. She hadn't thought it would fall out so quickly. She looked like a molting bird. Fortunately, with her hair being so blond, it wasn't as noticeable as it could have been. But she didn't want to wait until it was apparent, and she certainly didn't want to find clumps of hair stuck to her pillow or on her clothes. Flimsy reminders of what she was losing: an essence of her womanhood.

She knew what she had to do.

Frances climbed the stairs, then quietly shut her bedroom door, making certain to lock it before she crossed the room to the bathroom. With a shaking hand, she touched the wall and found the light switch. She hesitated before flicking it on. Bright light filled the room, and she was caught off guard when she saw her illuminated reflection. There were more areas where her hair had thinned than she had noticed in the downstairs mirror.

For a moment she shut her eyes and fought the urge to cry. She simply couldn't afford any more tears. Her emotional energy could not be depleted, and she vowed to remain strong, if not for anyone else, then for herself.

With a new, if not forced, determination, Frances opened the cabinet and removed a fresh towel, which she set on the counter. Then she knelt down and fished around under the sink for the dog hair clippers. The last time she'd used this tool was just before the summer had begun, when she'd trimmed their long-haired retriever. When she inspected it closely, there were still traces of the golden dog hair on the blades.

When she looked up to find the outlet and plug in the clippers, she avoided her reflection in the mirror. The clippers buzzed and vibrated in her hand. Carefully, she lifted them to her head and then, with a deep breath, she reluctantly looked into the mirror and held the clippers to her scalp. With a single-minded focus, she concentrated on the task at hand: shaving off the rest of her hair. It fluttered down to the towel, wispy locks of blond hair that—thanks to her foresight—were short instead of long. For some reason, that seemed to help ease the pain of shaving her own head.

It was hard to see the back, and she only hoped that she didn't leave any patches. But after she finished, when she ran her hand over her scalp, it just felt a little like day-old razor stubble.

She stood there and took it all in. Her scalp was paler than the rest of her face. Without her hair, her face looked plump and more round. She noticed how her cheeks appeared puffier than usual and wondered if that had anything to do with the antinausea medicine. As if it wasn't bad enough to have cancer, she was now bald and puffy.

Swallowing, Frances yanked the cord from the socket and threw the clippers back under the sink, not even bothering to return them to the case. She'd worry about that later. Instead, she gathered up the towel with the remnants of her hair and carried it over to the toilet. She knew better than to throw it in the trash can. If Carrie or Andy wandered into her bathroom and saw it, they'd ask questions that she wasn't prepared to answer just yet.

When she flushed the toilet, she watched as her hair spun around before disappearing into the sewer.

To her surprise, when it was all over, she didn't feel a great sense of loss. Not like she had anticipated. She had thought she would mourn her hair; after all, it had been something that had defined her since she was a young girl and had refused to let her mother cut it before each new school year. The fact was there had been something liberating about having taken control of this aspect of cancer. She had removed her own hair. Instead of letting cancer remind her, one lost lock at a time, Frances had stood up and fought back. It had been her choice. And astonishingly, it made her feel stronger. Empowered.

With a deep breath, she left the bathroom and hurried over to her dresser. In her bottom drawer, tucked behind her pajamas, she'd hidden the wig she'd purchased last week. After she pulled it out of its box, she gave it a little shake, then put it on and adjusted it with the sticky tape, just like the saleswoman had instructed. Then, she wandered across the room to Nicholas's closet and hunted for an old baseball cap. Now, at least, Carrie wouldn't be able to tell that she was wearing a wig.

"Mom?" Andy yelled from downstairs.

Frances stared at her reflection one last time before she called out, "Getting changed, Andy. What's up?"

"What time is dinner?"

Frances smiled to herself. That very normal question—one she must have heard hundreds, if not thousands, of times—was why she was doing this. Keeping a sense of normalcy in the lives of her children. It was the one thing she didn't have in her own life now, but she just wanted them to be happy.

CHAPTER 13

When she walked into the chemotherapy center, she felt as if everyone was staring at her. With her short wig and thinning eyebrows, she knew that, for the first time, she actually looked like a cancer patient, and the feeling made her very self-conscious. Even though it was a wig and not a thinning or patchy head of hair, she could see that *they* knew. The nurses, the patients, the family members waiting for their loved ones—they all knew. To their trained eyes, it was easy to tell the difference between real hair and hair meant to hide the fact that she, too, had become part of the exclusive Cancer Club; no invitation needed to join, thank you very much. No discrimination here. Age, gender, ethnicity: none of this mattered. No one chose to join; instead, cancer chose its members. The Cancer Club might be open to all, yet it came with an exorbitant price tag attached.

Of course, they weren't really *all* staring at her. It was mostly in her imagination. Still, when some looked up to see who had walked in, she felt uncomfortable. Perhaps even vulnerable, a feeling she wanted to avoid at all costs.

The Chemo Cocktail Lounge was unusually quiet for a Thursday afternoon. Frances walked past the nurses' station and greeted Eddie. He smiled at her and held up his hand, indicating that he needed to finish something before he would take her vitals: temperature, weight, pulse, and blood pressure.

Frances took another glance around and wondered why it had been so busy her first time. This time, however, the nurses were lingering around the main administration desk, chatting away as they plucked chocolates from an almost-empty Russell Stover box.

"Good morning, Mrs. Snyder," Eddie finally said as he motioned toward the chair. "How are you doing today?"

She had barely sat down before he popped the thermometer into her mouth and asked her to roll up her sleeve.

"Phf-ine," she managed to mumble while attempting to keep the device held steady under her tongue. *Why do they always do that?* The dentists, the doctors, the nurses. Always sticking something in their patients' mouths, then asking the same silly questions, expecting an intelligible answer. Or, perhaps, not expecting any answer at all. It was just part of the routine, she guessed.

"Good, good. That's just what we like to hear!" He smiled at her and began pressing buttons on the blood pressure machine.

For an instant she found it amusing that "Phf-ine" was *just* what they liked to hear. Indeed, these people had become adept at interpreting medical grunts! A silly image crossed her mind: She visualized an austere classroom chock-full of newly recruited medical students, all wearing white medical gowns and stethoscopes, each one sitting in a chair with a thermometer stuck under their tongue. Eddie was standing in front of them, like an orchestra conductor, a huge scalpel in his right hand in place of a baton. At his prompt, they were all, in unison, repeating the same sentence, "Aheh hamm phf-ine," over and over again.

She might as well have answered, "The sky is blue," and he probably wouldn't even have noticed! But the vision made her relax a little, and she fought the urge to chuckle under her breath.

While the sleeve was inflating and becoming tighter on her arm, Frances glanced around at the row of chairs that lined the back windows near where she sat. One was occupied by an elderly woman who looked sound asleep, perhaps due to the monotonous humming of the machine she was hooked up to. Another chair was occupied by a young man in his twenties, with an even younger woman seated by his side. Down the row, at the very back in the corner chair against the wall near the window outside of which a bird feeder hung, sat Madeline.

And like the last time, she was alone.

"Hmm." Eddie pressed some more buttons on the blood pressure machine. "Let's try this again."

She waited until he took the thermometer from her mouth before she asked, "Something wrong?"

"No, no. It's probably the machine. Acting up." He winked at her. "As usual."

But when the machine beeped again, he frowned.

"What is it, Eddie?" she asked with a little more urgency in her voice.

"Your blood pressure is quite elevated, Mrs. Snyder. You feeling all right?"

Truth was she had been feeling tired and worn-out for quite a few days now, even though the nausea had ended shortly after the third day following her first treatment, conveniently when Nicholas had departed for Chicago.

"Fine, just fine," she lied. "I . . . uh . . . I walked up the stairs instead of taking the elevator, though. Maybe that's what did it?"

He didn't look quite convinced.

"Why don't you go and find a chair, Mrs. Snyder? We'll take your blood pressure again in a little bit. See if it goes down."

"What does that mean?"

He leaned forward and touched her knee. "It's 195 over 100. That's too high, Mrs. Snyder. So go relax a little and take some deep breaths. Let's see if it's better in a few minutes, after you rest from that flight of stairs and your pulse comes down a bit."

That wasn't something she wanted to hear. Even though he didn't say it, she knew that it could translate into a problem, something that would hinder her treatment.

Despite not feeling social, Frances walked over to the empty chair next to Madeline. At least it was more comfortable than sitting next to a stranger. And perhaps Madeline might understand exactly what high blood pressure meant in relation to her treatment. The older woman's eyes were shut as if she was asleep. Over her right shoulder, the chemotherapy pump churned, the toxins systematically pushing their way through the narrow plastic lines that ran to Madeline's chest.

If she had any luck, Madeline would sleep throughout the entire treatment and she wouldn't be bothered with any social discourse. Yet, she couldn't help but wonder why she had been so drawn to sit beside her if she wanted to avoid making conversation. Perhaps it was familiarity; it was the same chair she had sat in last time, and Frances tended to prefer the comforting feeling of routine. At work, she used to occupy the same stall in the women's restroom, and on the few occasions it was unavailable, she found herself quite distraught by the thought of having to decide between waiting or taking another unfamiliar stall.

"Ah, Mrs. Snyder!" a cheerful nurse called out as she practically bounced on the balls of her feet toward Frances. "How did everything go after the last treatment?"

"And you are . . . ?"

It was a pet peeve of Frances's: people not introducing themselves, especially when they pretended to know who she was. Proper decorum always dictated that a person extend an introduction. That was what her mother had taught her.

"Laura." She didn't stop working as she began hanging bags and checking the machine. "I noticed that you were here the week before last, but another nurse snatched up your case."

I'm a "case."

"Now why would she want to do that?" Frances asked, only partially trying to hide her sarcasm.

Laura glanced over her shoulder at Frances and raised an eyebrow. For the first time, Frances really looked at the nurse and realized that she had a cheerful face, her big brown eyes illuminating her entire expression. Even her heart-shaped lips seemed full of life, an invitation for adventure.

"Well, that is a good question, isn't it? Perhaps she was just eager to meet you and get you started with treatment." Laura paused and gave a mischievous smile to Frances. "That *is* our job, isn't it?"

Now it was Frances's turn to wonder about the level of sarcasm in the nurse's comment. From the looks of the people in the Chemo Lounge, there wasn't much to know about the patients. They appeared tired, miserable, and weak. While admittance was by invitation only, it was an invite no one wanted to receive.

As the nurse walked away to gather some more supplies for Frances's treatment, Madeline stirred in the corner seat.

"Back for more, eh?" she said with a small smile.

"Couldn't seem to stay away," Frances quipped, her sarcasm somehow masked in humor, which caused Madeline to chuckle.

"Better than the alternative," Madeline said.

Frances took a deep breath and turned to look at Madeline. "Mind if I ask you something?"

"Seems like you just did."

It took a second for Frances to understand, but when she did, she gave a small laugh.

"Eddie said I have high blood pressure."

"Oh." It came out like a whoosh of breath. "They won't give you treatment if your blood pressure is too high. I would take some long deep breaths. Shut your eyes and try to think of pleasant things." She paused. "That's why I like the bird feeder, you know. Keeps me calm during all of this"—she explained while gesturing toward the machine and tubes—"this horrible stuff."

Taking Madeline's advice, Frances leaned back in the chair and shut her eyes. She concentrated on her breathing, making certain each breath was long and deep. She couldn't possibly put off her treatment. She had cleared her schedule and precooked four meals so that she could deal with any post-treatment sickness and side effects. Mentally, she had psyched herself up for facing round two. Any delay would be devastating to her psyche.

"Is it OK if I ask you a question now?"

Frances kept her eyes shut and nodded her head.

"I've never seen anyone come here alone for their first chemotherapy treatment," Madeline said. "In fact, most people always have someone with them."

Frances tried not to smile. "That's not a question."

This time Madeline laughed.

"But if you are pointing out that people usually have a support team with them, and I don't, my comment would be that it seems you, too, are alone," Frances said calmly, still trying to focus on her breathing. "You have family?"

"A son." The crisp manner in which Madeline said the word *son* made Frances open her eyes and look at her.

"I take it he's either not local or . . ."

That was the moment when Madeline's face changed, the sparkle in her eye fading and her smile disappearing. Gone was the look of concern that she had worn just a few seconds earlier. In its place was a look of sorrow.

"It's the 'or,' I'm afraid," Madeline said softly and turned to look out the window. "He's too busy."

"Hmm." Frances wanted to mention that she knew the feeling of being neglected in favor of work. "Does he know?"

"Yes."

Deep breath in. Deep breath out. Frances had to shut out Madeline and the image of a son knowing but not caring enough to support his mother. It was a similar image to the one Charlotte had painted for her the previous week when they had met for coffee. Someone in the family knowing and not reacting was the worst thing Frances could imagine. Family members who loved each other supported each other. And it wasn't a one- or two-shot deal. Family members made meals for, comforted, and helped each other when a crisis arose. It was the one time when people needed to push aside their own self-absorbed needs and focus on providing strength to the patient.

And that, not her fear, was the reason Frances had procrastinated telling Nicholas. She didn't want him to push aside his needs, at least not yet. Her husband would not be like Madeline's son, no matter what Charlotte said.

"I'm sorry," Frances whispered, and for a quick second, she wondered if she actually said those two words out loud or to herself.

"Me, too," Madeline responded with a deep sigh. She still kept her eyes on the window. Frances followed the older woman's gaze. She noticed that there were birds perched on the feeder outside of the window. Three nuthatches eagerly pecked seed, flying away to a nearby tree, and then miraculously another bird would appear as if they were taking turns.

Frances hadn't paid close attention to the bird feeder during her previous treatment. In fact, she hadn't even paid much attention to anything outside that window. Now, as she observed the birds, she realized that the small parklike seating area on the other side of the windows must have been designed specifically to add endless natural light to the chemotherapy center. While it was a thoughtful gesture by the architects, Frances noticed that all of the chairs in the Chemo Lounge faced away from the windows with the exception of Madeline's.

"Is that why you sit here?" Frances heard herself ask. "To watch the birds?"

"Hmm?" Madeline turned around. "Did you say something?"

Frances leaned over and repeated her question.

"Well, I suppose I do," Madeline answered. "I've been doing this for over two years, you know. The birds have become my friends, I reckon."

"Two years!" The thought of undergoing chemotherapy for such an amount of time startled Frances. What could it mean other than the fact that Madeline's cancer had never gone away and probably would not ever? "Surely you had friends accompany you in the beginning? Family? A sister or brother, perhaps?"

Madeline shook her head. "My sister's dead, and my son put me into a nursing home." Her expression darkened. "Or, as he liked to call it, an assisted-living facility. I call it a prison, no matter what he says about how wonderful the place is."

To Frances, Madeline didn't appear as if she needed a nursing home. She seemed functional and perky enough. But, of course, she knew Madeline only from these two treatment times and only while the woman was receiving chemotherapy.

"I'm sure they have fun events and nice amenities at the home," Frances said, hoping to shift Madeline's gloomy mood.

Waving her hand at Frances, Madeline scoffed at her comment. "Fun events? Why, I'd rather be in my own home with my cat, watching television from my own sofa." She clicked her tongue and shook her head. "Nothing is like being home. Your real home. The one that you invested your body and soul into making the heart of your family."

Frances understood only too well what Madeline meant. Her role in the family was to provide that beating heart to her children and husband. And she knew that it centered around the house. It was the foundation on which the family dynamics rested.

"When he talked me into moving to Pine Acres—forced me, to be perfectly honest—it ripped out my heart," Madeline admitted. "There's nothing fun or exciting about living in a small room, sharing your meals with complete strangers, and having busybody staff members checking on you every thirty minutes. It's as if they are waiting for you to die."

"Oh, Madeline!"

"Makes me wonder what I've been fighting for these past two years." Once again, she shook her head and remained silent.

There was nothing that Frances could think of to say. She didn't know Madeline well enough to have any words of advice.

"Well, Mrs. Snyder," a cheerful voice said. Frances turned and saw the nurse Laura approaching her with a blood pressure machine. "Let's see what's going on here, shall we?"

Frances redirected her attention to the blood pressure sleeve, watching as the nurse gently wrapped it around her arm. "I'm sure it's because I was walking up the stairs. Just made me out of breath."

Laura gave her a funny look. "It's just one flight. Besides, a quick pulse does not affect blood pressure that much."

"Well . . ." She was at a loss for words.

Laura chuckled. "I know, I know. You just want all of this over with. But we, Mrs. Snyder, want you better. Hypertension is nothing to play around with."

A few presses of buttons and the sleeve tightened, once again, around Frances's arm. The machine clicked, and red numbers began to display. When it finally stopped clicking and the rest of the pressure released around her arm, Laura pursed her lips and seemed to be thinking.

"What is it?"

"Well, it's come down somewhat. Just not a lot. But," she said, turning to look at Frances, "I think we can give you another ten or fifteen minutes and try one last time. If it comes down enough, you should be good to go." She stood up and pushed the machine to the side. "I'll be back in a few."

With Madeline staring out the window, watching the birds, Frances shut her eyes and began her deep breathing again. She didn't know Madeline, and although her heart broke for anyone in pain, she knew that her focus had to be on herself and her own family. Every person currently in the chemotherapy center had their own problems and their own worries. They, too, needed to concentrate on their personal healing and not fret over the problems of the other patients in the room.

Like the nurse had said to her, their job was caring for the patients. It was, however, the job of the patient to take care of herself.

CHAPTER 14

"Mom! Your phone keeps ringing," Andy said as he walked into the kitchen with her cell phone in his hand. He slid it down the length of the countertop toward where she was standing.

It was Sunday, and the week had gone surprisingly well. Despite feeling fatigued, she hadn't gotten as ill after her second treatment. Taking the medicine before she felt nauseated had definitely helped thwart an adverse reaction.

"What's for dinner, anyway? It smells good."

Frances wiped her hands on a dish towel and reached for her phone. It wasn't ringing now, but she could see that she'd missed five calls, all from the same unknown number. "Chicken *piccata*, Andy."

He made a face. It was expected.

Mealtimes at the Snyder household had always been among the toughest parts of her day. Even at a young age, Andy had been a fussy eater, not to mention stubborn as well. Vegetables rarely crossed his lips, and the main ingredient for most meals was inevitably carbs. Pasta, potatoes, and bread seemed to be his foods of choice. Fortunately, he was active in sports, and it didn't show on his frame. But Frances worried about his future, especially when he would begin working full-time and exercising less. She knew that he would eventually put on weight if he maintained the same poor eating habits.

On the other hand, Carrie was even worse. Whenever Frances tried to introduce something new to her diet, she would sink her heels into the ground and refuse to touch it. As a toddler, she wanted only chicken nuggets and Tater Tots drowned in ketchup. There was one night, when she was five, that Carrie had fallen asleep at the kitchen table. Frances had told her that she couldn't be excused until she tried one bite of creamed corn. Nicholas walked into the house at ten o'clock, and upon seeing his daughter asleep, still seated in the kitchen chair, just shook his head and walked upstairs to bed.

Ever since then, Frances had decided to make what the children wanted. She might have lost the battle, but she justified her decision as having won the war: no child of hers would ever go to bed hungry at night.

She pressed the "Call Back" button, then lifted the phone to her ear.

"Pine Acres," a woman said.

Frances frowned. Pine Acres? It took her a minute to place the name. "The retirement home?" *Why on earth would someone from Pine Acres call me?* And then, it dawned on her: Madeline. "I'm returning your call. Is this about Madeline? Has something happened to her?"

"Are you Frances Snyder?"

"Yes."

"As a matter of fact . . ."

Andy walked over to the refrigerator and opened the door, pulling out a can of soda. "Who's Madeline?" he asked.

"Shh!" Frances shot him a look. "I'm sorry. Could you repeat what you just said?"

"She has a fever and won't agree to be admitted into the hospital." The woman hesitated. "That's our policy, you know. For cancer patients."

"I understand that." Fever was enemy number one for patients undergoing chemotherapy treatment. She had heard that preached to her time and again, especially from the nurses, who systematically reminded her after each treatment that should she have a fever over 101 degrees, she should go immediately to the emergency room.

But what Frances didn't understand was why they were calling *her*.

"Madeline's son didn't respond," the woman explained. "She gave us your number. So, will you come?"

Frances wanted to ask how Madeline had known her phone number, but she figured she'd save that question for when she saw her in person. "Of course. I'll be right over."

When she hung up the phone, she stood in the kitchen, staring out the picture window that overlooked their backyard. As the weather continued to change, cold and flu season would rear its ugly head. Somehow she'd have to avoid getting sick. It was something she hadn't considered. Now she was going to a nursing home, putting herself right into the thick of germs. Of course, she put herself at risk every time she went to the hospital for treatment. The irony wasn't lost on her.

"What's wrong, Mom?"

Her train of thought broken, Frances turned and looked at Andy. "Nothing. But I have to go somewhere for a bit."

He frowned. "Go somewhere? But it's Sunday night!"

"A friend is sick."

Carrie darted around the corner, one of the dogs nipping at her feet, and slid across the tile floor, laughing as the dog ran into her. "When's dinner, Mom?"

"It's chicken *piccata*," Andy mumbled.

"Yuck."

Frances ignored their comments. "You two will have to deal with this tonight. It'll be ready in . . ." She leaned over and looked at the oven clock. "Twelve minutes. Carrie can set the table, and, Andy, you can take it out of the oven, OK? Use oven mitts or you'll burn your hands."

"No duh!" Carrie said as she rolled her eyes.

Frances took a deep breath. Part of her wanted to shake Carrie, to scream out that she could be dying at that very moment, that she was fighting cancer in order to live, not for herself but for them. Whether they wanted to admit it or not, they still needed her. She knew that . . . *had* to believe that. Why couldn't Carrie just drop the tween attitude and get beyond this rebellious, snarky hump once and for all?

"And leave a plate for your father if he doesn't get home in time to join you," she said as she hurried upstairs to quickly change her clothes and put on some makeup.

Thirty minutes later, when she walked into the nursing home, Frances wrinkled her nose at the distinct odor of disinfectant mixed with death. At least that was how she defined it: the smell of aging people who clung to life until their last breath.

She hated nursing homes. Always had. Her grandmother had lived in a nursing home toward the end of her life. Frances had been only fourteen at the time, but she had been old enough to realize that the frail, wrinkled people that lay in those metal hospital beds were at the tail end of their lives. Most of the time, the residents were alone in their rooms, their eyes glued to the television set that hung from the corner of the ceiling or, even worse, just staring at the ceiling. It was as if they were lying on those beds or sitting in a vinyl recliner just waiting for someone—anyone!—to visit them. Or perhaps they were just waiting to die.

After all of those years raising families, working in corporations, and volunteering at the church, what was the point of prolonging life only to be neglected by the very people—children, colleagues, and friends—whom they'd spent their entire lives supporting and nurturing?

After signing in at the front desk, she headed to the elevator, pressed the button, and waited for the doors to open. A man in a wheelchair rolled beside her and, even though the button was illuminated, he pressed it. Not once but twice. Frances glanced at him, taking in his stooped back with a thick mass that made him hunch forward. His face was wrinkled, and his skin looked paper-thin. And, not surprisingly, there was a distinct stench of urine surrounding him.

She took a step away.

"Slowest elevator on the planet, I say," the man grumbled. He lifted his hand and pointed behind her. "Better option might be the stairs."

Frances turned around and saw a sign for the stairs screwed onto the wall. A much better option than traveling in the elevator with the wheelchair man and his urine smell.

"Thank you," she managed to say before she hurried over to the door.

By the time she got to the third floor, she needed to pause and catch her breath. Before chemotherapy, she wouldn't have even been winded. Now, however, she gulped for air as she clung to the railing. It took her at least two minutes to calm down her beating heart. Only then did she open the door and emerge on the third-floor landing. She walked down the long hallway, glancing into each room that she passed. Most of the doors were open. Frances was surprised to see that each room appeared comfortable, some with plants and books on the window ledge, and almost all of them decorated in some unique way. Unlike her grandmother's nursing home, it was almost as if they were trying to mask the fact that the rooms were in a nursing home.

At the end of the hallway, she stood in front of room 313 and, taking a deep breath, knocked gently, then opened the door and entered.

"Oh, Frances!" Madeline cried out when she saw her. She sat up in her bed, a white knit blanket pulled up to her waist. She looked frail with a small gray cap on her head and wearing a floral-print nightgown. Frances was happy to see that a spark of life still gleamed in her eyes. With a concerned frown, Madeline shook her head apologetically. "I don't know why they called you!"

"Now, Madeline," a nurse said, brushing past Frances, "you told us to call her when your son didn't answer."

"I didn't think you would make her come here! He lives only five minutes away. He probably just stepped out for a minute. You could have tried him again in an hour before bothering my friend."

Frances hesitated before she walked farther into the room. She suddenly realized that she didn't know much about the woman at all. She set down her purse on the recliner next to Madeline's bed and walked up to her side.

"Well, they called and I came, Madeline," she said. "Fever is not good. You know that with the chemo your body is in no condition to fight it alone. You need antibiotics."

"Pssh!" She waved the air as if dismissing Frances's comment. "I feel fine. I keep telling her that."

The nurse looked at Frances. "Over 104 degrees. I contacted her oncologist, and he wants her over at the hospital at once for blood work and observation. Perhaps you can talk some sense into her."

Frances gave a slight nod of her head, understanding the situation but not understanding Madeline's reluctance to follow the doctor's orders. She waited until the nurse left them alone before looking at Madeline, who was watching her with mild curiosity.

For a moment Frances wasn't certain what to say. She barely knew Madeline, having been in her company only two times during chemotherapy. Despite her curiosity about Madeline's son, after their discussion at the last treatment, Frances knew better than to ask. There was bad blood between mother and son, and the last thing that she wanted to do was upset Madeline if she wasn't feeling well.

"How did you get my number, anyway?" she asked, moving toward the chair. She pushed her purse to the side and sat down, leaning forward so that her hands almost touched the railing of Madeline's bed.

"Those nurses always leave their charts lying around," Madeline replied. "I have a photographic memory. I saw it and remembered it."

Frances caught her breath. "I've never met anyone with a photographic memory! How interesting!"

"It's like having a superpower. It can be put to use for good or evil."

Frances laughed. "That's one way to look at it."

"I am sorry that they contacted you. And on a Sunday night. I hope you weren't interrupted?"

Of course she was interrupted, interrupted from making dinner for her children, who barely spent any time with her and did not appreciate it anyway. Interrupted from waiting for her husband, who always seemed to prefer spending time away from his home. Interrupted from listening to sassy comments from her kids and cleaning up after them. Interrupted from making a home for people who would much rather spend time away from it. In fact, Frances couldn't remember the last time that she had gone out socially at night alone. Charlotte was usually busy with her boyfriends or other friends, most of whom were single. In a way, it felt liberating to have somewhere to go. Someone to see.

"Don't think twice about it," she said. "Now, what are we going to do with you?"

"I feel fine, Frances. Honest."

"But a fever, Madeline," Frances said patiently. "You know what the nursing staff says. You have to contact them if you run a fever."

Madeline waved her hand at Frances. "Bah! I've been doing this for two years. I'm tired of the hospital."

After just a few weeks, Frances felt the same way. But she knew that fevers were not something to be trifled with.

"Even so, I think it's best that you go, Madeline. How about if I accompany you? If it's truly nothing, we can come right back."

Reluctantly, Madeline eventually agreed.

Frances hadn't considered how to get Madeline over to the hospital. She also hadn't figured that the staff at Pine Acres had a plan for such situations and it didn't involve merely walking out the front door and crossing the street. Instead, an ambulance had to be called, and Madeline needed to go on a stretcher. After all of the fuss and delays, she was almost sorry that she had talked Madeline into going. After all, the older woman did, indeed, look fine.

Sarah Price

.It took almost an hour for Madeline to get situated in the emergency room. Fortunately, because she came in from the nursing home and they had called ahead, Madeline received preferential treatment. Frances waited with her in one of the back rooms until someone came to check her vitals.

"Let's just get some blood drawn before we check your temperature and blood pressure," the young man said. He didn't get into any personal conversation, and Frances thought briefly about Laura from the Chemo Cocktail Lounge. Surely it took a special person to be a nurse in the oncology department, someone with great compassion and love for other people. This man, however, was all about business, and his business was about moving on to the next patient. *Draw blood, send to the lab, continue with the next case.*

"Blood pressure is a little high but not too bad," he said, jotting something down on a form before he wrapped up the equipment. "I'll send this to the lab, and someone will be in shortly." Without another word, he left the room.

"Pleasant fellow, eh?" Madeline commented. "Any wonder why I hate coming here?"

Frances straightened out the white blanket that covered Madeline's legs.

"Now, now, Madeline. ER staff is different. It's not like they have time to establish a relationship, not like the nurses we are used to dealing with." She smiled at her friend. "Would you like something? Water? Ginger ale?"

When she returned from fetching Madeline a can of ginger ale and a cup of ice, a nurse was already in the room and setting up an IV. Frances frowned and glanced at Madeline.

"What's this?"

The nurse glanced over her shoulder. "Fluids. Her fever is too high." Her eyes fell down to the can of ginger ale in Frances's hand. "Oh, that's great. If she can drink that, too, it will help."

Frances nodded, opening the can and pouring some into the cup. She handed it to Madeline as her cell phone rang from her purse. Setting the half-full can on the counter, Frances dug into her purse to retrieve the phone. Someone from home was calling.

"Where are you?"

Frances glanced at the clock, surprised to see that it was already nine o'clock. "A friend of mine is sick, Nicholas. I'm with her at the hospital."

"Charlotte?"

Even though he couldn't see, she shook her head. "No, someone else. You don't know her."

He didn't ask any further questions. "You know that I'm leaving in the morning, right? I'm trying to find my suitcase."

Her heart ached. Perhaps she had thought he actually had missed her. At least worried about her. It was rare for him to return home and not find her. But his question quickly corrected that misguided notion. With a deep sigh, she turned her back to Madeline and lowered her voice.

"It's in the guest room. I put it away after I unpacked it on Friday night."

"Thanks." He barely said good-bye before he hung up, leaving Frances with the phone pressed against her ear and a lump in her throat. Just once, couldn't he say something kind to her? A word of endearment? Ever since she had gone to his office, he had been acting even more cold and detached, leaving her to wonder what, exactly, was going on.

Madeline cleared her throat. "You don't have to stay with me, Frances. I suspect you have your family waiting for you."

Shoving her phone back into her purse, Frances turned to face Madeline. "No, it's fine. The children will be going to bed soon, and my husband is packing for a trip."

"Children? How old?"

It struck Frances as odd that here she was, in the emergency room with a woman who had used her as an emergency contact—despite claiming that she hadn't thought Pine Acres actually would contact her!—and yet, they knew so little about each other.

Sitting down in the chair next to Madeline's bed, Frances took a deep breath. "Let's see. My son Andy is sixteen and goes to Morristown High School. He plays football and gets decent grades. Carrie is twelve and goes to Frelinghuysen Middle School, also in Morristown. She likes ballet and is in that stage where she's a bit mouthy. Knows everything, and I, her mother, am just a foolish older woman who couldn't possibly have any knowledge about anything relevant to her."

Madeline smiled in a knowing sort of way.

"How about you? I know you have a son . . . ?"

"James, yes. He's about your age, maybe a few years older. Fifty-two."

"More like ten years older," Frances was quick to point out with a smirk.

"Cancer ages us." It was an apology for having overestimated Frances's age. "I also have two daughters, but one lives in Texas and the other over in London with her family. I haven't seen them in years."

"That's a shame."

Madeline shrugged her shoulders. "Ever since they were teenagers, they weren't as close to me as they should have been."

Frances wondered why but didn't want to ask.

"My husband died ten years ago, and that was the beginning of the end of any relationship with the girls. James lingered on for a while, but his wife, Dina, worked her magic." She grimaced. "I became the evil mother-in-law that every wife loves to complain about."

"I find that hard to believe."

"Me, too." Madeline winked at her. "But James's wife loves to create her own reality. And I did not fit into it. Although, I confess, it wasn't as if I really tried. We just don't see eye to eye on things."

Frances hadn't thought about her own mother-in-law for a while. She did not particularly care for Ellen Snyder. She was abrupt and judgmental, quick to share her opinions and even quicker to dismiss others', especially if they came from Frances. With only sons, Ellen always favored anything and everything that Nicholas said and Andy did. Fortunately, she did not live close enough to just pop in unexpectedly, and more often than not Nicholas visited her rather than her traveling to visit the family in Morristown.

"How about your own children? How have they taken the news about your cancer?" Madeline asked.

Frances startled at the question. "My children?"

Madeline raised an eyebrow and waited expectantly.

"Oh, uh . . ." Frances didn't know how to admit the truth. Fortunately, she didn't have to, as someone interrupted their conversation.

"Ah, Mrs. Cooper," a young doctor in a white jacket said as she walked into the room. Two younger women trailed behind her, their blue coats clearly delineating their status as interns. "How are we feeling?" she asked as she reached down to touch Madeline's wrist.

"I feel fine. But I don't know about you," Madeline quipped back.

The doctor nodded, her eyes on the clock behind the bed. When she finished counting, she gently released Madeline's arm. "Well, your blood work does not say the same, I'm afraid. Your white blood cell count is very low. We'd like to admit you. Between the low white cell count and your high fever, we want to keep you on fluids and under observation. If the white blood cell count doesn't increase, we'll need to administer a blood transfusion."

"Can you make it a young woman?"

The doctor blinked. "Excuse me?"

"Blood from a young woman, preferably smart and gorgeous, please."

Frances smiled at Madeline's teasing comment while the doctor appeared to realize that her patient was making light of the situation's severity. Finally she smiled.

"I can see what we can do to accommodate your request," she said and pressed her hand on Madeline's shoulder. "In the meantime, you'll need to rest up and take it easy. We don't want you getting an infection that your body can't fight." She motioned to the two people with her. "They'll take you to Franklin Four. Fortunately, we already have a room ready. It's private, so I want to move you there right away. You never know when someone might steal it away from you." She winked at Madeline and turned to talk to the two interns. "Transport is coming, yes?"

They stepped outside the door to finish conferring about Madeline.

"See? It's good that you came here," Frances said, trying to sound cheerful. "And you said you don't like Pine Acres anyway."

But Madeline was clearly not jubilant.

"I'll come visit you tomorrow. How's that?" It was, after all, going to be Monday. With Nicholas gone and the children at school, it wasn't as though Frances had too much else on her schedule.

She waited until the transport person came to move Madeline, one of the interns making certain that the IV fluids did not get tangled as the man moved the bed. Frances watched as the hospital bed was pushed down the hallway, the team of medical people following close behind. It saddened her to think about Madeline, a fine woman with a good sense of humor who had no family to fuss over her.

And then Charlotte's words floated back through her mind, yet again. Lifting her chin, Frances shoved the memory away and started walking toward the exit. After all, she did have family waiting at home for her, even if everything wasn't exactly the way she would have liked it. But she had family at home, something both Charlotte and Madeline did not.

CHAPTER 15

"Good morning, Mrs. Snyder!" the nurse said immediately as Frances stepped out of the elevator. For the fourth day in a row, she was visiting Madeline at the hospital. It had become part of her routine. By this time, she was convinced that everyone thought she must be the older woman's daughter, and for some reason she didn't bother correcting them.

"Good morning. How is she today?" Frances asked as cheerfully as she could muster.

"She's ornery as always." The answer came with a slight laugh. "But definitely doing better."

Frances knocked on the door before opening it, a habit that she'd developed at home. Privacy was important for teenagers, and since she'd never had any as a child, she knew how much a simple knock meant.

When she pushed open the door, Madeline greeted her with a warm smile. "To what do I owe this honor?" she asked. Frances managed a small laugh. "Three weeks ago I couldn't get you to talk, and now I've seen you four days in a row?"

"Oh now, don't be so sassy, Madeline," Frances countered. "It's not like I'm doing much, anyway."

Madeline said, "Hmm," and Frances immediately wished she could take back those words. She didn't mean to imply that it was only because she had nothing to do that she was visiting. She meant only that coming to sit with Madeline was not an inconvenience. Rather than continue to call attention to the blunder, Frances walked across the room.

"The nurses tell me you're feeling better?" At the window a bouquet of flowers, purchased from Kings Food Market just two days before, was already wilting. She put her finger into the pink pitcher and then, realizing it needed water, carried it over to the sink. "That's wonderful news!"

Just like people, even cut flowers needed attention and care.

Madeline smoothed imaginary creases in the blanket, watching Frances as she put the flowers back on the windowsill.

"I never thought I'd say this, but I want to go back to Pine Acres."

"Pine Acres can't be *that* bad," Frances said, even though she knew it wasn't the most pleasant place.

"I miss my birds," she said in a quiet voice. When she looked up, Frances was staring at her with a quizzical look on her face. "I have a bird feeder just outside my window. The night orderly fills it up for me, almost every day now." Madeline gave a small smile. "He doesn't have to do that, you know. Awful kind of him."

Something about the wistful way that Madeline spoke felt bittersweet to Frances. "That *is* kind of him," she said.

"When I was younger, my son gave me a bird feeder for Mother's Day. Every weekend, he would fill up that feeder so that I could see the birds while I worked in the kitchen."

Ah. Frances pulled the chair closer to Madeline's bed. *That explains a lot.*

"So what happened?" she prodded.

"My sister died and a family battle ensued."

"And that has to do with the bird feeder? How?"

Madeline shrugged her shoulders and, with just a brief flicker of her eyes, glanced up at the ceiling. Frances immediately recognized the movement because it was the same gesture that both Nicholas and Carrie made when they were trying to avoid telling her something.

"No one filled that bird feeder ever again."

That didn't make sense. Not to Frances. "I don't think I understand."

Madeline sighed. "It's a long story, Frances, and I'm not feeling up to talking about it right now."

From the bedside chair, Frances reached out to pat Madeline's hand. "Understood. That's fair enough." She, more than anyone else, knew what it was like to avoid certain topics. And from the sound of it, Madeline's family dynamics had created a rift that had negatively affected her relationship with her son, if not others. Although Frances didn't understand the correlation between the death of a sibling, a family argument, and a bird feeder, it was clearly a subject that Madeline didn't want to pursue.

"It's a beautiful day out." Frances looked out the window again. "A little crisp, but a sweater works just fine."

"Autumn is my favorite season," Madeline said.

"Mine, too." Looking for a way to distract Madeline from the boredom of being in the hospital room, Frances began talking about the seasons and how she used to love summer because that meant no school and then, when she had her own children, she came to prefer the beauty of spring. Now, especially since winter—with its frigid temperatures and dreary gray feeling to it—was right around the corner, she relished autumn.

"Change. That's what autumn is all about," Frances said, feeling as if she needed to explain her reason for the preference. "Change can be good, I guess. At least when it comes to seasons."

"Most of the time." Madeline's voice sounded bored and flat. Frances wondered if she was still thinking about her children. "It's no different than life. We change, just like the seasons."

Frances looked at her. "What do you mean?"

Madeline gestured toward the window. "Young children are spring, and as they grow, they become summer. And then, as they age, they become autumn. You're in the autumn of your life."

Frances frowned. "I don't want to think of life in such a way."

Waving her hand at Frances, Madeline scoffed. "You might not like it, but it's true. Just wait until you hit winter. Like me. There's nothing left after that."

"Madeline!"

But Madeline shook her head. "It would be a shame if we didn't change, wouldn't it? Age gives you the wisdom to recognize that we have no choice but to change. Otherwise, you end up like me. Alone." She paused and looked at Frances with a stern expression. "Don't leave autumn without facing the need to change, Frances. It's lonely enough when winter comes along. It might be too late for me to mend my ways, but it's not too late for you."

Frances did not have a chance to respond, although she had several comments she might have made. She didn't need to change. She just needed to work harder to bring her family together. But before she could say that, their conversation was interrupted.

"Good morning, Mrs. Cooper!" A middle-aged man walked into the room and approached the bed. He extended his hand to Frances before turning his attention to Madeline. "The good news is that your numbers are coming back up."

Madeline made a face. "What's the bad news?"

The doctor frowned. "What makes you think there's bad news?"

"There's always bad news that follows any statement that starts with 'The good news is . . .'"

He laughed. "Ah, I see. Well, there is some bad news. Nothing too bad, however. We would like to keep you for another day or two, just to make certain."

"I don't want to miss my chemo."

"Understood. I don't think there will be any delays," he said as he glanced down at her chart. His eyes flickered back and forth while he read through the notes. Then he shut the file and smiled at her. "Well, pending no further complications, anyway."

After he left, Frances tried to think of something to talk about. She didn't know Madeline well enough to keep the visit filled with in-depth conversation, and over the past four days, she had used up all of her small talk.

"I wonder if my bird feeder is being filled at the home," Madeline sighed. "Poor creatures, if it's not."

Frances tried to ignore the flashback of her mother always calling the sick and downtrodden "poor creatures."

"How's that, Madeline? They certainly have enough insects to eat."

Madeline held up a finger as if to make a point. "There's a difference, Frances. Those birds come every day to my window, looking for their food. They leave fed and happy. Now they will leave disappointed and hungry. There is nothing worse in the world than disappointment and hunger, don't you think?"

"Well, I can't say that I've ever been hungry . . ."

"Of course you have!" Madeline perked up and straightened herself in the hospital bed. "We hunger all the time. We hunger for love. For affection. For sunny days during a spell of rain. We hunger for God's love. We hunger for earthly treasures, something that we should put a little less emphasis on, in my opinion."

Frances was surprised by Madeline's words, for she hadn't taken her to be a woman of faith.

"I didn't know you were so . . . religious."

Madeline frowned. "I didn't say I was religious. I am, however, in a personal relationship with God. I just don't care for those organized churches."

"And why is that?"

"Do you?"

Realizing that Madeline had answered a question with another question, quite possibly to moderate her own response based on Frances's, she spoke slowly and tried to select her words carefully. "Growing up, we went to the Catholic church every Sunday. My children have both gone through their sacraments. But we have stopped attending, especially now."

"Why especially now?"

How could she possibly explain the changed dynamics of her household?

"My husband works a lot. My children have activities. The only time that everyone can relax a bit is on the weekend, although they usually have something to do anyway. Church just fell out of the equation."

"What about you?"

Feeling uncomfortable with the focused question, Frances shifted her weight on the seat. After the children fought her about getting up early on Sunday and balked at attending a Saturday mass instead, Frances had given up on attending with them. For a few weeks, she went alone. But she could not help but notice the odd looks she received from the other parishioners, many of whom were in Nicholas's network of "acceptable" friends.

She worried that they would gossip about her marriage, as she knew they were prone to do with other people. Without any discussion with Nicholas, she merely stopped attending.

No one ever inquired about her absence.

"I have a personal relationship with God, too, I suppose," she admitted. "Although I used to attend church regularly."

"So you see? You can still love and honor God without a church involved. Some people prefer to be involved with a church community. Others insist it's the only way to salvation. I, however, am more inclined to not follow the masses and still maintain that personal relationship with him. It doesn't take much more than studying his word and speaking to him, directly to him." Madeline paused, a cloud appearing to cover her eyes. "I've had a lot of private conversations with God over the course of my life, and I'm at peace that he has forgiven me many times over for the sins of my past."

Frances could hardly envision Madeline as a sinner. And she was about to comment as such when she heard something in the hallway that caught her attention. It was a man speaking to someone at the nurses' station. The word "Madeline" was uttered, first by him and then by someone else, probably a nurse.

"Are you expecting anyone?" Frances asked, curious as to who would be visiting her friend.

Madeline gave a short laugh. "Me? No, unless you have a double who wants to also grace me with her presence."

Frances smiled and was about to respond when she saw Madeline's face change. Her eyes looked past Frances's shoulders in the direction of the open door. For just the briefest moment there was joy etched on her face.

"James!"

Frances spun around in her chair, staring at the tall man with thinning dark hair who walked through the doorway. He barely glanced at either one of them as he took off his overcoat and casually slung it onto the empty chair by the bathroom door. His demeanor spoke of entitlement, and Frances suspected that she wouldn't like him.

"Mother." It was nothing more than a cold acknowledgment. Frances noticed that Madeline's expression of happiness immediately faded. He pulled another chair to the side of the bed and sat down, his eyes falling on Frances as if noticing her for the first time. "And you are . . . ?"

"Frances Snyder. A friend." She held out her hand to shake his. "You must be her son, James. Your mother has told me so much about you." She tried to sound lighthearted when she said it, but he snickered in a disagreeable way. Rather than comment, she moved on to another subject. "Your mother is doing much better now."

"So I understand."

Frances glanced at Madeline, who looked pale. Nothing that Madeline had shared with her about the family rift could have prepared

Frances for such an icy greeting. Clearly, she'd miscalculated the severity of the discord between mother and son. It made her briefly wonder how much worse it might be with the two daughters.

James turned his attention to his mother, leaning forward with his hands resting on his knees.

"I understand you didn't want to go to the hospital. And with a fever?" He made a disapproving noise with his tongue. "Very irresponsible, Mother. That's exactly why Dina and I made the decision to put you in Pine Acres."

Madeline rolled her head to the side of her pillow, her eyes fixated on the window and her lips pressed together.

Her son didn't seem to notice or, rather, simply did not care that his mother was less than thrilled with his statement.

"Clearly, you can't take care of yourself. That's what we were telling you all along." He reached up and adjusted his collar, tugging at it as if the room was too warm. "I hope you see that now."

"It's not home."

"You haven't given it much of a chance. If you participated in more activities and interacted with the other people, you'd see that it's a much better lifestyle for you."

Frances didn't like the way James emphasized the word *you*, as if Madeline was some special case, different from other people.

"And it's quite an exclusive place, Mother. They even had a waiting list! I cannot tell you the strings that Dina had to pull to get you into that facility." Done fiddling with his collar, he dropped his hand back onto his lap. "It would go a long way if you could just acknowledge what she has done for you!"

Frances bit her lower lip, wondering about this odd exchange between mother and son. If Madeline had been at Pine Acres for so long, at least a year, why would this still be a topic of discussion? Of course, Frances knew that Madeline didn't like having been forced into Pine Acres. The Pollyanna statement from James did not mask the truth that her son, and apparently his wife, had a different vision of what Madeline needed.

The tension in the room made Frances feel as if there were pressure building inside her chest. As bad as things were at home, she could never imagine either of her children talking to her in such a manner. And immediately she realized she'd been correct: she disliked Madeline's son.

She started to get up. "I'll leave you two alone for a bit."

Quickly, Madeline turned her head and stared at her, a pleading expression on her face. "Please. Don't."

James smiled, but there was no happiness in his expression. "You see, Frances, we don't always see eye to eye. Isn't that right, Mother?"

Silence.

"She resents that we wanted to move into her house, and she opted to move into Pine Acres," he continued.

"It was my home." The words came out in a soft breath. "And you took it away from me."

James shook his head. "You couldn't live there alone anymore. You know that." He looked over at Frances again. "She didn't want us to move into the house, you see. Felt that we were trying to push her out, rather than care for her. As usual, she thinks about herself first, never about others."

Abruptly, Frances stood up, the chair pushing back and making a loud squeaking noise against the floor. "I . . . I need to get some coffee." She didn't wait for either one of them to respond. Instead, she left the room and walked as fast as she could away from the open door. She could hear James's deep voice, but she fought with herself to not pay attention to any of his words.

What could possibly drive a son to be so shameless and cruel toward his mother? She pressed the button to call the elevator. Part of her felt guilty for leaving Madeline alone with her son. But another part knew that she couldn't stay and listen to his insulting words and disrespectful behavior for one minute longer.

At the sound of her name, she turned around, surprised that some-one had recognized her. Even though she'd grown up in Morristown, she had always kept to herself. Besides time with Charlotte, Frances didn't socialize much, unless it was with the other volunteers at the Museum of Modern Art or the occasional lunch at their country club, even though she wasn't particularly fond of most of the women there. For some reason, MoMA was the charity of choice at his organiza-tion, and Nicholas had insisted that she become involved. To her sur-prise, the women's luncheons at the local country club were ten times more presumptuous than the social events associated with MoMA. She dreaded those luncheons which were full of women seeking one thing and one thing only: to keep up with each other or, even better, outdo the others in their quest to dominate the climb for superior social status.

Frances dreaded those country club meetings more than anything.

Sure enough, the woman who walked toward her, her dark-brown hair perfectly coiffed and her outfit definitely from Nordstrom's, was the wife of a member of Nicholas's golfing group.

They were A-listers; that's what Nicholas called them. If Frances could speak her mind, she'd call them something a little less amiable. They drank too much, spent too much, were too noisy and full of them-selves and, above all, far too concerned with social status for her taste. But Frances kept those feelings to herself, especially because Nicholas had never sought her opinion or her approval. Instead, he had merely encouraged her to be friendly with the woman and accept her invitation to be a part of the fund-raising committee.

Frances suspected his request was more for social positioning rather than just social interaction.

"Debbie Weaver!"

They leaned forward, air-kissing each other on the cheek.

"What a pleasant surprise!" Frances could only hope that her voice sounded sincere, given the location of the encounter.

"I was just dropping off some paperwork to a client of mine," she said casually. Her eyes swept over Frances as if she were appraising an object, not a person. "He just sold his house before he was admitted. Needed to get this signed quickly. What are you doing here?"

Two years back, Debbie had become a real estate agent. Frances was reminded of that fact almost every week when a slick postcard would show up in her mailbox, announcing the houses that she had either just listed or sold. Usually, these were mini-mansions in upscale neighborhoods. It was easy to see that Debbie was doing quite well in real estate.

What she couldn't figure out, however, was why Debbie would waste any marketing efforts on her, when she clearly knew that Frances and Charlotte were friends.

When Charlotte and Gary had been married, they were often part of the social circle at the country club. But once Charlotte had filed for divorce, it was almost as if she didn't exist anymore. Frances often wondered if her unspoken shunning came from the women who feared their husbands might be interested in the soon-to-be-single-again young woman, or the men who feared she'd influence their wives to do the same and go for a large share of their assets. Probably both, she thought.

With appearances at the country club meaning everything, Debbie had led the pack in determining what was socially acceptable or not. Divorce was clearly on the not-acceptable list, as was a working wife, the latter ranking next to children attending a public school. So it had surprised everyone when Debbie started to work in real estate. Suddenly, being a simple housewife and stay-at-home mother wasn't enough. The other women began talking about revamping their careers. But Frances refused. Even if Debbie wanted to change the rules, Frances had refused to follow her back into the workforce. The irony of the situation, Debbie's flip-flopping on the subject, wasn't lost on many people. Even Nicholas had wondered if the Weavers were having money problems, but Frances turned a deaf ear to his comments. It wasn't that she didn't like gossip; it was that she didn't particularly like the Weavers.

And it wasn't just Debbie. It was the others: the Campbells and the Jacksons. Darcy with her weight obsession, which was odd considering her husband was four times her weight and a prime candidate for diabetes, and Jennifer with her denial that she had married her husband because they both needed a spouse to advance in their careers. Both of those women were similar to the woman who now stood before Frances: self-centered and in denial, at least in public, that their lives were structured in a way to fit the expectations of society, rather than fulfilling the dreams of little girls fantasizing about a knight in shining armor.

In either event, they had all failed.

Debbie was still staring at her as if waiting for her to say something. And while she wanted to comment on Debbie's subtle remark about getting the papers signed quickly—a typical self-serving attitude displayed by the entire group of fellow A-listers—she managed to hold her tongue.

"Oh! I, uh . . . I'm visiting a friend of mine."

"On the cancer floor?" The way Debbie said the word *cancer* was almost with the same level of disgust as she had uttered *divorce* when she had contemptuously mentioned Charlotte and Gary's split.

Frances glanced around. She hadn't realized that there was a cancer floor, not beyond the chemotherapy center. "Is that what this is considered? The cancer floor?"

Debbie gave her a look that immediately made Frances feel ignorant. "Well, I'm sorry for your friend, whoever he or she is." Then she peered down the hallway. "This place is so forlorn! It just reeks of death, doesn't it?" She turned back to Frances. "Poor creatures. Cancer will kill half of them, no doubt. Such a pity they don't know it. Or, rather, cannot accept it."

The elevator dinged and the doors opened. Frances made no movement to step forward.

"Aren't you waiting for the elevator?" Debbie asked as she started to step inside.

Frances shook her head. There was no way she wanted to spend one more second with that woman, even for just a short elevator ride. "I was just stretching my legs for a minute."

As the doors shut, Frances turned and leaned against the wall. Her chest heaved as she gulped for air. She hadn't realized she was holding her breath until the moment Debbie Weaver disappeared from her sight. A chill traveled up her arms, so she rubbed them with her hands. How could people be so cold and callous? Cancer was not a form of corruption. Not the result of deviant behavior by social standards. It could target anyone at any time. The shadow of its hand lingered over everyone. Why did it carry such a stigma, almost as if it was a disgrace to contract the disease? Couldn't people look at it like they would renal failure, diabetes, or emphysema?

And while she could excuse her family, she could not excuse people like James or Debbie, who didn't understand that the people in those hospital beds on Franklin Four, the so-called cancer floor, were not *poor creatures* to be pitied. They were people who needed to be uplifted and loved. Past differences needed to be set aside. And people needed to think about the patients' needs, not their own.

If these were examples of the type of support cancer patients would receive, then Frances was beginning to think that God *had* placed all of the obstacles in her path so that she didn't have the opportunity to tell Nicholas. She could hardly imagine how he would have reacted. Even now, he was barely any help on the two days she'd been sick. Why would learning about her cancer make him any more attentive?

CHAPTER 16

She never would have believed that she'd actually look forward to Thursday, chemotherapy cocktail day. But after the grueling weekend and added stress over the upcoming holiday, Frances breathed a sigh of relief when she sat down next to Madeline, who faced the bird feeder as usual.

"That bad, eh?"

Frances nodded her head. "And then some." Plopping her bag onto the floor, she turned to face her new friend. "I hope you'll fill me in on what, exactly, happened the other day with your son James."

"It's nice to see you, too," Madeline said. "Where have you been?" Clearly, she wasn't responding to the question on purpose.

"I'm terribly sorry. I was volunteering at Carrie's school for a two-day book sale and forgot to mention it to you." Frances hadn't felt up to working the book fair, but had committed to it the first week of school when Carrie brought home volunteer slips for her to fill out. She did not want to breach her obligation. And, of course, rather than appear grateful for her mother's assistance, Carrie had merely rolled her eyes when she saw Frances in the gymnasium standing in front of the book display and taking orders.

"So, what happened with your son last week? I tried waiting until he left to say good-bye, but it was getting too late and I had to get home to the children. I hated to leave without letting you know."

"The nurse gave me your note," Madeline said. "I understand."

"I felt awful. He seems to have a big chip on his shoulder."

Madeline appeared unfazed by Frances's comment. "That he does," she said. And then, as she turned her attention toward the window, her eyes sought the birds that were usually flying about and fighting for a turn at raiding the feeder.

Only it was empty and there were no birds to be seen today.

"I wonder who fills that?" Frances asked, more to herself than to Madeline.

"Whoever fills it should be fired," she replied in a resigned voice.

A silence fell between them, so Frances turned her attention to the other patients. As usual, most of them had someone at their side. Madeline and Frances seemed to be the only two who consistently arrived and departed alone. Yet, even though the others had company, it seemed there was little, if any, conversation taking place, at least not between the seasoned veterans and their visitors.

By now, Frances could easily identify the Chemo Cocktail Lounge newbies. Whoever accompanied them seemed to talk incessantly, often to the point of being overbearing and tiresome to the other patients, who would much rather go through their treatments in peace and tranquility than overhear the usual banalities. Frances had noticed that by the end of the first treatment, the patient would usually transform from a scared cancer victim to an irritated chemotherapy survivor. And as they transformed, their visitor would slowly become aggrieved at being an underappreciated companion.

The next treatment, that patient might show up with the same person, but there would be less fussing and conversation. And by the third visit, there would be silence.

Far from being clairvoyant, Frances could almost read the minds of the visitors. On the one hand, they were grateful that they weren't the ones sitting in the recliners. But on the other hand, they were offended that their sacrifice of time and attention was not elevated in status. The lack of appreciation and gratitude was clearly an affront of the gravest kind. As Frances always said, everyone wanted to be a superhero.

The truth was, however, that the superhero was the person seated in the recliner, a clear plastic tube running into their chest, neck, or arm. An hour or two of companionship did not override the twenty-four-seven battle that each cancer patient had to endure. The valiant nature of the war against cancer could never be supplanted with a frozen dinner, bouquet of flowers, or chair-side companion. Those were offerings that people were just supposed to give, with no expectation of glory. Unfortunately, Frances knew far too well that glory played a part in the reward; without gratitude, people too often became disgruntled with their role as caretakers.

As she stared at the back of Madeline's head, the wiry and thinning gray hair poking out from beneath her scarf, Frances felt guilty. She didn't know much about her, at least not much more beyond the fact that she, too, had cancer. But she'd learned, rather abruptly, that there were problems brewing beneath the surface, problems that clearly pained her new friend.

"Why doesn't your son come with you, Madeline?"

The words just popped out of her mouth. Frances blinked, surprised that she'd blurted out such a private question. She hadn't even been thinking about Madeline's son.

"He's too busy," Madeline said, her voice flat and emotionless.

"He lives nearby?"

Madeline pursed her lips together and nodded her head. "James and his wife, Dina, live in Madison."

Frances raised an eyebrow when she learned that Madeline's son and wife lived in the next town over. "Oh?"

"In my house."

"Oh."

"And with my cat." Another pause. "At least I hope."

Taking a deep breath, Frances tried to think of something to say. Nothing came to mind.

"They moved in after my husband died," Madeline went on. "I always heard that no one should make rash changes after the death of a spouse. Apparently, James hadn't agreed, and kept trying to convince me that Pine Acres would be a much better place for me to live than my own home."

"I'm . . . I'm sorry," Frances said quickly. "It's none of my business."

Madeline glanced at her. "You have the right to ask."

Another wave of guilt.

Every person around them with toxic chemicals dripping into their veins had their own set of problems. Madeline was no different. As a friend, Frances wished that she could provide a better support system for Madeline. Obviously, she didn't have one, and neither did Frances.

She felt as if she owed Madeline an explanation, an excuse for her prying behavior.

"My curiosity," she said slowly, "comes from the fact that I have a situation with my family."

The only reaction from Madeline was the shifting of her body so she could sit back and listen to Frances rather than watch for the birds. Her facial expression, however, didn't change.

"I . . . well . . . they don't know."

Madeline's eyes opened wide. "They don't know?"

"About the cancer."

"So I gathered."

Her lack of further inquiry did not discourage Frances into silence. Instead, she suddenly felt like she needed to explain. In some ways, confessing the truth to Madeline was making her feel liberated, much like she had felt when she had shaved her head. "I mean, it's just cancer, right? Why should everyone's lives be disrupted? Millions of people go through it every year, and most of them survive. Cancer destroys enough by itself without causing more collateral damage in its wake."

"Collateral damage." Madeline repeated those two words softly. Frances looked up.

This time, it was Madeline who broke the silence. "Every war has collateral damage, Frances. Whether it's cancer or divorce or bankruptcy, or some other tragedy. Wars can bring people together, just as much as they can tear them apart. Families are supposed to stick together and support each other through those events, not avoid leaning on each other."

"It's not that . . ."

Madeline frowned. "Your nurse is coming," she said, turning her head back toward the window.

It was Laura, sunny and bright Laura, who greeted Frances with a big, happy smile. "Hello, gorgeous! How're you doing today?"

Frances watched as Laura began to unpack her sterile kit of instruments to connect the AC line to her port.

"Fine, I guess. Eddie said my blood pressure is better?"

"It's still a little high, Frances. Moving forward, we need to keep an eye on it, maybe check it at home a few times a day, OK?"

Frances made a mental note to stop by the pharmacy for a blood pressure monitor. "Check it from home. Got it."

Laura began unwrapping the sterile kit and slipped on her gloves. "But at least it's low enough that we can administer your chemo." She gave a little laugh. "Thank God for small favors, right?"

Not certain how to respond to that comment, Frances remained silent. She felt, rather than saw, Madeline peering over, most likely paying attention to what Laura was doing.

"OK, you ready for the needle?"

Frances nodded as she shut her eyes. This time, she barely flinched when Laura broke skin.

"Easy, right?"

"Hardly." But Frances smiled at the young woman.

"I can only imagine," she replied while flushing the port.

After she turned on the machine and the saline drip started to pump, she hurried away to fetch the AC drugs. They were always mixed fresh just after the saline drip had started. Frances suspected it was to ensure that no medicine was wasted.

"You take a young gal like that," Madeline said in a slow, reflective voice. "What drives her to be around dying people all day long?"

Frances shook her head. "We're not dying."

"We're all dying," she corrected. "It just so happens that the people in *this* room are fighting to delay the inevitable for a little while longer." She paused for a few drawn-out seconds. Frances could tell from the pensive look on her face that she had more to say on the subject. "I never liked being around old or sick people. In fact, I avoided it. When my grandparents and parents were sick, I refused to visit them."

She fought the urge to catch her breath. "Do you regret that?"

"No."

It was impossible for Frances to imagine not having the chance to say good-bye when her grandparents fell ill. Perhaps if her mother lived closer, she might have confided in her about her cancer. Her mother would have insisted on being by her daughter's side. She would have flown to New Jersey and taken over the house as well as Frances's treatment. As she envisioned her mother's reaction to the entire chemotherapy center, she cringed. Her mother would take one step into the Carol G. Simon Cancer Center and she'd begin organizing a crew of volunteers to deliver newspapers and magazines, water and ginger ale, or even to bring patients blankets and pillows. She was, no doubt, a take-charge sort of person, only she preferred to lead and leave the dirty work to others.

"What about your sister?" Frances asked.

"Who?"

"Your sister."

Madeline made a noise deep within her throat. Then, rather than answer Frances's question, she asked one of her own. "You have any siblings, Frances?"

"Two, a brother and a sister, but I'm not close to them."

Madeline perked up, apparently gaining new interest in the conversation. "Why's that?"

She shrugged. "They think too much about themselves."

At first, Madeline didn't react. Her eyes glossed over and she took a deep breath.

"Is it the same with your sister?" Frances asked tentatively.

"No." That one word came out fast, spoken in a clipped tone. "Not at all," she added.

They didn't have time to continue their conversation, because Laura appeared, waving two large syringes, one filled with red liquid and the other clear, as if she were holding a coveted door prize in her hands.

"You look so happy," Frances said lightly.

"Someone has to look happy around here," Laura answered while making a silly face. For a moment she looked ten years younger, and Frances found herself appreciative of the woman's happy-go-lucky attitude. As if reading her mind, Laura said, "Seriously, though, it does help. A positive attitude goes a long way in making this whole ordeal more manageable. You know, over the years I've found there are two kinds of patients: those who give in, and those who fight on. I can tell you're a fighter." She glanced at Madeline. "Like her."

"Ha." Madeline scoffed dismissively. "A fighter. Right. For two years now!"

If Laura detected the sarcasm in Madeline's voice, she ignored it. "Exactly. Fight on, ladies. Fight on." She snapped the syringes into the machine and pressed two buttons. It began to make a whirling noise and then started clicking. "There you go! You're all set. Sit back and relax for a spell."

Relax. Frances didn't know the meaning of the word anymore.

"Easy for them to say, eh?" Madeline quipped after Laura walked away. "They aren't the ones sitting here getting poked and prodded!"

Frances didn't respond. She didn't need to; it was understood. After all, they were members of the same club.

"All that talk about family," Madeline said, returning to their previous conversation. "What are you doing for the holidays?"

It wasn't something that Frances had thought too much about. Holidays in the Snyder house were usually fairly low-key. There was often some arguing over who would travel to visit Ellen and Dan Snyder, Nicholas's parents. Over time, however, the brothers had developed the habit of alternating years. Fortunately, this was not Nicholas's year.

Indeed, Frances was more than glad. She was looking forward to a little quality time with just her family. "Staying home!" she said breathlessly. "Hallelujah!"

"Oh yes. I know! Those holidays are never easy," Madeline said. "I'll never forget the family problems that always seemed to evolve around a well-planned but poorly executed Thanksgiving table." She paused, thinking for a moment before adding, "Christmas, too."

Frances smiled. "Glad to know I'm not alone."

"Siblings?"

"No. In-laws."

"Ah!" Madeline chuckled. "It's always been a curiosity to me how we worked so hard to get them to like us when we were courting, and then, once married, those in-laws became out-laws."

"Out-laws. Yes, that's a perfect description." She shut her eyes for a moment. "Will you go to your son's house for Thanksgiving, Madeline?"

Another laugh, only this one was without mirth. "Pine Acres will have a nice dinner, I'm sure," she said quietly.

Their conversation ended abruptly as Frances's chemo machine began to beep. Within seconds Laura was back, pressing buttons and mumbling about the machine.

"I hate this machine. We just had it serviced, and already it's acting up." She pushed more buttons, and within seconds, the whirring sound began again with the rhythmic clicking following shortly thereafter.

"There! Now you should be all set," Laura said, then smiled.

After a while Frances looked over at Madeline. Her face was turned toward the window, eyes on the empty bird feeder, indicating that she didn't feel like talking anymore.

By the time Frances got home, it was later than usual. She wouldn't have a chance to take a nap, which she desperately needed, before the kids got home from school. Instead, she started on some of her chores that she'd been neglecting. Between visiting with Madeline and volunteering for the school book fair, Frances had let the laundry pile up, and the house needed thorough cleaning, especially with Thanksgiving the following week.

"Mom!" Carrie called out the moment she barged through the front door. "Where are you?"

The question, practically screamed out as if Frances should have been standing at the door, ready to greet her and cater to Carrie's needs, sent a shiver down her spine. For some reason her nerves were on fire. When she heard the sound of the front door slamming shut and the book bags being tossed on the floor, she felt a wave of anxiety that she couldn't explain. While she recognized that no one knew the sacrifice she was making in order to keep harmony within the household, it wouldn't have killed them to just hang up their backpacks.

"Can you two please pick those up?" she called out in a sharp tone.

"Jeez!" Carrie bounded into the kitchen. "Someone's having a bad day, or what?"

"Or what," she responded, not trying to hide her derisive remark. "You know, without your father home, I have even more on my plate. Both of you could chip in a bit and try not to leave your stuff all over the place."

Carrie headed toward the refrigerator, flinging open the door and pulling out a bowl of freshly washed grapes.

"Well, it's not like you have other stuff to do!"

"Carrie!" The audacity of her daughter's comment caught her off guard. "That's uncalled for!"

But Carrie seemed unconcerned with the scolding as she popped a grape into her mouth and stared at her mother.

"What?" she asked with feigned innocence.

"Manners wouldn't kill you, you know," Frances snapped. "And I'm not here to serve you. I have a life, too."

Carrie gave a little laugh and took the bowl over to the table.

"Hey, Mom! Guess who's starting quarterback on Sunday?" Andy walked into the room, carrying both of the backpacks, and set them on the floor near the table. "Coach told me today. And if I play well, he said he'd consider starting me for the Thanksgiving game!"

"That's great, sweetheart."

Carrie made a face.

Ignoring his sister, Andy looked at his mother. "You think you might make the game?"

Once again, her nerves fired up. For so many years, she'd struggled through countless baseball, basketball, soccer, and football games. Sports had never been her thing. She knew she hadn't been attentive this year. In fact, she wasn't certain she'd been to more than one or two games.

But to commit to this Sunday? She had no idea how she was going to feel after her chemotherapy, although she had been taking the antinausea medicine. But those pills didn't help with her fatigue. With the weather being colder, the last thing she wanted to do was sit outside on a metal bleacher for over two hours watching a football game.

"We'll see," she managed to say.

Her answer did not please him. She could see that by the way he frowned. "Come on, Momma!"

"Please don't call me that," she snapped. "And maybe I'd be able to go to more games if you two helped out around the house! I mean, seriously, Andy. You, too, Carrie. We have Thanksgiving next week."

"So what?"

"Yeah, it's not such a big deal. It's just another family dinner," Carrie chimed in.

Frances shut her eyes and shook her head. They all had so much to be thankful for, more than they knew. How could she possibly explain this to them? How could she let them see that it was important to *her*?

"I'm tired of this conversation," she mumbled.

"Seems like you're tired all the time," Andy shot back. "You're always going to bed right after dinner. You never watch a movie or spend time with us anymore."

"Where is this coming from, Andy?" She stared at him, surprised by his outburst. If anything, he was normally the one who kept the peace instead of making waves. And it wasn't as if she wasn't trying. Despite everything that she was going through, she was still making certain that there was food in the house, the dry cleaning was picked up, and everything was as normal as she could possibly make it. "You know how much I do. It's a lot of work cleaning up after four people and keeping a nice house."

"It's better to have a nice family than a nice house," he retorted angrily. "Never mind. Don't go to my game. I don't care, anyway." He leaned down, grabbed his backpack, and stormed out of the kitchen.

Carrie looked after him, her mouth full of grapes.

"Wow. He's mad."

Frances took a deep breath, counting to ten when she wanted to toss something at her daughter instead.

"That's a teenage boy for you."

"At least I'm not the one on your bad side this time," Carrie commented before adding in a snarky "for once."

Frances looked at her, speechless.

With a contemptuous smile, Carrie stood up and grabbed her bag. She slung it over her shoulder and grabbed the grapes.

"Guess I'll go to my room now."

Standing at the counter, Frances raised her hands to rub her temples. She knew she'd been short-tempered with the children, something that she always tried to avoid. For a second, she contemplated apologizing to them. But then she noticed muddy footprints tracked across the freshly washed floor.

Please God, give me the strength to get through this.

Then, as if on autopilot, she walked over to the laundry room and grabbed a mop. With a new sense of calm washing over her, she wiped away the muddy footprints left behind by her children.

CHAPTER 17

"God, Mom! Take a chill pill!"

Frances stood in the center of the kitchen, her hand on her hip and a frown on her face. One Mississippi, two Mississippi, three Mississippi . . . This time, however, counting didn't work. "How is it possible that you're failing both math *and* science? Those were your two favorite subjects last year!"

"It's a progress report," Carrie said.

With her light-brown hair twisted into a messy bun on top of her head, Carrie looked older than her twelve years. And the look of disdain that she wore aged her even more. Frances wondered if this was what she would have to deal with for the next five years until she went off to college.

"I just have to hand in a few missing assignments. It's no big deal. Stop making a mountain out of a molehill like you always do."

But it *was* a big deal, especially if Nicholas found out. Part of her job was monitoring the children's progress at school. Only As and an occasional B were acceptable; everything else was not. And an F was unheard of, at least in their family. He'd be angry with Frances, not Carrie, for failing to provide the proper supervision, especially since a good portion of the progress report made it clear that her missing homework was the main reason Carrie was in danger of failing. Nicholas expected both of their children to attend Ivy League schools and made no bones about letting them all know that he would accept nothing less from them. It had been his own dream to go to Princeton, but his parents hadn't been able to afford the tuition, so he went to Boston College instead, where he had been offered a scholarship. He still harbored a bitter resentment toward his mom and dad, although in Frances's opinion, his degree from Boston College was nothing to complain about.

Therefore, excellent grades and extracurricular activities were more than important; they were expected. And this was just one more thing that she'd let slip.

"Your teachers want me to come in for a meeting, Carrie. I don't have time for this!" She gestured to the letter on the counter. "I've enough to do around here, don't you think?"

Carrie rolled her eyes. "That's all you think about. Housework. There's a world out there, Mom. Besides, like I said, I just have to hand in a few missing assignments. No biggie."

"It is a 'biggie,' Carrie Anne Snyder. School is *your* work, need I remind you? Your responsibility. It comes before ballet, before socializing, and before social media. It would be quite beneficial if you began to think about *your* work more. It needs to be a priority, not an afterthought. Maybe put down the cell phone for an hour or two each night and get that homework finished."

"Like *that's* ever going to happen . . ."

There was something about the way Carrie said that. Frances felt as if battery acid were coursing through her veins.

"Well, you're going to make it happen, Carrie," she said in a clipped, even tone, "or you can say good-bye to that iPhone!"

"Mom!"

Frances turned away from her, not wanting to engage anymore. Her heart was still racing, and she started to feel short of breath. Carrie stormed out of the kitchen, stomping her feet on each step as she made her way up the staircase, then slammed the door with such fury, a picture frame in the foyer toppled off the wall. Frances could hear the precise moment when the glass shattered against the hardwood floor. She didn't even have enough energy left to yell for her daughter to come clean up the mess. Instead, she picked up her cell phone and angrily texted her about picking up the glass before her father got home from work, or worse yet, one of the dogs got glass in their paw. In hindsight, Frances knew exactly what had happened. It had been weeks since she'd asked Carrie about homework. Usually, after dinner, she would spend some time with her daughter, reviewing her schoolwork. But in the chaos of dealing with cancer, and her never-ending exhaustion, she'd been too tired to handle it. Fatigue had been her only after-dinner company, it seemed. Most nights, she retired to the comfort of her bed, reading a book until she fell asleep, sometimes with her glasses still perched on the tip of her nose and the book lying open on her lap.

How could I have neglected to follow up with Carrie? Perhaps I had too much faith that she would be responsible enough to maintain her straight As? Clearly, that had been a misplaced expectation.

Frances was still standing there when she heard the front door open. Quickly, she looked at the oven clock. Six thirty. She grabbed the letter from the counter, folding it before putting it into her purse. She'd have to call the school in the morning to figure out if they could do a teleconference instead of a face-to-face meeting. In the meantime, there was no sense in getting Nicholas involved until she learned more about Carrie's situation.

"What's going on?" Nicholas asked, concern in his voice, as he walked into the kitchen. "There's broken glass in the foyer." His eyes swept over the unset table and the unwashed dishes in the sink. "No dinner?"

Frances looked up, irritated at his greeting. "Good to see you, too," she snapped.

"Whoa!" He backed away from her, holding up his hands as if warding off an attack.

She raised her hand to her forehead, taking a moment to calm down.

"I'm sorry," she said. "It's just been a bad day."

"I can see that."

"Bad few days, actually."

He reached up to loosen his tie. "What's going on?" He pulled off the tie, a silk Salvatore Ferragamo that she'd given him last Christmas, and tossed it onto the chair back. "You seem tense recently. Did you ever get to the doctor? Maybe you still have a touch of the flu."

If she were in a better mood, she might have laughed at the irony of his comment. How was it possible that he didn't realize that she was, indeed, still sick? So sick that she was fighting for her life? She knew she was partially to blame for not telling him. Perhaps she should have just blurted it out instead of trying to find a perfect way and time to do so. Still, it struck her that she was so invisible to the family that no one even noticed on their own that she was, indeed, very sick.

"I'm fine." It was her mantra these days. *No. Years.* Repeating it was the only way that she could believe it to be true.

"Good."

He walked over to the liquor cabinet and pulled out a bottle of vodka. Without being asked, she reached for a glass and put ice into it. She wasn't a fan of his after-work drinking, but as per usual she kept her thoughts to herself.

"Oh, I meant to tell you. My parents called and are coming for Thanksgiving."

Frances caught her breath. *Thanksgiving?* It was only a week away, the Thursday between chemo weeks. That was how she measured her time: before chemo and after chemo as well as chemo weeks and non-chemo weeks. She'd forgotten that he had mentioned wanting to invite his parents for Thanksgiving, just as she'd forgotten about checking Carrie's homework.

"They never visit on the holidays, no matter how many times we ask them," she managed to say, the closest thing to a complaint that she could muster. "Why now?"

He sighed and took a long, slow drink. When he lowered the glass, he stared at her with dark eyes that flashed at her question.

"Why not now, Frances? We did invite them, you know. Did you forget?" Before she could respond and defend herself, tell him that she knew—*just knew!*—that they had never actually discussed his parents coming for Thanksgiving, he shook his head and shot a glare in her direction. "You aren't going to start that again, are you?"

"I'm not starting anything, Nicholas," she countered, although she could think of a dozen reasons why they shouldn't come, number one on the list being how his mother sat around and waited for Frances to serve them, never once offering to lend a hand. "It's just that—"

He interrupted her. "Just what? They are my parents and your children's grandparents. They have the right to visit us once in a while."

"My children?" She felt that increasingly familiar pounding inside her chest and a viselike tightening that made her start to gasp for air yet again. "Our children."

He ignored her comment, raising his glass to take a long sip. Even the sound of the ice cubes when they clanked against the side of the tumbler made her cringe.

"You aren't going to start *that* again, are you, Nicholas?" she asked, tossing his own words back at him like a boomerang.

She saw the anger building inside of him. His nostrils flared and his eyes narrowed as he stared over at her. Over the years she'd learned to pick and choose her battles carefully. Nicholas was very adept at carrying a grudge. Better than anyone else she'd ever met, if she had to be truthful. And while he hadn't particularly wanted children, arguing that they would interfere with his career, once they were born, he took credit for all of their accomplishments. Yet when things went wrong and they didn't meet or exceed his expectations, he tended to conveniently forget that he'd been involved in the baby-making process. They became "her" children, as if he'd had nothing to do with their existence at all.

"You're barely home anymore. Wouldn't it be nice to have a small dinner with just the four of us?"

"Frankly, no." The definitive way he said that made Frances wince. "You've been acting strangely, Frances. What's going on with you?"

Again, she contemplated blurting out the truth. She tried to imagine his reaction to the words *I have cancer*. Would he suddenly embrace her, crying on her shoulder for fear of losing his wife and the mother of his children?

When she didn't respond, he glowered at her.

"Fine."

She snapped out of her thoughts. "Huh?"

He merely shook his head. "If there's no dinner tonight, I'm going out to grab a bite."

That's right. Just walk away. It was Nicholas's specialty: turning off and tuning out. Disgusted, she slid a glass across the counter, which fell into the sink and broke into pieces. Between the frame in the hallway, the glass in the sink, and her nerves, she felt shattered, too.

"Debbie Weaver?"

Frances nodded and Charlotte made an overly exaggerated eye roll. "She was ambulance-chasing a deal," Frances said. "Poor man wasn't doing well, but she was more concerned about closing the deal."

"Disgusting. Typical, but disgusting." She sipped at her wine, then questioned, "Did she ask why you were there?"

"I just told her I was visiting a friend. It was the truth, anyway." Frances thought back to her meeting with Debbie and added, "Not like she cared."

"I don't miss those people. Big phony fish in fake little ponds."

Frances laughed at Charlotte's description.

"What about that mousy little thing? Darcy Campbell? Have you heard anything about her?" When Frances shook her head, Charlotte added, "I'm surprised you didn't run into *her* there. As a patient! Her bulimia has to be catching up to her."

"Charlotte!"

But Charlotte merely waved away her mock outrage. "Oh please! It's almost ironic that she's so frail and pale, puking her way to nonexistence as if it will hide the fact that her husband is beyond obese! And let's not get started on the Jacksons with *their* marriage. I still say that he's using her for a figurehead to hide his closet inclinations so that he might get to be attorney general one day!"

Frances couldn't help but enjoy Charlotte's perceptions of the country club group that both of their husbands had hung out with. While Gary no longer could afford the club, Nicholas still chose those men as his comrades on the golf course. And Frances couldn't understand why.

Figuring it was time to change the subject, Frances picked at the salad that she had no appetite to finish.

"Different topic, please," she said. "What are you doing for Thanksgiving?"

"Me? Nothing, really. Might go to the Shore with some friends, maybe play in a poker tourney at the Borgata."

"Nicholas dropped a bomb on me last night. His parents are coming in for the holiday." She didn't need to tell Charlotte what she thought about that. Over the years, Ellen and Dan Snyder had been the subject of numerous discussions over wine or coffee.

"Reminds me why I got divorced. At least I won't have to suffer at Gary's parents' for any more dry turkey and boring conversation. His mother used to cook that darn bird for days! It was like chewing on leather."

They both laughed, just a little. But, in reality, there was nothing humorous about either set of in-laws. Frances could only hope that one day when Andy married, she would have a better relationship with his wife and not be viewed as overbearing or imposing.

"So, how are you feeling?" Charlotte finally asked.

"Tired on most days. Short-tempered, too. Last night I snapped at Carrie and then at Nicholas."

"Bravo!" Charlotte practically cheered at the news.

But Frances didn't feel like celebrating something that she considered unpleasant. *There should be harmony in one's home,* her mother had always reminded her. "Carrie's grades have slipped, and Nicholas was angry that I hadn't cooked dinner."

Charlotte rolled her eyes again. "He's a big boy. I'm sure he didn't suffer."

"That's the thing." Frances leaned forward. "I thought that I was protecting them. At least until this merger is over. But instead of everything staying the same, it seems to be getting worse." She didn't want to mention that things were falling apart and she couldn't help but think that the cancer had nothing to do with it. "That woman at chemo. Madeline? She was telling me about her family, too. Only she didn't really tell me anything at all, just that no one talks to each other anymore."

"So?"

Clearly, Charlotte didn't get it.

"What if that's the way my family turns out? No one talking to each other? No one caring about one another?" It was a worry that had kept her awake on the many nights she couldn't sleep.

"Frances, not all families get along. Family dynamics are a tricky thing. There's jealousy and pettiness in all families. One kid is smarter or has a better job, so the other tries to show their sibling up. Parents age and start turning into old people, focusing on what they're having for dinner or some other banality like that. People change. It's normal to have an abnormal family relationship. We can't all like each other all of the time."

But Frances didn't want that for her children. She didn't want them to be estranged from each other. Her idea of a good family was one that shared meals together, talked about their days, and maybe even discussed their problems. Instead, Nicholas was never home, Carrie sulked in her room, and Andy . . . well, he tried on his good days.

"I guess," she said, acquiescing to her friend rather than belaboring her perspective.

Charlotte glanced at her cell phone. "Oh! I have to run. I need to pick up some papers and a lockbox at the office, and then I'm headed over to the gym."

"The gym?"

She ruffled through her purse for some cash and tossed it onto the table. "You don't get this body by sitting around all day long," she quipped, which made Frances laugh. "Maybe when you're finished with treatment, you'll consider coming with me."

"Maybe." But they both knew that she wouldn't.

Scoffing, Charlotte stood up. "When a lady says *maybe*, it usually means no."

Frances leaned forward so that Charlotte could kiss her cheek before she hurried down the sidewalk and turned the corner.

CHAPTER 18

With as much patience as she could muster, Frances tried to calm her daughter. "It's important that the table looks nice, Carrie. Your grandparents are coming up for Thanksgiving."

"I don't understand why you're freaking out!" Carrie cried out as she practically slammed the good china onto the oval wood table. "It's just Thanksgiving! You're always making such a big deal out of nothing!"

"Just Thanksgiving," Frances repeated as if the words tasted as dirty as they felt.

"That's what I said." Carrie tossed a knife and spoon next to a plate. "Just another dinner, right? Only with Grandma and Grandpa coming."

"It's a holiday, Carrie! And one that we should all pay more attention to. It's not just about turkey and mashed potatoes. It's about reflecting on what we are thankful for. And it's about family. Our family."

Carrie shrugged. "It's not like you really care about them anyway!"

Frances spun around and put her hands on her hips. "What did you just say?"

"Oh please, Mom!" Carrie gave a little laugh. "Everyone knows that you can't stand them. It's not like I blame you."

Frances took a deep breath and watched as Carrie continued throwing the china onto the tabletop. "Can you please be careful with those?

They were from my wedding," she scolded. "And I don't know why you would think such a thing."

"Because it's true?" Another laugh. "She's never been really nice to you. Or me either, for that matter." Carrie looked up, and for a split second Frances thought she saw a look of resentment cross her daughter's face. "She sure loves Andy, though. But she treats the both of us like we have the plague."

Frances's temper immediately dissipated. All of these years, she had tried to shield Carrie from the acrimony between herself and Nicholas's parents, especially his mother. After all, none of this was Carrie's fault. While she could hardly argue with Carrie's observation, she had hoped that Ellen's indifference toward her granddaughter might have gone unnoticed. It wasn't as if they visited frequently, anyway.

But Carrie had noticed, and despite her front of indifference, it bothered her.

"She doesn't treat us like we have a disease," Frances said softly, but the words sounded lame because, in truth, she did. "She doesn't have any daughters or sisters. She's just more comfortable with boys, I suppose." It was a lie. Frances knew that. But over the years, she'd tried to make excuses for the way Ellen treated them.

"Yeah right."

Frances sighed. She could no more convince Carrie of that than she could believe it herself. "Look, why don't you go upstairs and get changed? They'll be here any minute. I'll finish setting the table."

"Thank God!" She tossed down the final plate and hurried out of the dining room before Frances could change her mind.

The quiet that followed was a welcome change. All morning, Frances had been cooking and cleaning, trying to juggle everything while Nicholas went to watch Andy's football game. Frances had remained quiet when they left, resenting that she had to miss it but far too aware that neither of them seemed disappointed.

When they finally returned, it was only an hour before his parents were due to arrive. Andy hurried upstairs to take a shower while Nicholas escaped to his office to check his e-mail. Frances bit her tongue. She could hardly believe his firm expected him to answer e-mails on Thanksgiving.

When the oven timer beeped, she hurried into the kitchen to check on the turkey and stuffing. As she opened the oven door, the comforting aroma wafted into the room, filling the entire kitchen with childhood memories. She stood by the counter, recalling how her mother's house always smelled during the holidays: warm, inviting, and calming. *Picture-perfect,* her mother would say. In hindsight, whether or not that was true, Frances had wanted to duplicate that feeling for her own children, but each year it seemed to take more and more of an effort. No one wanted to help prepare the meal she inevitably made alone.

"Wow! That smells like a family dinner!"

She looked over her shoulder at Nicholas. He stood in the doorway, dressed in freshly pressed tan slacks and a burgundy sweater over a white turtleneck. The perfect image of a country club man. Her mother would have approved.

He walked over to her and pulled her into his arms. She could smell the citrusy undertones of his aftershave—Jo Malone, another gift she had given him the previous year. The grapefruit scent that she usually found so attractive made her feel nauseated now, so she turned her face away from his cheek.

"I know you've been under a lot of pressure," he said, the first words of tenderness that she'd heard in a long time. "I want you to know how much I appreciate all that you do."

As he pressed against her, she felt his chest rub against her port. It was just one more reminder that he hadn't touched her in weeks, nor had he displayed any interest in intimacy. For if he had, surely he would have noticed the small quarter-size disk that bulged from the upper-right corner of her chest. Even now, he felt nothing or, rather, chose to feel nothing. In a way, there was a bitter irony to his words.

"I need to check the oven." She turned her back to him.

By the time the doorbell rang, Frances felt her heart racing. The kitchen was hot and her forehead was sweating. She dabbed at her brow with a paper towel, mindful of where her wig met her skin. The synthetic fabric made her scalp perspire and itch. She hated it.

"Where's my grandson?" The singsongy voice of Ellen calling out for Andy made Frances's skin crawl.

"Hey, Granny!" Andy walked down the stairs. Frances wondered at that. Usually he came charging down like a bull in a china shop.

Wiping her hands on the dish towel, she took a deep breath and walked toward the foyer to greet her in-laws. When she reached the small gathering, she stood by the foot of the stairs, leaning against the handrail.

Ellen noticed her. "Oh!" she gasped. Confusion registered on her face. "Frances! Oh . . ."

For once, she was speechless. Frances wasn't certain why.

"Happy Thanksgiving, Ellen," she said and moved to embrace her mother-in-law.

The returned hug was brief.

Holding Frances at arm's length, Ellen stared into her face. "Are you well, dear?" She didn't wait for a response to turn toward Nicholas. "You didn't tell me that she was sick!"

Nicholas frowned and glanced at Frances. "She's fine, Mother. Why would you think that?"

Ellen pursed her lips and returned her gaze to Frances. Her eyes flickered back and forth. Frances saw Ellen's mouth open as if she wanted to actually respond to Nicholas's question. She couldn't help wondering what she would say. Would Ellen point out her pale skin and hollow cheeks? Or perhaps she'd comment on how thin her eyebrows looked? Or maybe just point out the overwhelming sense of general fatigue that Frances knew lingered around her entire body?

"I'm fine," Frances said with as much forced happiness as she could.

To her relief, Ellen dropped the subject.

"Now there's our big football player!"

Frances took a step back as Dan walked into the house, carrying a large suitcase that he promptly dropped on the floor. Frances looked at the bag, then Nicholas. He hadn't said they were staying. Or had he? She couldn't remember. What she did remember was that she didn't have the guest room ready for company. It needed a fresh set of sheets, a dusting, and a vacuum, and it would take a miracle to pull that off without anyone noticing.

She heard Carrie's footsteps trudging down the staircase. Each slap of her heels on the hardwood sent a dagger through Frances's head.

"Please, Carrie," she said in a low enough voice so no one else would hear. "I have a splitting headache."

"You always have a headache," Carrie said softly. Only this time, her words were not spoken in a sharp or unkind tone; they were more of an observation. "Want something, Mom? Water? Tylenol?"

Frances gave her a smile and reached up to put her hand on top of Carrie's, which was sitting on the smooth oak railing. "Thank you, sweetheart. That would be nice."

As they snuck past their guests, Frances realized that no one had said hello to Carrie. It dawned on her that her daughter, too, was invisible.

While Frances reached for the Tylenol in the cabinet by the sink, Carrie fetched her a glass of cool water. When she handed it to her mother, she stared at her, that same look of concern that she'd had a few weeks past when she noticed her mother's hair falling out.

"I can help you with dinner," she offered, a dejected tone in her voice. "It's not like they'll miss my company."

Frances swallowed the tiny white tablets and set down her glass. "That's not true, Carrie. I told you that earlier."

"They didn't even say hello to me, Mom!" This time, her voice sounded bitter. "I don't exist. And neither do you."

"Please stop, Carrie." She raised her hand to her head and shut her eyes. She needed a break from what seemed like incessant complaining. At this moment she frankly didn't care if her in-laws neglected her. It was probably better that way. She just needed to go through the motions and get through the rest of the day. "If you want to help me, why not sneak upstairs and tidy up the guest room?"

"*What?*"

Frances put her hand on her hip as she faced her daughter. "That would be the most helpful."

"They're staying here? Overnight?" Carrie asked, although Frances suspected that the question was mostly rhetorical. She rolled her eyes and mumbled something under her breath. "Get Andy to do it. He's their 'favorite football star' grand*son*." The way she emphasized the word *son* made Frances sigh.

Andy appeared in the doorway. He made a face, but Carrie just glared at him.

"There she is!" Ellen said. "Where've you been hiding, Carrie? Not coming to greet your grandparents!" She looked at Frances. "Honestly, Frances. Her manners . . ."

Carrie crossed her arms over her chest in defiance.

"Excuse me . . . ?" Frances felt the familiar tightening in her chest; she gripped the side of the counter.

"Andy came right down. Such a good boy!"

Frances wanted to defend her daughter, felt the urge to speak out, but Nicholas emerged and lovingly wrapped his arm around his mother's shoulders.

"Doesn't everything smell wonderful, Mother?" He didn't wait for an answer. "Hey, Pop. Beer? We can catch the tail end of the game."

"All right!" Andy hurried into the family room with Ellen close on his heels, asking him questions about who was playing and which team was his favorite. Within seconds, the noise of a football game filled the air.

Frances would have preferred soft music and meaningful conversation.

Carrie turned toward her mother.

"I'll go do the guest room," she said and slipped out of the room, her shoulders sagging in defeat.

Frances looked around the kitchen and wanted to cry. Her heart ached, and the pounding in her head was making her feel light-headed. A family holiday, indeed. And at that moment she remembered Charlotte's two words, just after she'd finished her first chemotherapy treatment: *What family?* The jarring truth to that simple question caught her off guard, and she suddenly understood exactly what her friend had been trying to tell her for over a month: she had no family.

"Frances?"

Frances turned in the direction of Nicholas's voice. He gave her a smile, too long overdue, and handed her a glass of wine.

"You going to watch the game?" he asked.

She almost declined the wine. She wasn't supposed to drink alcohol during treatment. But she needed that glass to get her through the day. Taking it from him, she bit back her anger and resentment.

"In a minute," she said with a forced smile. "Let me just baste the turkey one more time."

During the meal she found herself short of breath. Somehow she'd managed to cook the entire meal by herself. The only "help" that she'd gotten was when Dan had offered to carve the turkey and Ellen helped to carry a few serving bowls from the kitchen to the dining room table.

They weren't where Frances would have put them, but at this point, she didn't care. *Just eat. Eat and let me go to bed.* Her father-in-law was on his seventh beer, and his words were slurring just enough to tip off

Frances that his eighth beer must definitely be his last. Nicholas and Ellen were deep in conversation about something work related; Frances had no desire to be a part of that conversation. She was sick of hearing about the big merger. Andy was teasing Carrie about something, probably a boy from the way her face was turning red, and she was elbowing him, whispering for him to shush.

"Pass the carrots, Fran?"

She looked up and realized that Nicholas was talking to her. "Hmm? I'm sorry. What?"

He narrowed his eyes and studied her. "You all right?"

"I'm fine!" she snapped. "Why does everyone keep asking me that?"

Ellen leaned toward Nicholas. "I told you she looks sickly. So puffy and red." The whisper would have been easily overlooked if anyone else had been talking. However, that wasn't the case.

Frances glared at her mother-in-law. "What did you say?"

"Nothing, dear. I'm just concerned."

"About what?" Frances felt her heart rate increase as her breaths came in short, quick bursts. "Certainly not about your granddaughter, who, by the way, came downstairs to greet you, but you overlooked her once again!"

"Frances."

She ignored Nicholas. "Certainly not about your husband's excessive drinking problem!"

"Calm down, Mom," Andy urged.

But Frances couldn't stop. She pressed her hands against the tabletop and forced herself to stand. "And certainly not about lifting one finger to help me with this meal. So why, Ellen Snyder, would you have any reason to be concerned about me and my well-being, except to point out, yet again, to my husband how imperfect I am!"

Ellen blinked twice and let her mouth fall open. "Where on earth is this coming from?" She gave a nervous laugh and looked at Nicholas. "Has she lost her mind?"

He frowned. "Frances, what's going on?"

"Mom?"

Her daughter's panicked voice broke her concentration. It sounded as distraught as it had the day she noticed her hair had fallen out. Frances turned toward her daughter just in time to see the color draining from Carrie's cheeks.

"You're . . . you're bleeding!"

At first, Carrie's words didn't make sense. *Bleeding?* She backed away from the table, intent on leaving the room and letting the rest of the family gorge themselves on the fruits of her labor.

"Frances!" Nicholas jumped to his feet and hurried down the length of the table. "Your nose!"

She lifted her hand to touch her nose, then looked at her fingers, which were covered in blood. She took a step backward and turned, her leg catching the foot of the table. In what felt like a suspended moment in time, Frances felt herself falling toward the floor, and then, as she landed, her head hit the edge of the sideboard. The last thing she noticed before she blacked out was Nicholas hovering over her and Carrie screaming, "Mom!"

CHAPTER 19

When she opened her eyes, it took a minute for her to place where, exactly, she was. Her head hurt and her mouth was dry. She tried to lick her lips, but there was no moisture in her mouth. She looked around, but with fuzzy vision she couldn't clearly see anything. Still, she could tell that someone was seated near the window.

"Water," she managed to whisper, barely recognizing her own voice.

"Frances?"

She heard the sound of the chair legs against the floor as Nicholas hurried over to her side. He sat on the edge of the bed and reached for her hand, holding it in his.

"I need water," she said again, feeling as if her lips were practically glued shut.

"Oh! Of course! Yes." He hurried out of the room, and she thought she could hear him calling for one of the nurses. Within seconds, he returned and sat back beside her.

She was in the hospital. That much she could figure out. But she didn't know why. "What happened?"

Nicholas stared down at her and smiled. It was a sad smile, and as her vision cleared, she thought she noticed tears in his eyes.

"You gave us quite a scare, Frances Snyder." He reached out and straightened the thin blanket that covered her. "You passed out during dinner. Don't you remember? You hit your head and"—he paused, swallowing deeply as he struggled to tell her—"your wig came off."

She shut her eyes and groaned.

"The paramedics came and brought you here."

For a length of time they were both silent. The sound of someone walking into the room stirred Frances to open her eyes.

A nurse smiled at her as she carried a white Styrofoam cup and a dark-pink pitcher. "I hear someone woke up thirsty!" she said in a loud, happy voice. She set the items down on the hospital tray before reaching up to adjust something on the drip line connected to her Port-a-Cath. "How are you feeling?"

"Thirsty." Frances started to reach for the cup.

"Just a little to start, OK?" the nurse said. "I'll be back in a few minutes. Need to check your vitals. See if that fever's come down at all."

Fever. Was that why she was here? But Frances couldn't form the words to ask. She was too busy trying to drink as much water as she could. The coolness of the liquid did little to quench her thirst.

"Just slow down now, OK?" the nurse said, reaching for the cup and taking it from Frances. "Too much too soon and you'll know it."

As quickly as she had entered the room, she hustled back out, leaving Nicholas and Frances alone once again.

He leaned forward and reached for her hand, holding it gently in his. His eyes, shadowed by dark circles, searched her face.

"Why didn't you tell me?"

Frances shut her eyes and turned her head so that he couldn't see her face. How many times had she tried to tell him? How many times had he made up excuses as to why he didn't have time to listen? How could she explain to him that his inability to make her a priority in his life had thwarted every attempt she made to include him in hers?

"I have to tell you," he said slowly, picking his words carefully, "we were all shocked, Fran. The children, my parents, me."

Quickly, she turned her head back to stare at him, her eyes wide with fright. "The children? Oh, Nicholas! How are they?"

He squeezed her hand. "Fine. Or, rather, they are fine now, anyway. Carrie had a terrible time understanding why you were bald. My mother nearly fainted, and while Andy tried to put on a brave front, I could see how shaken up he was. Between Carrie's hysterics and my mother's reaction, it wasn't easy."

She almost chuckled at his comment, but couldn't muster the strength.

"They said you had almost no white blood cells, Frances," he said at last. There was a tenderness in his voice that she hadn't heard in a long time. If she didn't know any better, she would have thought she saw tears in his eyes. "You could've died."

That was the one thing she didn't want to hear. It was the only thing she hadn't considered during this solitary journey she had unwittingly embarked on.

"You should have told me," he said, a disapproving tone sneaking into his words.

She felt a flash of anger and did her best to repress it. She reminded herself that, for Nicholas, this was new. He would have to go through the same stages of denial, regret, and acceptance that she had gone through. And apparently in a much shorter period of time.

"I tried. At least in the beginning" was the best response she could give without sounding too critical.

"I . . . I never thought you were unfaithful to me," she whispered. "Not really. It's just that . . ." How could she explain how she felt? In the past, she never did. Now, however, she needed to share all of those feelings she had hidden for so long. "Every time I wanted to talk to you, something else came up. Something else *always* comes up."

"Frances . . ."

"Maybe I could have tried harder. Maybe I should have told you after that first phone call." She raised her eyes and met his. "But I really thought it would be nothing, and I know how you hate hospitals. How you hate waiting and wasting time."

She watched as he slumped into the chair, his shoulders sagging, his face looking drained.

"When I found out, there were so many things going through my mind. So many questions, and I thought I'd get the answers first, you know? So that I could tell you everything at once. I know how you like efficiency."

Deflated, he made a noise, a low groan from deep in his throat, and shut his eyes.

"But you were too busy, Nicholas. I tried before my first chemo treatment, but my dinner attempt failed. And then you left for Chicago. After that, I just didn't know how to tell you."

Reluctantly, he nodded his head but averted his gaze from hers. She felt she could read his thoughts as he remembered the times when she had tried to talk to him, but he had simply been too busy to listen. Too busy to spare even five minutes of his day to listen to his own wife. So partially because of her own procrastination but also because of his inaccessibility, she had faced cancer and its treatment by herself. It was clear that the guilt weighed heavily on his shoulders.

He leaned forward to take her hand. Awkwardly, he clutched it, squeezing it gently before he lowered his lips to her skin. She shivered at the gesture, unable to remember the last time he had kissed her anywhere, never mind just her hand.

"I should've been there, Frances." He took a deep breath, his chest rising and falling as he exhaled. "I . . . I don't know what got into me. Or when it all changed."

"Carrie . . ."

He grimaced. "Maybe yes. Maybe before that. You wanted more children, even though I didn't. You didn't want to work, and that made me angry. How much harder would I have to work to support another child? How many more years until I could retire and we could do all those things we wanted to do? I tried to tell you how I felt. But you didn't listen and you got pregnant anyway."

Frances bit her lower lip.

"Work became everything, and I lost sight of what's really important." He glanced at her and forced a small smile. "Family. My family. When I think back to all of those wasted years spent working sixty-, seventy-hour weeks, all of those recitals and games that I missed. And for what? A job? A promotion? A raise?" He removed one of his hands from hers and rubbed his eyes. "What does all of that matter, Frances, if my world is upended?"

She blinked her eyes, hoping that she could hold back the tears. She had been so strong for so long; she didn't want to break now.

"I mean, you've been there for me at every step," he continued. "I realize that now. Maybe I always did, but I didn't want to admit it. Or acknowledge it." Abruptly, he stood up and began to pace the narrow width of the room. "Or maybe I felt you owed that to me."

"Owed it to you?"

He avoided looking at her. "The more I dug myself in at work, the more I took on, the more you took on at home. Without complaining. Why didn't you ever complain, Frances? Why didn't you call me out?"

Frances stared at him, her mouth agape. Did he truly not remember the arguments? The ruined weekends or nights out because he was late and she fought with him? The tears? Somehow, though, over the years she had stopped arguing and crying.

"And despite all of that . . ." He choked back a sob and raised his hand to his mouth as if to hold back another. "I wasn't there for you when you needed me most."

"Nicholas . . ."

"I wasn't there for you at all, was I?" He didn't fight it anymore; the tears fell freely. He sat back down in the chair, an expression of emptiness on his face. "I wasn't there for you after Andy was born and certainly not after Carrie. I just spent my time focusing on myself and my career. Oh, Fran! How could you have put up with me? How could you have possibly stood by me?"

His shoulders slumped again as he sobbed. There was nothing Frances could say or do to help ease his suffering. Mostly, he had painted an accurate picture of their lives together, and when he said it in such simple terms, Frances had to agree that it was an ugly portrait of a dysfunctional family. Yet she couldn't let him shoulder all of the blame. After all, she had been a willing participant.

"Please, Nicholas. Stop," she whispered. "I could've spoken up. I could've said something."

Yet, in truth, she knew that it wasn't in her DNA to push back against her husband. From birth, her mother had trained her to keep harmony in the household, all the while reminding her that it was the woman's place to serve the husband. If she really wanted to blame someone, she knew exactly whom to point the finger at.

But even that wasn't the truth.

If she wanted to play the blame game, there was only one person she could truly hold responsible: herself. She could have spoken up and said something, just as he had said. The only problem was that she hadn't. She saw the folly in her decisions, not just about the cancer but about everything else that she had remained silent about in their marriage.

Charlotte sauntered into the hospital room wearing a suit and carrying a vintage Louis Vuitton bag that screamed success. She must have been at a closing for one of her real estate deals, because Frances rarely saw her friend pull out her most expensive outfits unless there was money involved.

"Well, well," Charlotte said. "For someone who didn't want to tell the home team, you sure had a way of hitting it out of the ballpark!"

Frances gave a soft, tired laugh. "Point well taken."

Setting her bag down on the floor, Charlotte slid into the chair and leaned forward. "So tell me what happened, Fran. You feeling all right?"

"I am, I guess. It's just the white blood cell count is so low, and my blood pressure is so high," she said. Individually they were dangerous. Combined was even worse. "I'm going to need a blood transfusion." She paused, remembering Madeline's comment to the doctor when told that she, too, needed a transfusion. "Maybe I should request a young, smart executive's blood."

Charlotte shook her head in disbelief. "What?"

But Frances merely laughed again. "Nothing. It's just something that Madeline said."

Charlotte glanced around the room, most likely noticing that there were no flowers or cards on the windowsill. "Hasn't Nicholas been here?"

"Of course!"

"Well, you say that as if he's been Mr. Wonderful throughout this entire crisis."

Frances didn't want to argue with her friend, but felt the urge to set the record straight. "Charlotte, remember that he hadn't known. And he's surprised me with how supportive he's been since he found out. He hasn't left the room much, the nurse told me. And he got very emotional today when I woke up."

Arching one of her eyebrows, Charlotte leaned back in the chair. "Tell me more."

"Everyone was shook up, especially the children." Frances tried to push away the fuzzy memory of their reactions when she'd fallen to the floor and hit her head. Even worse was the imagined picture of how her children had reacted when they learned the truth about her condition. She shut her eyes and shook her head, fighting back tears. If only she had told them. If only she had thought this through. Swallowing, she took a deep breath, willing herself to be strong. "They can't visit me here. Andy and Carrie. Infections are too risky, especially with children."

Charlotte inclined her head and gave Frances a knowing look. "So I gathered. They practically sprayed me with antibacterial soap before they'd let me in," she quipped. "I thought I'd have to put on a hazmat suit!"

Frances almost smiled. The nurses had been obsessive about washing their hands before touching any of the plastic bags of medicine or lines that connected to her port.

"No flowers or anything that could bring in germs, either."

Once again, Charlotte's eyes flickered to the windowsill. "Ah." Charlotte nodded and changed the subject. "I'm sure not visiting you is causing extra stress. How are they? The children, I mean. Carrie in particular?"

Carrie. Unlike Andy, during times of crisis, Carrie preferred to isolate herself under a false mask of bravado. It was a defense mechanism that she had created in order to hide her feelings. And that meant that most people assumed that Carrie was stronger than she actually was. They tended to forget that she was still a little girl who needed hugs and a sympathetic ear from time to time. Something Frances seemed to have forgotten lately, too.

"I . . . I'm not certain how she's doing," Frances admitted.

Charlotte ignored Frances's uncertainty and persisted. "Tell me that Nicholas isn't ignoring her again."

It wasn't a subject that Frances liked to discuss with Charlotte. It had taken her five years to finally admit to her friend that Nicholas hadn't wanted children and, after Andy was born, was adamant that they have no more. But Frances hadn't wanted an only child, and despite his protests, she had stopped taking her birth control pills. When she became pregnant again, Nicholas had been furious. That, too, was something Frances had been reluctant to confide to Charlotte, even after she admitted that there had been an issue about having children.

In hindsight, Frances knew that was about the time when Nicholas started working more, and she suspected it was to avoid participating in the child rearing. She had promised him that she could handle two children and he would not be inconvenienced. *Perhaps there are some promises that should never be made.*

The second-child issue had lingered, woven deeply into the fabric of their relationship. Yet as much as she had tried to shield Carrie from the truth, surely she had sensed the resentment built into their father-daughter relationship.

"I don't think he's ignoring her, although he's been here when he's not at work," she finally acknowledged. "Not with the children."

Frances could see the disapproval in Charlotte's expression when she shook her head. "I'll stop by the house, then. She can't be left on her own. This must've been a shock for both of your children, but you know that I worry especially about Carrie. She's more fragile than she lets on and might need some one-on-one time with a person who cares."

Frances gave her friend a grateful smile. The vision of Carrie sitting alone in her room, worrying about her mother, was not a happy one. Leave it to Charlotte to consider the needs of her children. No one else would share that concern; people were usually too absorbed in their own needs or unwilling to be inconvenienced by someone else's children.

It was at times like these when Frances realized what a blessing Charlotte was in her life.

"I'd really appreciate that, Charlotte. Perhaps you could take her out for a bite to eat. Both of them."

"Of course. That's what friends do, right?" Charlotte reached out her hand to cover Frances's. "We take care of each other *and* each other's families, especially during a time of difficulty."

Frances nodded her head, blinking back the tears that threatened to spill over. How could she ever thank her friend for everything that she had done?

"Don't get all weepy-eyed on me," Charlotte said, reaching over with her free hand to grab the small box of tissues. Gently, she placed it on Frances's lap. "I can't stand that crying stuff. You know that."

Frances gave a soft laugh, even as some tears trickled down her cheeks. She reached for a tissue and dabbed at her eyes. "No. No tears. I haven't cried yet, have I?"

"You have not!" Charlotte proclaimed like it was a badge of honor. "So don't start now!"

Again, Frances laughed. She squeezed her friend's hand and gave her a loving smile. "Thank you, Charlotte. Thank you for everything."

Charlotte tried not to smile back, pretending to roll her eyes. But when she looked at Frances again, she had tears in her eyes, too. "Anytime, my friend. Anytime."

CHAPTER 20

The house felt unusually peaceful. After nine days in the hospital, Frances was glad to be coming home. Behind her, Nicholas set down her bag. Somehow she had accumulated things while at the hospital: a new robe to wear over her hospital gown, fuzzy pink slippers for her feet, and, of course, her toiletries, books, and magazines.

"Where is everybody?" she asked, more than disappointed that the children were not there to greet her.

Nicholas, however, called out for them.

To Frances's surprise, both Andy and Carrie poked their heads around the open kitchen door.

"Come," Nicholas instructed. "Say hi to your mother."

They looked nervous as they approached her, both lacking color on their cheeks. Carrie looked thinner than ever. Standing before her, both children stared, wide-eyed, at the scarf she had wrapped around her head.

Nicholas cleared his throat.

In one swift movement, Andy reached out to embrace her as Carrie flung herself into Frances's arms. The hug from her son was surprisingly protective, while Carrie's seemed apprehensive but genuine.

"How are you feeling, Mom?" asked Andy.

Frances reached out her hand and pressed it against Andy's cheek. "I feel fine, honest."

He didn't look convinced.

"We wanted to visit you in the hospital," Carrie blurted out, her arms still wrapped around Frances's waist. "Someone wouldn't let us." From the look of the glare that she gave to Nicholas, it didn't take much imagination to know who that someone was.

Frances leaned her head so that it was pressed against the top of Carrie's. "Now, now, sweetheart. I had an infection, and they wouldn't let anyone visit." Truth be told, Frances had been glad to have a break from the children so that she and Nicholas could deal with the situation without the risk of interruption.

"Why didn't you tell us?" Andy asked, his eyes searching her face. "How could you keep that from us?"

Nicholas interrupted. "Let's not bombard Mom with those questions right now, eh? Let's get her situated in the family room so that she can relax." He placed his hand on her shoulder and gently guided her away from the foyer.

The house was spotless, and the family room had been set up for her. A pillow, a fluffy white blanket, and her slippers had been placed on the sofa. Carrie hurried into the kitchen to fetch her some ice water while Nicholas helped her sit down.

"Honestly," she laughed. "I'm fine."

Andy fiddled with her pillow. "I guess you can let us pamper you some."

"We even made supper!" Carrie announced as she bounded back into the room, spilling some water on the carpet.

It was overwhelming, their sudden change of attitude toward her, and as she took the water from Carrie, she fought the urge to cry. How was it possible that, buried so deep within her family, there was such decency that had been hidden from her for so long? Even more important, how long would it last?

◆ ◆ ◆

"I spoke to your oncologist today," Nicholas said. She had been home for only a few hours when he came into the family room with this announcement. "He won't speak to me until you sign a HIPAA form." He handed it to her with a pen. "He's going to call me in fifteen minutes, Frances, so please sign it. I need to get it back to him right away."

She sighed and took the paper. "I can tell you everything you need to know. And I have a folder upstairs in my nightstand with all of the reports from the biopsy." But she signed the form anyway.

"Thanks." He took it back from her. "It's always good to have a second person hearing what they're telling you, Frances. And I have a lot of catching up to do."

"Nicholas . . ."

He stood there, the paper in his hand, staring at her. His eyes seemed to study her face, and she wondered what he saw. Gaunt cheeks? Thinning eyebrows? Was he realizing that all of the signs had been there and he simply hadn't noticed?

"They . . . they want me to get a double mastectomy," she said softly.

He paused and stared down at the paper. For a long time he seemed to study her signature. But she knew that he was actually pondering what she had just told him. How would he feel about his wife losing her breasts? The recovery? The multiple surgeries to reconstruct them? She couldn't imagine what he was thinking, especially since she couldn't begin to wrap her own head around it.

Finally, he looked up.

"That's probably a good idea," he said, even though his face had drained of color. "Avoid any possible recurrences, I guess."

Slowly she nodded.

"We don't want to go through this again, right?"

Neither one had to comment on the irony that, so far, only she had been going through it.

"But we can cross that bridge when we get to it, right?" He rolled up the paper and tapped it against his hand. "You need anything before I get on the phone with him?"

"I'm fine," she said.

"I've put off calling your mother," he said. "But I feel it's time that she knows."

Frances took a deep breath. She'd have to mentally prepare herself for the ultimate arrival of her mother. Once she learned about Frances's cancer, she'd be flying to New Jersey in no time. The house would fall under her domain, and Frances would become the poor, pathetic patient that she certainly didn't want to be.

"Please, Nicholas. I don't want her to come here."

He gave her a helpless look. "I don't see how you—or I—can stop her. You know how determined she is. A woman who doesn't take no for an answer."

"You don't need to remind me." She shut her eyes and raised her hands to her rub her temples. "I just don't want to be another one of her charity cases. Like when I was growing up. She always made such a big production out of everything. Like that time with our neighbor."

"Your neighbor?"

She nodded. "Mrs. Bentley. She lived down the street, and my mother made me pose with her for Christmas because Mrs. Bentley had no children and she was dying of cancer. I was horrified, standing next to her, but mostly because my mother kept calling her a poor, pathetic creature."

He frowned.

"Exactly. I don't want to be that person, a person to be pitied, to my mother. You know how she wants everything to be perfect, even if it's in appearance only." Frances dropped her gaze and stared at the floor. "And cancer clearly does not make a person perfect in her eyes."

"Frances." He spoke her name in such a soft, low voice that she looked up. He gave her a reassuring smile. "It'll be different, Frances.

216

She's older and this is her daughter, not some neighbor living down the street. People can change, you know. Trust me on that. She will see the error of her ways, and everything will be all right. As for now, you just rest up. Let us take care of you, the way we should have been all along."

She watched as he slowly backed out of the room and then, turning, disappeared down the hallway toward his office. He shut the door gently and locked it, most likely so that neither Andy nor Carrie would bother him.

The silence in the room—no, the house—was so loud that it was deafening. Even the dogs seemed on high alert to be extra quiet. They hadn't even greeted her when she came home. Most likely, Andy had locked them in his room so that they wouldn't jump on her.

When she had checked out of the hospital earlier that day, the nurse had reviewed a list of follow-up procedures, including visiting Dr. Graham for a review before returning to the chemo center for treatment. Nicholas had listened intently, taking notes on a pad of paper. This new, nurturing side of her husband would take some getting used to. But over the past nine days she had noticed that he had thrown himself, full force, into this new responsibility. It was almost as if his addiction to work had been transferred to a new role: being a husband to a sick wife.

The doorbell rang, and Frances was about to get up when she heard a voice.

"Hello?"

Frances smiled to herself and called out, "In here, Charlotte."

The sound of high heels and the crinkling of a bag grew louder as Charlotte walked to the family room. She set down the bag. "Well now! Look who is home!" She leaned down and kissed Frances's cheek. "How's it feel?"

"Odd."

"I bet." Charlotte glanced around the room. "Where is everybody?"

"The kids are upstairs, and Nicholas is making some phone calls."

Charlotte frowned but said nothing.

"I think they're trying to give me some space, Char. Everyone is acting as if I'm so fragile," she said, a hint of displeasure in her voice. "Andy was pale as a ghost with worry."

"Of course he is! They all are. This was a bolt from the blue for them, Frances. But it was also a rude awakening. Nothing in life is guaranteed. Any one of us could be gone tomorrow." She moved over to sit in a chair, crossing her legs as she leaned forward. "I didn't tell you, but I took Carrie out to dinner two nights ago."

"Again?"

Charlotte nodded. "She was so upset the first time I took her that I promised to take her out again. Besides, the kid has to eat! She was living on macaroni and cheese."

"I really appreciate that, Charlotte." She had heard about Charlotte helping with the children, bringing meals to the house and spending time in the evenings with both Andy and Carrie while Nicholas had been with her at the hospital. There was great comfort in knowing that Charlotte was such a support during her time of crisis. Unlike others who could have stepped up after her diagnosis was known by all. She felt that tightening in her chest as she thought of Ellen and Dan. "I would've thought that Nicholas's parents might have stuck around to help with their grandchildren."

At this comment, Charlotte performed the old eye roll. "Please, girl. It's better that they hightailed it home."

Frances nodded. There was some truth to that.

"You know," Charlotte continued. "I still don't agree with how you handled this, but some unexpected good may come out of it anyway."

Frances hadn't expected such an admission from her friend, especially since Charlotte had always been far too outspoken against Nicholas and even her children. "How so?"

"Carrie." She leaned back in the chair, a thoughtful look on her face. "She recognized that she doesn't always treat you with the respect you deserve. She cried to me, Fran, that she always thought you were weak because of how her father treats you. And her. She resented that."

A gasp escaped Frances's lips. "She said that?"

"She did, indeed." Charlotte tapped her fingers against the arm of the chair. "You think that your children don't see things, but they are more astute than you'd imagine. She observed the neglect, and rather than comfort you, she struck out. Sometimes, when pushed into a corner, we lash out at those we love the most."

Charlotte's words were bittersweet. On the one hand, she was telling Frances that Carrie loved her, despite being rebellious and passive-aggressive. Yet, on the other hand, her heart broke for the weight of suffering that she had unknowingly placed upon her daughter's shoulders. All of those years, she had thought she was shielding them from the problems in her marriage. But Carrie had seen through that. Her reaction was one of self-preservation in order to survive.

And that thought troubled Frances.

What if Nicholas's new attempts to comfort and support her were too little too late? What if he reverted to his ways after a few weeks or even months? While she knew that, in the face of crisis, people often amended their behavior, she also knew that a tiger's stripes rarely changed, even if they faded for a while.

"I think you'll find a new Carrie in the house," Charlotte said with a satisfied sigh. "She wants a relationship with you, but just isn't certain how to go about it. I think she fears rejection."

"She's had too much of that from her grandparents and her father," Frances said in a soft voice. "But I would never reject my children."

"She'll come around—trust me on that one." Charlotte stood up and looked around the room. "They told me they were going to clean the house when I stopped by last night."

Frances had noticed how everything was tidied up and there was the faint scent of oranges in the air. "That was definitely a nice surprise."

"I've brought some dinner for the family," she said as she retrieved the shopping bag.

But Carrie had told her mother that she had made dinner.

"I believe they already have something planned."

Untroubled, Charlotte walked into the kitchen and set the shopping bag on the counter. "Then in the fridge it goes!" She began taking food out of the bag, placing each item on the counter. "And you also have some frozen dinners that people dropped off." She paused and glanced over her shoulder at Frances. "Imagine the surprise on that Debbie Weaver's face when she stopped by with a lasagna and I answered the door."

Frances couldn't help but laugh. "Oh, do tell!"

"I'm sure she was expecting Nicholas. Well, you should have heard her gush over with concern, wondering if she could do anything. She even offered to take Carrie to a holiday party at the country club with her own daughter and friends. Can you imagine?"

Frances shut her eyes and shook her head in disbelief. How could anyone possibly think that a twelve-year-old girl who just found out that her mother has cancer would want to go to a holiday party with another family she barely knew?

"Carrie doesn't even know her children."

Charlotte waved her hand before her. "My thoughts exactly." She shook her head disapprovingly. "Oh, I'm sure Debbie wanted to paint herself the hero, helping you out. A change to make herself the center of the story, not you. Typical." Charlotte folded the bag, the crinkling noise loud in the otherwise silent room. "Sometimes even the best of intentions on the surface carry deeper non-altruistic designs. But there's good ole Debbie, wanting to parade your daughter around at some hoity-toity country club holiday party, just to show off what a great friend she is."

"She's not my friend."

Charlotte laughed. "I thanked her for the offer and declined on Carrie's behalf. My finesse would have impressed you."

Frances could barely imagine Charlotte having any finesse with someone like Debbie Weaver, especially after the abrupt postdivorce dissolution of their own friendship. "I suppose I should be appreciative of the offer, no matter how self-serving it might have been. After all, she was kind enough to bring some food."

But Charlotte held up her hand. "Oh, trust me, my dear, that lasagna was not homemade. I'm certain it was pulled from her own freezer; there was an inch of ice on it! She dug it out and dropped it off so that she could tell everyone the gossip while touting how charitable she is. Why, I bet that lasagna she brought over was recycled from when she had those twins four years ago! Can you imagine her actually making lasagna? For someone else? Ha!"

That made Frances laugh.

Laughing made her feel better, even though she felt a minute sense of guilt that it was at the expense of another. Still, it was a relief to realize that all families had problems, a river of dysfunction running through their lives despite their best attempts to display a public facade of perfection. What mattered was how people chose to handle those obstacles that kept them from crossing the hills and mountains to get to the valleys.

She only hoped that she was now in a valley, for the mountain she had just climbed had been far too long and high. It was time for peace in her life. If her family was ready to tackle the challenge of working together instead of in isolation, Frances knew she could face anything.

CHAPTER 21

An overwhelming sense of peculiarity washed over her as she walked into the chemotherapy center with Nicholas at her side. Something felt strange. Very strange.

For starters, over the past eight weeks, she had dealt with her cancer on her own. Without any support, at least not from her family, she had become self-sufficient and, in her own mind, stronger. Now, however, she couldn't seem to shake them from her side. Especially her husband.

As soon as they walked into the main waiting room and Frances checked in at the desk, Nicholas thrust his hands into his pockets and began jingling his spare change.

"Where do we go?" Nicholas asked in a way that sounded like he was nervous. He wore freshly pressed khaki pants and a pristine pink shirt that he, not Frances, had picked up from the dry cleaner's. She wondered if he had worn pink on purpose, and rather than ask him, she decided to believe the gesture was symbolic of what she was going through. "Do you see the doctor or . . . ?"

"Not today. I just get blood work and then go into that room back there." She pointed toward the long row of recliners. "It's really nothing, Nicholas. I told you that you . . . you didn't need to come."

He appeared to cringe at her words and pressed his lips together. She wasn't certain if it was because she had mentioned blood or because she had said he didn't need to be there. Either way, he looked unhappy but didn't respond. Instead, he merely looked away.

"Mrs. Snyder?"

She smiled at the man in the white coat who opened the door and called out her name.

"Ready for your blood work?"

She nodded and followed him into the back, pausing to see if Nicholas was behind her. When she saw him hesitate, she motioned for him to come.

In a way, his timid approach to dealing with her cancer was endearing. For once, he had to defer to her experience and knowledge. She had two months' head start on him in regard to researching, questioning, and living with her diagnosis. He, however, was still in shock and trying to come to grips with everything.

"Did you have a nice holiday?" the man asked as she sat in the chair.

Without being asked, she laid her arm down so that he could take her hand and stick her finger to draw blood.

"It seems so long ago," she commented. Almost two weeks to be exact. She had missed her chemotherapy appointment the week after Thanksgiving because she had still been in the hospital. The doctor had rescheduled it for the following Tuesday to get her back on track.

"And Christmas will be here before you know it!" He smiled at her as he pressed a bandage against her fingertip.

"It will," she said, although she didn't want to think about the upcoming holiday. Was she expected to decorate? Organize presents?

"Now hold that for a minute, all right?"

He turned his back to organize the tubes of blood. Frances caught a glimpse of Nicholas's face, which blanched at the sight. For a moment she almost found it comical, given the amount of blood work, poking, and prodding that she had gone through. But this was all new to him.

"You're all set. Have a great rest of your day!" he said.

Nicholas walked beside her to the back room. He leaned over and whispered, "Have a great day? You have cancer, for crying out loud!"

"It's not a reason to be miserable, Nicholas." She wasn't certain that allowing him to accompany her to her chemo treatment was the greatest idea after all. At first she had said no, but he had insisted. Reluctantly, Frances had given in.

He stood at the nurses' station and looked around the room at the chairs that lined the back wall. She could read his thoughts, far too apparent in his expression and probably not too far from what she had thought on her first day there: every one of those chairs was occupied by someone fighting a battle for their life. Not all of them would make it. She wondered which ones were going to lose.

Ignoring her husband's reluctance, Frances moved forward.

"Hi, Eddie," she said and sat down in a chair, extending her arm for him to take her blood pressure. "I think you'll be happy today with my blood pressure," she said.

Eddie glanced over at Nicholas and back to Frances. "Oh?"

"This is my husband," she said, trying to keep her voice cheerful. Still, something dark crossed Eddie's eyes, and she knew exactly what he was thinking: *Where have you been, Mr. Snyder?*

"Nice to meet you, Mr. Snyder," Eddie said as the two men shook hands, but Frances could still see the quizzical look in his eyes.

Just as she had during her other visits to the center, Frances sat down and waited for the thermometer. Sure enough, as Eddie popped it into her mouth, he began talking to her.

"We missed seeing you last week," he said. "I was surprised to not see your name on the list for Thursday." He paused as he began wrapping the blood pressure band around her arm. He waited a few seconds for the temperature machine to beep, and then he removed the thermometer. "Your temp is a perfect 98.7." He popped the protective covering off the thermometer. Only then did he begin pressing buttons on the blood pressure machine. "Now, let's see how you surprise me today, hmm?"

Nicholas shifted his weight on his feet as he stood beside her. "Has there been a problem with her blood pressure? She was just in the hospital for hypertension and low white blood cells."

Eddie raised an eyebrow. "Did they put you on more medicine?"

Frances nodded. "Blood pressure medicine and a water pill."

He nodded and looked at the machine. "Looks like it's working: 140 over 100. Still high, but much better."

"Maybe we should alert the doctor," Nicholas said. "I mean, 140 is above normal."

Frances reached out her hand and touched his arm. "It's all right, Nicholas. Chemotherapy increases the blood pressure, anyway."

He glanced away, either from nerves or irritation that she had corrected him; she couldn't be certain which. Having him so involved in her treatment made her feel as if she were walking on eggshells. But she wasn't about to let him become a hysterical husband. She had gone through enough to know that she had a voice, and unlike before, she wasn't afraid to use it.

"All set," Eddie said as he removed the armband and handed her a white slip of paper. "Just take an empty seat, and one of the nurses will be right over to get you situated."

She thanked him as she stood up and started walking around the nurses' station toward the back corner of the center. Nicholas followed her and paused at an empty chair.

"Here, Frances."

But she shook her head. "I always sit with Madeline. She's here on Tuesdays and Thursdays, too."

"Who's Madeline?"

"She's a friend," she explained as she continued heading past a few more empty chairs.

But when she got to the back corner, Madeline's chair was occupied by another patient.

Nicholas leaned over and whispered, "I hope that's not Madeline, because if it is, he has more problems than just cancer."

She swatted at his arm and hushed him.

"She probably doesn't come on Tuesdays after all," she said as she sat down. But something was missing. Madeline was her companion in this journey, the one person who had been there to cheer her on during each chemo session. Now Frances had Nicholas, but from the way he reached into his pocket for his smartphone, she wasn't certain how much support he would provide.

She cleared her throat and waited for him to look up.

"Maybe you might go to the cafeteria and get me a Diet Coke? The bubbles help my throat."

He looked relieved to be given something to do. He never had been one for sitting around and waiting. "Sure thing. Anything else?"

"Maybe two Diet Cokes?"

He laughed and leaned over, planting a soft kiss on her forehead. His face brushed against the scarf that she wore and he quickly backed away as if afraid he might knock it off her head.

She raised her hand and straightened it. "All good."

He looked relieved and started toward the door marked with a red "EXIT" sign. "I'll be right back."

Once he was gone, she breathed a sigh of relief.

"Where's Madeline?" she asked when Laura started to sterilize her port. She was used to having her friend next to her, but the seat by the window was empty and the bird feeder unfilled. "She's always here."

"Oh!" Laura looked at her with wide eyes that immediately filled with tears.

"What? What's wrong?"

"I . . . um . . . Didn't you . . . ?"

But Laura's words left a hollow in the conversation. After all, no one was supposed to share information about the patients.

Frances, however, didn't care. "What? What happened to her? You have to tell me!"

"Oh, Frances," Laura said. "I'm so sorry."

Frances stared at her, her eyes wide with apprehension.

"She's gone."

For a moment Frances didn't know what to do or say. *Madeline is gone? Just like that?* Surely, she had been mistaken. Laura just meant that she no longer needed chemo and was gone from treatment. "I don't understand you. What do you mean 'gone'?" she asked at last. "Where is she?"

"She . . ." Laura opened her mouth but didn't say anything else.

Frances could understand Laura's hesitation to mean one and only one thing: Madeline was dead.

"When?" she whispered.

"Monday." Laura glanced around as if to make certain no one could hear her. Laura knew that Frances and Madeline had become friendly, even friends, during their chemotherapy treatments. "She had a fever again, and apparently she collapsed on Thanksgiving morning. She passed in the hospital early Monday morning. I'm so sorry, Frances."

Sinking into the empty chair beside Madeline's, Frances stared out at nothing. *Is that how it happens? An infection that can't be managed? And suddenly the cancer wins?*

They had both been in the hospital at the same time. Only, upon her admittance, Frances had been taken to a different wing of the hospital, since Franklin Four had no available rooms. Apparently, Thanksgiving had more on the menu than food and festivities for cancer patients. If only Frances had known that Madeline was there, she could have visited her and, perhaps, been with her when she passed away.

The thought dawned on Frances that Madeline had probably died alone. Her daughters hadn't come to say good-bye to their mother. And James . . . Frances wasn't certain whether he would have visited again.

Alone.

Her eyes couldn't focus on anything, and her heart pounded against her chest.

"You all right, Fran?" Nicholas asked when he walked over to her, his hands laden with a tray of drinks and snacks.

She shook her head, and as she did, she realized that the reason she couldn't see was because her eyes were filled with tears.

"Hey. What's going on?" He set the tray down on the floor and quickly pulled up a chair next to her. "I'm here, Frances," he said as he reached for her hand. "I'm here for you."

But she couldn't talk. She couldn't even breathe. Even her arms shook as her shoulders were racked with sobs, each one causing her to fall deeper into hysterics. It was as if all of the tears that she had been holding back for the past two months had suddenly been released. She let them fall, not caring if other people were watching.

Two months of dealing with cancer, worrying about other people, arguing with Charlotte, hiding things from the children, and fearing Nicholas's reaction. Everything combined had built up inside of her, and now the floodgates had opened.

"Let me close this," Laura said in a soft voice as she pulled the curtain around the chair, giving both Frances and Nicholas some privacy.

Nicholas rubbed her hand as he looked at Frances, his eyes laden with guilt. "I'm so sorry, Frances. Please. You have to forgive me."

She tried to wave her hand at him, wanting to let him know that her tears were not really about him, but she couldn't even do that.

He pulled her into his arms, pressing her cheek against his shoulder. "Shh. Everything is going to be all right. You'll see. I promise, Fran, you do *not* have to walk one more step in this awful journey without me beside you. You will never be *alone* again."

Just the word sent her into a new round of sobs.

Until she had collapsed at the Thanksgiving table, she had been alone. The only difference was that she hadn't known it. Andy with his sports, Carrie with her attitude, and Nicholas with his work obsession had created a large void in her life. Each day she had moved through her routine with no one showing her any love or tenderness. Instead, everyone had just focused on their own needs, not realizing that Frances had been just barely treading water in a sea of neglect.

While life had pushed them apart, cancer had brought them back together.

And now that her family had the pieces in place to work on their relationships, Madeline was gone.

CHAPTER 22

No one at the Carol G. Simon Cancer Center knew any details about when the service was being held, so Frances had contacted Pine Acres to inquire about Madeline's funeral. When she learned that it was to be held on Friday, she thanked them and took down the rest of the information. But after she hung up the phone, she sat at the kitchen table, alone and staring at the wall. The finality of life, so neatly wrapped up by a single day of recognition before lowering that casket into the ground, struck her as being particularly depressing. Why didn't a person's life require more than just one day to say good-bye?

After the children left for school on Friday morning, Frances managed to take a shower, letting the hot water cascade down her back. With her eyes shut, she tried to shake the lingering nausea from the previous night. She had forgotten to take her medicine and had spent a good portion of the early evening vomiting in the bathroom. This time, Nicholas was by her side, dabbing a cool cloth at the back of her neck and rubbing her back. She had been surprised at how comforting it had actually been to have someone telling her that everything would be all right.

She shut off the shower and stepped onto the soft bath mat. One glance in the mirror told her all she needed to know: she looked as bad as she felt. Her face looked puffy; whether from the chemotherapy treatment or the sleepless night, she was not certain. And her bald head was a constant visual reminder of what she was battling, the very battle that her friend had just lost.

"You OK?"

She looked at the closed door, glad that she had remembered to lock it. "Yes, thanks. Just drying off."

"We should leave soon, Fran."

As she wrapped the towel around herself, she avoided looking at her reflection again until she found her wig and situated it on her head. She tried to apply some makeup, hoping to look halfway decent for Madeline's funeral.

Her mind reeled with what little she had learned about Madeline's death. Her white blood cell count had dropped again. Only this time, she had caught an infection in the hospital. On Sunday she had lost consciousness, and Monday she'd slipped away in the early hours of the morning.

Frances still couldn't believe it. One minute Madeline was here. The next she was gone. And never far from Frances's mind was the fact that it could have been her who'd caught the infection and died.

As she sat in the church, wearing her black dress and black high heels, she looked at the casket, a plain brown coffin, and the truth suddenly sank home. She reached out and grasped Nicholas's hand, clutching it in hers.

He had insisted on attending the funeral with her even after Frances had told him that she didn't want him to accompany her. Ever since she had awoken at the hospital, she had been greeted by a new Nicholas, one that seemed much more like the Nicholas from their dating years: attentive, concerned, loving. And while she was thankful for his 180-degree turnaround, she needed some space as well as time to get used to the new Nicholas. She had told him as much, something she wasn't used to doing. But despite her protests, he had insisted. He hadn't wanted her driving alone, and she finally agreed. Her last chemotherapy treatment had made her extraordinarily fatigued.

But as her eyes took in the sight of the casket, she was beyond grateful that he had been so persistent.

"What is it?" he whispered.

"That could have been me." She swallowed and looked at him from the corner of her eye.

He pressed his lips together and slowly nodded his head. "I'm well aware of that, Fran." He squeezed her hand.

If there were twenty people at the church, Frances would have been surprised. She refused to count, horrified at how few people had shown up. She recognized one of the Pine Acres staff members from her sole visit to the nursing home. There were two older people seated next to the staff person, and Frances suspected that they, too, were from the nursing home. That warmed Frances's heart. Perhaps Madeline had truly not given the place a fair chance.

Other than those people, there were just a few others, most of whom Frances did not know. Older people who sat by themselves in the different pews scattered throughout the sanctuary, which made it look as if even fewer people were there.

She thought it was odd that James had arranged for the funeral to be held at a church, especially after Madeline had told her that she didn't attend church. But the Methodist pastor had apparently been quite familiar with Madeline, for when he spoke, he referenced several different occasions when they had been together for fund-raisers, church socials, and even Bible study.

"What's wrong?" Nicholas whispered.

"That pastor," Frances whispered back. "He's talking about how Madeline was involved with the church. But she told me that she didn't believe in organized religion."

"So?"

"It just doesn't ring true." Frances tried to return her attention to the service, but she still had a niggling feeling that something wasn't quite right.

Up ahead, in the second, not first, pew, she saw the back of James's head. Seated next to him was a woman with long, straight hair. It was a mixture of brown with gray, and she wore it in a classy blunt cut that reminded Frances of the country club women. Both of them stared straight ahead, their eyes riveted on the pastor. Not once did Frances see them tilt their heads in grief or dab at their eyes in sorrow.

In the next pew, two women with dark-brown hair sat so close together that their shoulders touched. Frances wondered if they were her daughters. Was it possible that they had made the journey to New Jersey to finally visit their mother, even if it was only to say good-bye to her body, for her spirit was already long gone? That seemed like a waste to her. How much more meaningful it would have been had they visited Madeline during her lifetime, rather than after death!

She leaned over and nudged Nicholas. "I don't want to stay afterward," she whispered.

"Are you feeling all right?" The concern in his voice, so different from the previous months—no, years—of contempt was such a change that Frances wasn't certain if she could get used to it. Not as fast as he had been willing to offer it to her.

"I feel fine, but I get the sense that something isn't right here."

At that moment the pastor asked for James to step forward to the podium because he had some words about his mother.

Immediately, Frances gave her full attention, forgetting about how uncomfortable she'd just felt.

James took his time sliding out from the pew and walking to the front of the church. He nodded toward the pastor and took his position at the podium, pausing to gaze around the room. Frances wondered if he felt the same way that she did when he saw how few people were in attendance. If so, he did not show any signs. Instead, he cleared his throat and moved the microphone so that it was positioned better to carry his voice.

"When I was a child," he began, "my world revolved around one and only one person: my mother. During the course of her life, Madeline Cooper had that effect on many people. She was both the rising and setting sun for so many that have come and gone before us. As Pastor Ralph said, her involvement in the church made her a beacon for many during the storms of life. She was always there for people in need." He paused and glanced toward the two women who Frances thought were his sisters. After he looked at them, he averted his eyes. "What is a *beacon*? I looked up that word in the dictionary and was not surprised to see it defined as a light set in a prominent position to serve as a warning or guide for others. My mother was certainly that: a beacon.

"Yet, like so many others, the time comes when spring turns to summer and then autumn to winter. And like those changing seasons, so, too, do people adapt and adjust. We have no choice but to accommodate the seasons of life. Yet my mother fought those changes, refusing to accept the fact that she was not only aging but ailing. She tried to defy the odds by fighting her diagnosis, and when offered only two years to live, she decided to engage in war with her cancer, rather than succumb to it.

"She lived for ten years, flouting the medical diagnosis with pride and dignity."

He cleared his throat, his eyes once more flickering in the direction of his sisters.

"But that was how she had lived her life, ignoring common wisdom and sometimes avoiding what was practical. During my youth, she did her best to protect us from the ugly side of life, to the point that she built a bubble that, once burst, was hard to repair."

James paused. He removed his glasses and wiped them with a handkerchief that he had pulled from the inside breast pocket of his jacket. When he replaced his glasses, he continued speaking.

"Standing on conviction is a dangerous thing, but my mother believed in her own opinions and love for her family so much that she was willing to do just that: live according to her own ideas. Some might say that it cost her more than she could have envisioned. Now that she is gone, we must all be at peace with some of the decisions and demands that she made in her life." His eyes swept the scantily attended gathering and landed upon his sisters. "We do that because we loved her."

Frances leaned over to Nicholas. "I can't listen to this anymore," she whispered. "Please. Let's go."

He took her hand and gently squeezed it, but remained looking straight ahead.

"None of what he's saying makes sense," she pleaded. "I need to get some fresh air."

She withdrew her hand from his grasp and quietly slid down the length of the pew. She knew that everyone could see her getting up, but she didn't care. Staring straight ahead, she walked toward the back of the church and out the front door. Outside, she took big, deep breaths and shut her eyes.

How could Madeline's son stand up there and speak about his mother in such a way? Nothing of what he said seemed to line up with what she knew about Madeline. Instead of speaking a proper eulogy, James seemed to have a hidden agenda, and that did not sit well with Frances. How could a grown man do such a thing? First, he forced his mother from the home that she loved, then he ignored her during her illness, and now he misspoke at her funeral!

Preposterous!

Fifteen minutes passed before the door opened and a few people began to step outside. As she waited for Nicholas to emerge, Frances moved to the side so that the other people could pass her. Most of them glanced at her and smiled as they passed. They appeared much happier outside of the church than inside.

The pastor emerged and, upon seeing Frances, walked toward her as if he had a purpose to do so.

"Excuse me," he said in a soft voice that Frances found rather soothing. "You're one of Madeline's friends?"

"I am."

"You left before the announcement that everyone is invited back to Madeline's home in Madison after we conduct the interment, for some coffee, sandwiches, and fellowship." He placed his hand in hers. "It would be a great comfort to her children, I'm sure."

Frances didn't know how to extract herself gracefully from the pastor's hand or request. The last thing she wanted was to go to Madeline's former—and James's current!—home. "I . . . I'll see what my husband says." It sounded dull and uncaring, but she didn't know what else to say.

"Excellent. I look forward to seeing you there after we leave the cemetery."

He stepped aside as a large black hearse drove up. The driver stepped out and opened the back door. Frances felt as if someone had punched her in the stomach. She almost doubled over when she realized that by saying *we* the pastor was including her. She was about to correct him, to tell him that she would not be going to either the cemetery or the small gathering at Madeline's—now James's—home. But a movement just inside the open church doors distracted her.

Several men were walking out, Nicholas included, each one positioned at a corner of the casket. They were carrying it outside to the hearse. Their faces looked forlorn, even her husband's. Despite not having known Madeline, accompanying someone on the final journey was a reflective, if not humbling, experience. How could anyone not think of their own ultimate demise?

Standing to the side, Frances watched, feeling a lump form within her throat. It was a passage that everyone would take, no ticket needed to step on board. She began to feel panic rise within her stomach, realizing that she could have been the one that Nicholas helped during those final steps to the shiny black car.

As they slid the coffin into the back of the hearse, Nicholas stepped back, his eyes moving to meet Frances's. His cheeks were pale and his eyes wide with a look of fright as he, too, seemed to share her thoughts. She wanted to turn around, to not see the expression on his face that mirrored her own anxiety. But she couldn't. Even after the pastor said a prayer just before the back door was shut and the driver got back into the car, she remained staring at her husband.

And without speaking to him, she knew that he would insist that they accompany Madeline to the cemetery. It was the least that they could do, especially since Madeline had kept Frances company during her cancer journey at a time when she had not invited anyone else to accompany her.

At that moment Frances understood that she, too, would have it no other way. She owed it to Madeline to see her through this final stage in life's journey.

CHAPTER 23

The house on Woodland Avenue took Frances by surprise. It was larger than she anticipated: a two-story white colonial with an addition on the side that looked like a sunroom. It sat on a section of the Madison street that backed onto parklands, behind which was Drew University. It was located in a nicer section of town, many of the residents being New York City commuters.

She felt a resentment building inside of her. If Madeline hadn't wanted to leave her home, she could now understand why. Moving from such a nice house into one room would, indeed, be a major setback for her independence and privacy. Why would her son force her to do something like that?

"Nice house," Nicholas commented as he parked on the street in front of another car.

"Surprisingly. I had expected it to be a small Cape Cod or ranch." She unbuckled her seat belt and opened the car door before carefully stepping onto the street. "I wonder what her husband did?"

They walked down the driveway to the front walk. Nicholas held her elbow, guiding her along the narrow walkway to the front steps. The gesture comforted her, mostly because she couldn't remember the last time that he had thought to do such a thing. Once again, she realized how grateful she was that Nicholas had insisted on accompanying her, even if she had been hesitant about his company earlier in the day.

James opened the door and stepped aside for them to enter. "Welcome, Frances. Nicholas. Glad that you could make it after all."

Frances couldn't help but avoid eye contact with him. She slipped out of her heavy coat and handed it to him, thanking him with her eyes still averted. She took a moment to look around. There were even fewer people at the house than there were at the church. But she recognized the two women that she thought were Madeline's daughters as well as one of the staff members from Pine Acres.

Nicholas went to fetch her a coffee, and Frances slipped into the room where the others were gathered. It was a large, comfortable room with white bookshelves lined with leather-bound books and family photos. A fireplace along the back wall glowed with a small, well-managed fire burning to add both ambiance and some heat to the room.

She walked up to the woman from Pine Acres and promptly introduced herself.

"Why, yes! I remember you from the night she went to the hospital," the woman said. "The first night, not . . . the last night."

"So sad," Frances said. "And so unexpected. I thought she was doing well."

The woman merely nodded her head, and Frances realized that, even after death, privacy laws were in effect. She would learn nothing about Madeline's passing from this woman.

Nicholas returned and handed Frances a coffee. He smiled at the woman, but made no attempt to introduce himself.

"Gladys. Marion. Come meet one of Mother's friends," James said as he joined the small group of people.

Frances turned and forced herself to smile as she was introduced to Madeline's daughters. She wondered which one lived in London and where their spouses were.

"It's good to meet you, Frances," the one named Marion said. She was tall and willowy; only the crow's-feet at the corners of her eyes indicated that she was well into middle age. Her light-brown hair was pulled back into a bun at the nape of her neck. Her diamond stud earrings glimmered in the firelight, as did her wide-band diamond-encrusted ring when she reached out to shake Frances's hand.

"It's so nice to know that Mother was not alone during her final days."

The other sister, who resembled Marion with the exception of her short hair, merely smiled. There was something sorrowful about her dark eyes.

"We were in chemotherapy together."

Gladys caught her breath. "Oh, dear. I'm so sorry. I . . . I didn't know . . ." She suddenly appeared very uncomfortable. Her hands fluttered before her, and she looked as if she might burst into tears, especially when she glanced at Nicholas. "At least you have a good support system, I see," she said in a meek voice and with a forced, nervous smile.

Marion pressed her lips together, giving her sister what could only be described as a look. *Get it together,* she appeared to silently suggest. "Some people need a good support system," she said drily. "Others don't."

It took a moment for Frances to realize what Marion had just said. She felt her chest tighten, just a little, as she fought the urge to scream at this well-manicured woman. *Everyone needs a support system,* she wanted to shout. Hadn't she just learned that the hard way? That people needed to care for the patient *and* their family during such a hard and trying time? Perhaps she had denied herself the comfort and care of her family because she hadn't been strong enough to make them pause to listen to her, but Madeline? Not one of her children had been with their mother during her years of treatment. Unlike Frances's family, Madeline's knew and had still denied their mother the consideration of being by her side.

James cleared his throat and glanced from Marion to Frances. "It isn't as if we didn't try," he said. "Mother wanted it this way."

At his comment, Frances's mouth opened in surprise. Once again, she thought that she had misheard him. "I'm sorry. I don't understand you. She wanted *what* this way?"

Gladys looked away as Marion reached out to take her sister's arm. Clearly, the one sister was upset and needed to be comforted. They walked to the side, their heads dipped close together as Marion spoke softly to her sister.

James gestured for Frances and Nicholas to step closer to the bookcase, out of earshot.

"Mother was diagnosed with cancer almost ten years ago. My sisters had already moved, and Mother had cut off any contact with them," he said. "In fact, she cut off contact with most of her friends and stopped attending church. That surprised all of us. She'd been so active in the church; it was her home away from home."

None of what James said made sense to Frances. Certainly, he was mistaken. "Why would she do such a thing?"

His shoulders lifted in a semi-shrug. "Who knows why my mother did most of the things she did? When we were growing up, she did the same thing to her sister when she was ill. Just shut her off from the rest of us. It was a terrible mess when everyone found out. We were all very close to our aunt Barbara."

Shut off her sister? Frances narrowed her eyes as she studied James, trying to decide whether he was telling the truth. "That doesn't sound like the Madeline I knew."

He shrugged again, a gentle reminder to Frances that she really hadn't known Madeline very well at all. "Sometimes I wonder if she didn't feel guilty for having abandoned her sister during her time of need. I never could figure out why she did that." He frowned and scratched at the side of his head. "Over the years, I believe she didn't want to upset us, so she avoided the topic as well as Aunt Barbara. It was selfish, really, but I suspect that she wanted to protect us from the ugliness of death."

Frances swallowed and avoided looking at Nicholas. Hadn't that been her own intention?

"But," James continued, "it backfired. Gladys and Marion couldn't believe that anyone could do that to their sibling. At the time, my father was on the rise as an executive at good old Ma Bell, and they were both focused on climbing the social ladder. A dying sister just didn't fit the image, I suppose."

"That's ridiculous! No one thinks like that!" But she knew it was the truth. There were far too many people in their own social circle who were exactly the same. Hadn't those people, supposed friends, merely disappeared when they learned that Charlotte had filed for divorce? And since news of Frances's cancer had begun to circulate through the country club circuit, only one person had reached out, and that had been a sparse attempt lacking any authenticity or genuine concern.

Maybe Madeline had cut off people before they could cut her off.

"Mother had an idea of what the perfect family was and what it wasn't," James explained. "She didn't want anything unpleasant in our lives, Frances. She sheltered us so much that we practically lived in a bubble. When I was younger, I thought she walked on water. But when I learned about Aunt Barbara, I realized that she wasn't a saint. In fact, she was cruel."

"*Cruel* is a very strong word." Her voice must have carried anger, for Nicholas reached out and pressed his hand against the small of her back.

"It is. I agree. But she abandoned her sister during the darkest days of her life. When Aunt Barbara needed someone to hold her hand and comfort her, my mother turned her back on her. It was almost as if she felt cancer was contagious. That it wouldn't exist if it was ignored." He gave a soft chuckle. "Cancer taught her a lesson there, I suppose."

"Is that why neither you nor your sisters talked to her?"

"For a while, yes," he admitted. "But when she was diagnosed ten years ago, we tried to rally around her, to reconcile our differences. We didn't want to repeat the cycle."

"And what happened?"

"She refused. Said that if we loved her, we would leave her alone." The doorbell rang, and James looked over his shoulder. His wife was answering the door, so he returned his attention to Frances and Nicholas. "We still tried, Frances. But she never relented. And then when Dina and I wanted to move in with her, she refused and insisted on moving to the home."

Once again, Frances was left speechless. This version of Madeline's story was creating a new visual of the character of her friend. While she had hoped for some answers, she only had more questions. Nothing made sense.

"Ah, the pastor's here." He smiled apologetically. "If you'll excuse me, I should greet him."

Frances wanted to know more. Unfortunately, she knew she was going to lose James's attention, as several other cars appeared to be pulling up to the house.

Quickly, she placed her hand on James's arm.

"Before you go," she said in a pleading tone, "I have something I wanted to ask you."

He smiled at her. "Of course."

"Her room. At Pine Acres. Has anyone cleared it out yet?"

He shook his head. "Not yet, no. We've ten days to go through her things. I'll be down there sometime this week, or Saturday at the latest."

She hesitated, trying to think of the right words to formulate her request. When none came to mind, she decided to just say it outright.

"If you don't mind," she said, "there is something in her room that I . . . I would like to take. It's small. Insignificant. But it'll remind me of her."

James gave a soft laugh. "Most of her things will go to the Salvation Army, Frances. What does she have there but clothes, bedding, and a few decorations? Feel free. It would please me greatly to know that something of hers is with someone who managed to be a friend at the end. We have, after all, enough memories of her here."

As he walked away, Frances glanced at Gladys and Marion. The emotions had subsided, for the moment anyway, but Frances knew better than to approach them with any questions. It was too soon to leave yet, even though Nicholas was beginning to jiggle the change in his pockets in that irritating way. Ignoring him, she wandered to the bookcase and looked over the titles. The books varied from leather-bound classics by Jane Austen and Thomas Hardy to leather cases of *National Geographic* magazines that dated back almost twenty years. It made for an impressive collection.

She looked at the many picture frames, all but one holding aged photos that showed different aspects of Madeline's life: a young wife, a young mother, a church activist, and, to her surprise, part of a women's group at the very country club where she and Nicholas belonged. Her eyes skimmed over an empty picture frame, and she wondered about it.

But Nicholas wrapped his arm around her waist, interrupting her thoughts. "Let's go," he whispered into her ear. "The children will be home from school soon, and I want you to have time to rest."

She agreed and set down her coffee mug on a nearby table. There was nothing more she could do to honor Madeline now. Besides, she was feeling fatigued and didn't know when the antinausea medicine would wear off. The last thing she wanted was to get sick in public. Within minutes of saying good-bye to James and his sisters, Frances was back in the car, Nicholas driving, and headed toward home.

Frances stared out the window at the houses, so unfamiliar to her but probably so familiar to Madeline that they had become a faded part of her everyday life.

This new side of Madeline shocked her. Yet, in some ways, it was parallel to what she had done with her family. While she had wanted to tell them in the beginning, she considered their not being involved in her illness a way of protecting them. In reality, there simply was no way to shield family from the inconvenience of cancer.

She took a deep breath and looked over at Nicholas. "Do you think . . . ?"

"Do I think what?"

"Maybe it's time we sit down with the children, Nicholas. And talk about the double mastectomy?"

He gripped the steering wheel, staring straight ahead until they came to a traffic light. When the light changed from red to green, the car did not move.

"Nicholas?"

He turned to look at her and slowly nodded. "There's no time like the present, I guess. But we'll do it together."

Leaning over, she placed a soft kiss on his cheek, not caring that the driver behind them was honking the car horn. "Thank you," she whispered.

CHAPTER 24

Frances walked into Pine Acres, thankful that, for once, Nicholas had gone into the office and given her some breathing space. She needed it. With her mother arriving for an extended stay, Frances knew that time alone would soon be a precious commodity.

She recognized the woman at the desk as the same one from the postfuneral gathering.

"Frances, right?" she said with a bright smile. "Mr. Cooper mentioned that you might be stopping in to gather up some of his mother's things."

Frances shivered, even though she wasn't cold. James hadn't hesitated when she had asked to take something, a small memento, from Madeline's room.

The woman walked around the desk and led her to Madeline's room. The door was open, and the sun shone through the window. Immediately, Frances looked at the bird feeder and saw that it was filled with seed, even though there were no birds eating there at that hour. The bed was made, and everything looked as if Madeline had merely gone to the dining room and would return at any moment.

"You two must've been very close."

Frances turned to look at the woman. She didn't want to admit that she had known Madeline for less than two months, and that all of their friendship was centered around cancer. So she gave a little shrug and said, "We had chemotherapy treatments together. But she was a great support to me in a way."

"Well, Mr. Cooper said that you should feel comfortable taking anything you want and he'll be by this week to collect the rest." The woman smiled as she backed out of the room and shut the door, giving Frances some privacy.

At first, Frances stood in the center of the room and looked around. After having been to Madeline's former house, she could understand the resentment that her friend had felt at being muscled out and put into such small, cramped quarters.

But then Frances quickly reminded herself that, according to James, that wasn't what had happened. Madeline had chosen to leave her home and live her remaining years in the small hospital-like room. Had she really been punishing herself for having abandoned her dying sister?

She took a deep breath and walked over to the dresser. There wasn't much to pack up, a few knickknacks on top of the dresser and some books on the nightstand. Frances moved to the bed and sat down near the pillow. She let her hand fall onto the bedspread as she studied the books: the Bible, daily devotionals, and an autobiography by C. S. Lewis. She tilted her head, surprised at the selection yet not entirely sure why. Hadn't Madeline talked about how she had a personal relationship with God but did not care for organized religion?

Curious, Madeline picked up the C. S. Lewis book and flipped through it. Several passages were marked, underlined in pencil or with a yellow highlighter. One of the passages jumped out at her: "Nearly all that I loved I believed to be imaginary; nearly all that I believed to be real I thought grim and meaningless."

Frances laid the book down upon her lap and stared at the wall. *What a gruesome thought that is.* What had compelled Madeline to underline it? Yet, at the same time, she knew it had been exactly what she, too, had felt during the past few months. Her thoughts on what family should be were nothing compared to what she had realized they were. What, exactly, had Madeline gone through to come to such a realization?

It disturbed her that she was uncovering a new side of her friend. From everything that had happened at the funeral and then afterward at the house, Frances realized how little she knew about the woman. Of course, she had known her for no more than a few months, but Madeline had seemed so open and honest.

With a sigh, she set the book back onto the nightstand, and with a mixture of both curiosity and hesitation, she opened the drawer and peeked inside. It was organized neatly: lotion, reading glasses, and a small pile of letters tied with a ribbon. Curious, Frances picked up the letters and glanced at the first one. It was dated five years earlier and addressed to Madeline's Madison address. The return address was from London. Most likely from her daughter.

Two other letters were from the same address. Curiosity got the best of her, and despite knowing that she was intruding, Frances opened the oldest letter, which was dated January of 2008. Her eyes scanned the neat handwriting of the short one-page missive.

> *Dear Mother,*
> *I hope this letter finds you well. It has been a while since we have heard from you, perhaps since Father's funeral. Both Ron and I have talked and we would like to visit in the summer. I know that you say you don't want visitors, but it's unhealthy for you to isolate yourself from friends and family. James has contacted us and expressed concern that you are not well. I trust that you will see the doctors and follow their instructions.*

While I know that we have talked about this in the past, I just want to remind you that God forgives, even when we cannot. He sees everything, including what is in your heart. And he forgives and loves us. Just as we forgive and love you, too.

With love,

Gladys

Frances frowned and reread the letter. Why hadn't Madeline told her the truth? Setting the letter onto her lap, Frances stared at the wall. She hadn't realized how much she had in common with Madeline. Even if it hadn't been Frances's original intention, she, too, had isolated herself from her family. Had she not fainted on Thanksgiving, how long would she have kept her secret? How would they have reacted later? Perhaps she, too, would have lost the very thing she cherished more than anything: her family.

And yet, while Madeline had hinted to Frances that the children had abandoned her, it was clear from this letter that Gladys had tried to stay in touch with her mother. The letter confirmed what James had told her at the funeral. So while Madeline told others that her children did not care about her, the truth was that Madeline had ignored her children's attempts to be a part of her life.

Frances continued rifling through the envelopes and saw one from James and two from her other daughter, Marion. And then her eyes fell upon the last envelope. It was yellowed with age, the postmark from December 1980. Almost forty years old. There was no return address.

She flipped the letter over and opened it, carefully extracting the contents. Inside was a two-page letter in the neatest handwriting that Frances had ever seen. It was as if great pains had been taken to ensure that the letter was meticulous in delivering its message.

Dear Sister,

The holiday season is almost upon us. I fear that this will be my last Christmas. Surely I will soon pass from this earthly life to my heavenly home.

When a person has a terminal disease, there are few things that bring them greater joy than surrounding themselves with the people they love. I have missed seeing my nieces and nephew. And I have missed seeing my only sister.

I don't begin to understand your reasons for avoiding me. However, I suspect it's better than having pity from you. I do have one last request that I hope you will honor.

When I breathe my last breath and ascend to be with God and Jesus, please take comfort in the fact that I have forgiven you. Later in life, if your decision to shun me during my final days returns to haunt you, it will be important for you to know that forgiveness was given long before you asked for it.

I wish things could have been different, Madeline. But I will die knowing that I have told you what is in my heart. Since I cannot have you beside me when I live my final days, I will relive the happier days from our youth and surround myself with people who neither pity me nor fear my illness. I shall continue to surround myself with true friends, people who care deeply for us—in both the best of times and the worst of times. I only wish you were included in that increasingly small circle.

It is the next best thing to having you, my dear sister and sweet friend of my childhood, beside me.

With all my sisterly love,

Barbara

Frances placed the letter upon her lap and stared out the window, her eyes falling upon the bird feeder. She felt as if she should cry, but the tears would not come.

She was beginning to understand what had happened, how Madeline had abandoned her sister during her illness and kept her children away from her dying sister. She couldn't begin to understand why, but she did understand that Madeline's decision had created a backlash among her family.

And yet they had all tried to reach out to her during her final years.

Madeline, however, had rebuffed them and let herself live in much the same manner as her sister had lived: alone. Only, Barbara had wanted to have her family around her, while Madeline had not. It was almost as if Madeline had punished herself for her own decision, almost forty years ago, to disavow her sister.

What Frances couldn't understand, however, was why.

She started to fold up the letter and put it back in the envelope when she noticed that there was something else in it. A photo.

Carefully, Frances withdrew the small photo with rounded edges. She flipped it over and looked at the image of two people: an older women and a child. The woman sat in a red sleigh with a child standing next to her. There was snow on the ground, and both of them smiled as if it was the happiest of times.

A chill ran throughout her body and goose bumps covered her arms as she realized that she was staring at the photograph of herself as a child standing beside Mrs. Bentley. In disbelief, she flipped the photo over again and noticed the same elegant handwriting on the back: *Merry Christmas, Madeline. Your loving sister, Barbara Bentley.*

Frances just stared at the elegant handwriting. The words shocked her more than the actual photo. How unbelievable was the hand of God to have made this come full circle! Memories came flooding back to her, memories of her mother bemoaning the amount of effort she had put into tending to Mrs. Bentley, a woman who now, almost forty years later, had a first name. Her mother complaining about having to help that *poor, pathetic* woman with no family to assist her when, all along, Mrs. Bentley had family who didn't even know that she was ill.

Her emotions began to pull her into a new dimension of understanding how the effects of disease affected other people. Madeline had run in fear of the very disease that ultimately took her life. Yet, in doing so, she had alienated the very people who she would one day need to call upon for support. She had supported that detachment through her own actions when she estranged herself from her sister and chose not to accept the support of her family. Instead, she had chosen to push them away, refusing to accept the very thing that she had denied Barbara.

Frances sat on the edge of Madeline's bed, tears filling her eyes. For the first time since her diagnosis, she understood. She understood her own cancer and her reaction to it. She understood her inability to forcibly tell her husband as well as her reluctance to inform her family.

Tears streamed down her face, and she did nothing to wipe them away. Instead, she set the letters down on the bed and stood up. Slowly, she walked toward the window and paused before she opened it. She reached outside to pluck the bird feeder from the other window, tugging gently so that the suction cups that held it released without spilling too much of the birdseed.

She cradled it in her arms and turned to walk toward the door. Then she stopped and glanced at the packet of letters that she had laid upon the bed. She left them for James to find in the hope that he, too, might better understand the pain and suffering that his mother had gone through when she had decided to live the end of her life in the same manner which she'd forced Barbara to end hers: alone.

Only, God had made a final decision for both Barbara and Madeline that they would not end their lives alone. Somehow God had set Frances in their lives to ensure that their final days would be in the company of one person who did not judge and would love them, whether the love came in the form of a small child willing to take a Christmas photo with a dying neighbor or a sick woman choosing to provide friendship to a dying stranger.

With the bird feeder tucked under one arm, she reached over to flick off the overhead light in the room, and then she shut the door behind her as she said her final good-bye to the one friend who had taught her to live during her fight against cancer.

EPILOGUE

Frances stood at the kitchen sink, washing the dinner dishes. The sun was just beginning to set behind the trees in the backyard, the golden rays shining through the glass and shimmering on the water in the sink. She didn't mind the glare that blinded her eyes when she lifted the dishes from the soapy water to rinse them under the faucet. It was just one more reminder that spring was finally there.

"Mom! Come look!" Carrie called out from the family room.

"Just a minute," she called as she finished the last dish, setting it on the drying rack. She much preferred washing the dishes by hand than putting them into the dishwasher. For some reason, it felt as if it was the completion of a routine, rather than the avoidance of a thankless task.

Drying her hands on a dish towel, she walked into the other room. "What is it, sweetheart?"

Carrie pointed toward the window. "Look! A nuthatch!"

Frances raised her hand to her head and peered out the window. Sure enough, at Madeline's bird feeder, a small nuthatch was plucking birdseed from the tiny holes. "Oh my! Look at how pretty he is!"

"Maybe it's a she," Carrie said.

"The males have the dark eye stripe, remember?"

Carrie thought for a moment and then nodded. "That's right."

Frances smiled. "But he sure is beautiful, isn't he?"

Nicholas walked into the room, a mug of coffee in his hands. "What's going on, girls?"

Frances didn't answer but pointed out the window.

"Ah. We have a visitor, do we?"

All winter, they had been watching the different birds that came to feed at the bird feeder that was affixed to the window. It had become a family event to identify new birds and look them up on the Internet. By now, they had counted over twenty different species and could identify them by name, although not always by gender.

Frances raised her hand to touch her newly sprouted crop of hair.

"His hair is almost as long as mine," she quipped.

Nicholas smiled at her. "But he's not as beautiful, is he, Carrie?"

Carrie made a gagging noise, which both of her parents teasingly scowled at.

"Finish up your homework now," Frances said gently to her daughter. "Andy will be home soon from baseball practice, and he'll want to watch a movie."

"With all of us?"

Nicholas gave her a stern look. "If you finish your homework by the time he finishes his supper. And take the puppy outside."

This time Carrie groaned. "It's so cold out!"

"Hey! A deal's a deal," Nicholas said.

"Aw, Dad!"

He gave an exaggerated sigh. "Fine. But just this once," he said. As he walked toward the back door, he whistled.

The three-month-old yellow Labrador emerged from behind the reclining chair in the television room. He stretched and yawned before looking up at Nicholas with bright eyes, his tail wagging happily.

"Let's go, Harley," he said as he opened the door for the puppy to trot down the steps onto the shoveled walk and toward the snow-covered grass. The other dogs bounded after them, leaping through the melting snow behind the puppy.

Both Carrie and Frances watched Nicholas with the dog. A late Christmas present, the little foster puppy from the Seeing Eye had been Nicholas's surprise for everyone in the family. And while the children were supposed to take care of him, it seemed that Nicholas was commandeering that role, by choice more often than necessity.

Turning away from the open glass door, Frances put her hand on Carrie's shoulder. "Finish that up," she reminded her daughter.

"OK, OK."

When Carrie tilted her head back over her textbook, Frances walked over to the window, looking at the nuthatch, which seemed undisturbed by her presence. She watched him until, at last, he had his fill of seed and flew off to hunker down for the night. Only then did she turn to look at the photo on her bookshelf, the one of her and Mrs. Barbara Bentley. She glanced at it almost every evening before she retired, considering it a constant reminder of how much a faded photo could change her past, present, and future.

Regardless of what the future held for her, she remained grateful for the reminder of how much her past had altered her present. And she remained grateful for the gift of Madeline, for having brought her family together at last. A gift from a woman who gave so much without knowing that she gave anything at all.

ABOUT THE AUTHOR

A former college professor, bestselling author Sarah Price began writing full-time after she was diagnosed with cancer in 2013. She has written more than twenty novels, but *The Faded Photo* is her first foray into women's fiction. Drawing on her own experiences as a survivor of both breast cancer and domestic violence, Sarah explores the issues that touch—and shape—women's lives. Sarah lives in Morristown, New Jersey, with her husband and two children.